ONCE PETER DREXLER HAD BEEN ENGAGED TO HER DAUGHTER. HER DAUGHTER HAD DIED.

"There's no sense prolonging it," Joanne Ellis said in a voice that was dry and trembling. "You and I know you killed her. That should be enough."

"Mrs. Ellis . . ." Peter warned her.

Maggie climbed another step and Peter hit back at the air between them, shouting "Get—!", breaking off when he saw the gun, his gun, in Joanne Ellis's hand.

Maggie gasped, her hands jerking up to her face and covering her mouth.

"Think of yourself as a very lucky woman," Joanne said to her. "Much luckier than my Susan." She moved closer to the top step, holding the gun with both hands now and pointing it at Peter's head. "Thank her for this, thank her memory. . . ."

PARLOR GAMES

ROBERT MARASCO

A DELL BOOK

Published by
Dell Publishing Co., Inc.
1 Dag Hammarskjold Plaza
New York, New York 10017

Dell ® TM 681510, Dell Publishing Co., Inc.
ISBN: 0-440-17059-1

Reprinted by arrangement with Delacorte Press.

Printed in the United States of America

First Dell printing–September 1980

CHAPTER ONE

The limousine turned into the driveway. Joanne Ellis looked straight ahead at the house in the distance, half hidden below a rise in the grounds. Another turn and the Hudson appeared, gleaming, and then disappeared again. Joanne leaned forward and felt Arthur's hand on her arm.

"You're home," he said. His hand tightened around her.

She nodded. She could feel him watching her silently. The grounds were vast and manicured and Joanne tried to distract herself with them, and with Stewart, the gardener, who was working in the rose garden, deaf to the passing car. But she was being watched by the chauffeur, too, in the rearview mirror. It wasn't her imagination, either, because she met his eyes and he looked away immediately. If she turned suddenly to Arthur she'd catch him as well; find the same look–furtive and uneasy, a surveillance really. But Arthur was more practiced with her than was Paul the chauffeur. He would smile to cover, his hand would tighten on her again, and his face would melt with compassion. Anything to put her off.

They didn't trust her–Arthur anyway; Paul hardly

mattered—didn't at all believe that the past eight months "away" could have changed anything. They would deny it, of course, but that's what the looks were telling her, and not just now but all morning, all the way from Pinehurst. Her release, they were saying, was premature; she would have to crack again, it was inevitable given what she had gone through; and they were watching for it already, all of them, all set for it.

She turned suddenly to face Arthur. He *had* been watching her just a second before, but he was looking away now at the house directly in front of them. The limousine came to a stop, and the smell of lilacs was overwhelming when Paul opened the door for them.

"They're still blooming," Arthur said, and then his voice deepened: "That was an order."

He laughed, too heartily, and Madge, the housekeeper, who was coming down the front steps with an uncertain expression, brightened when she heard it and laughed herself to ease her nerves. She stopped at the edge of the gravel drive and waited for Joanne to take Arthur's hand and step out of the car. To Madge she looked as elegant as ever, wearing the tan silk suit and gold jewelry, lots of it. Her hair was a deeper gray now and cut a bit differently, and she might have been wearing more makeup than usual, but otherwise Mrs. Ellis looked just fine to her; not at all what Madge had been dreading.

Joanne took a deep breath and looked up, at the mass of the house (her house, finally!) and the big shade trees. She closed her eyes for a long private moment, and when she opened them again she heard Madge's voice saying, "Welcome home, Mrs. Ellis!"

Joanne turned to her and said *"Madge"* so warmly that Madge had to stop and reach into the pocket of her white uniform for a tissue. Joanne walked up to her instead, opened her arms, and embraced her.

Arthur had taken two small leather cases from Paul. "She looks wonderful, doesn't she, Madge?" he said.

"She certainly does."

"Why not?" Joanne said. "I feel wonderful." She tried to move away but Madge kept one arm around her waist and walked with her to the steps. Arthur was on her other side now, shifting the cases to free one hand for her. Joanne climbed a step and halted. "What are you doing, you two? I'm not an invalid." She glowered at them and they smiled and released her.

"The boss is back, Madge," Arthur said. "On your toes."

The house, a nineteenth-century stone showplace, was large and formal. The windows were oversized and were fitted, several of them, with wrought-iron balconies. There was a stunning view of the Hudson and the Catskills, one which had been featured in several magazine articles about the house.

Joanne looked at everything hungrily, with Arthur and Madge keeping a step below her. She moved slowly, without any further assistance. At the door she stopped for another lingering view of the lawn and the gardens. From somewhere on the river side of the house there was the sound of a power mower. She listened to it travel down the slope, toward the edge of the woods. It faded to a hum, distant and relaxing—hypnotic almost, with the sun on her and the heavy smell of the lilacs.

Arthur called her name twice before she heard him. She saw him waiting with Madge, whose uniform had suddenly become too white for Joanne's eyes. She saw Paul, too, shifting under the weight of her luggage. For just a moment she was disoriented, felt as though she were back at Pinehurst; and then she was embarrassed to have been carried away so easily, so obviously. They had seen her distraction; signals had probably been passed that she had missed. She started to apologize.

"For what?" Arthur said. Joanne shrugged and gave a weak smile. Arthur moved in front of her. He pushed open the front door, then bowed slightly and said, "Mrs. Ellis?" in a gallant and formal voice.

Joanne went into the house. There were fresh flowers on the hall table, a huge welcoming bouquet. Arthur waited in the open doorway and held the others outside, watching Joanne walk across the hall and ease herself back into the house. She looked up the wide, curved staircase, and then moved more confidently into the living room. Arthur followed her, and when she turned and their eyes met, he thought he saw it finally—a smile, and an honest one this time.

"Well, how does it feel?"

"Like I've never been away!"

"That's my Jo talking!"

He moved toward her but she had turned away and was crossing the living room. The room was airy and bright; spotless, too. There were French doors at the far end, open, and on the terrace facing the river were large stone urns filled with young geraniums. She went to the balustrade and Arthur's voice, sending Paul upstairs with her luggage, faded behind her. A young man she didn't recognize was riding the mower in a neat pattern below the terrace. She looked beyond him at the view. It was a scene she had kept with her in her room at Pinehurst all those months—this view, this angle. Only this wasn't a photograph, this was real; she was on her terrace, home, and everything around her was familiar. And *real.*

When she went back into the house, Arthur and Madge were in the hall, and talking too quietly, it seemed to her. They stopped abruptly when they saw her. "Secrets?" she called out.

"What secrets?" Arthur was coming toward her, smiling, his arms spread wide. "No secrets here."

"They whispered all the time at Pinehurst," Joanne said, and then made a sibilant sound to parody it. "It makes me very nervous."

"Madge was telling me about some calls that came in," Arthur said. "All the usual crises." He looked at Madge, who reminded him that Mr. Mitchell's was *very* urgent. "See what I mean?" he said to Joanne. "Get used to it all again."

"With pleasure," Joanne said. Madge was coming toward her as well now, at the same pace as Arthur; one on either side of her. It wouldn't surprise her if Madge had something like a hypodermic needle hidden behind her back. She had that sort of look. Would they be amused if she said it, or alarmed? She was silent.

They *had* been talking about her, of course—that was obvious enough. Arthur was probably giving Madge her assignment; telling her what to watch for, what sort of behavior should concern her enough to make her call him immediately, no matter where he happened to be.

She let them come just so close, then held out her hands. "Stop hovering, both of you," she said, and it came out sounding playful enough. "Madge, what I'd love is some tea. And you"—she jabbed Arthur in the chest lightly—"make your calls."

"The calls can wait," Arthur said. "Let's get you settled."

"I am settled. I'm home."

She pointed him in the direction of his study and gave a slight push, and he loved it, saluting her and saying, "On the double!" She waved Madge away as well and saw her scurry off as Arthur had done. But then Joanne called out to her; Madge came back into the hall. Mrs. Ellis seemed to be inspecting her silently.

"Ma'am?" she said.

Joanne looked up at her face. "For a while at least, Madge," she said, and then hesitated, "—would you not wear that?"

Madge looked puzzled. She touched her uniform. "This?"

"White," Joanne said, very distinctly. "Thank you." She turned and started up the stairs.

Madge wasn't questioning Mrs. Ellis's authority or judgment, but she felt she should check first with Mr. Ellis. She had, after all, been wearing a white uniform during working hours for twelve years. Mr. Ellis thought it was a fine idea that she wear something less "institutional," as he put it. Madge nodded; no further explanation was needed. She would, he assured her, be compensated for any damage to her own clothes, as well as for all cleaning bills.

She went to her room and selected something reasonably cheerful, with shoes to match. As an afterthought she pinned a small piece of jewelry to her dress, an enameled flower. Mr. Ellis was on the phone when she carried the silver tea service past his study, but he smiled at her despite the heated conversation he was having, and gave her a thumbs-up sign of approval.

Joanne's bedroom door was open. Madge knocked and, when there was no reply, entered. There were more fresh flowers in the room (Mr. Ellis had ordered them), and yellow flowered drapes on the windows through which the sun was beginning to pour in. Madge set the tray down on a table in the windowed alcove. She looked toward the bathroom. It was empty, the door half open, the light on. On the edge of the sink was a small bottle of pills, uncapped. The label, printed in blue letters, read *The Pinehurst Foundation.*

Madge called, "Mrs. Ellis?" just to be sure, then switched off the light and pulled the bathroom door closed. A small overnight case was open on a chair and a larger suitcase on the bed. There were more Pinehurst Foundation bottles in the case. On top of the neatly packed clothes on the bed was a framed photograph of a young woman, very pretty with dark blonde hair and brown eyes. It was Susan Ellis—the last picture taken of her.

There were other pictures of Susan in the room: one, it seemed, for each of her twenty-six years. There was a painting as well of Susan as a child. Another portrait of Susan, at eighteen, hung in her old room—where Mrs. Ellis would be now, Madge was sure. She tried to think of a way to avoid searching her out there, but there were no replies when she called. She went out into the corridor, slowing as she passed Mr. Ellis's smaller bedroom. Just before she reached Susan's door she stopped and cleared her throat, but that didn't bring any response, either; there was no sound at all from the room.

She took another step and Joanne Ellis was suddenly there, in the room. She was standing so close to the open doorway and so lifelessly still that Madge had to catch her breath. She tried to cover the sound with her hand, but Joanne hadn't heard and wasn't moving, not even slightly. She was staring, her eyes moist, at the bed, at a delicate ornamental doll with a long, pale-yellow dress and a hairline crack in the face, propped against the pillows. Susan, stunning in the portrait, was at her mother's back, looking down, directly at her.

Madge waited without entering the room. Mrs. Ellis was still completely unaware of her.

It had been this way before. Madge had seen it more than a few times in the past—that same awful look in the eyes, and the sense, an aura almost, of something terrible about to happen, despite the silence and the stillness. Like a seizure. And usually it did happen. There would be a cry upstairs or something breaking violently, and then shouts and more cries, and the next day the drive to the doctor, if he hadn't already been called to the house. And explanations, lame ones always, when Madge was asked to clear the broken glass or the porcelain that had been shattered against the wall, of Mrs. Ellis's "bad night" or "bad dreams." They were breakdowns, Madge knew that even if she couldn't put it into technical terms; small ones, most of them, but then that terrible one when even the local police had had to be brought in.

In the long silence Madge's mind was working to alarm her and make her even tenser. But it wasn't the same now with Mrs. Ellis as it had been last spring. It couldn't be, not after the months of treatment at Pinehurst, and all those doctors whose judgment was certainly sounder than Madge's. They had released

Mrs. Ellis, after all, pronounced her cured. It wis ridiculous for Madge to be keeping this protective distance between them now—as though Mrs. Ellis were some kind of threat to her.

Madge entered the room, and it was like coming into a mausoleum; it always was. It must have been her movement that finally broke Joanne's stare. She looked from Madge to the ceiling with an expression of great distaste. "There's no air at all in this room," she said. "Open the windows."

Usually the windows were opened briefly once a week; or once every other week while Joanne was away. Madge would give the room a quick dusting. No one else entered it with any regularity. Not Arthur Ellis, who seldom walked farther down the corridor than his own room. It was too painful for him, even the few times he'd managed to anesthetize himself with a stiff after-dinner brandy. It was especially painful for him then, in fact—alone and stumbling his way through a house that was too empty; and then turning on the light and seeing Susan's portrait, which overwhelmed the room; hearing her voice even.

It was Joanne who kept the room alive, who would open closets and bureau drawers, and order curtains and linens changed. There were even times—just before Pinehurst—when she would spend hours in the room, waiting for Susan, or watching in the dark while she imagined her sleeping. Talking to her, to *Susan*.

Motes of dust whirled in the sun as Madge moved the curtains. She opened the windows wide. "All of them," Joanne insisted. When she had finished she heard Arthur Ellis's voice saying, "Thank you, Madge."

He was standing next to his wife, which was a relief to Madge, since it meant she wouldn't have the responsibility, like some spy or keeper, of summoning him up to the room. She turned to leave but he stopped her and made a flattering comment about her change of clothes, never once taking his eyes off his wife. And Mrs. Ellis, looking and sounding perfectly normal, agreed; told her how much younger she looked, how downright *summery,* and then laughed and embraced Madge gratefully, as she had done outside. Madge looked hard at Joanne Ellis's face, trying to find a hint of what had chilled her not more than two minutes ago. It couldn't possibly have been her imagination.

They were silent after Madge left the room, and then Joanne moved away from Arthur, letting her hand trail over the surface of a bureau and the small white rocking chair. The curtains floated on the steady breeze blowing in from the river. She held them open and looked down silently until Arthur was beside her again. He said, Joanne . . . ?" and his tone promised something that would be hard but honest and sensible.

"I know, Arthur," she said, and then she looked at him a long time without speaking. He saw her take a deep breath and close her eyes. "Susan is dead." It was the first time he had ever heard her say it. "I can say it as calmly as that," she went on dully. "So all those months—away, as we say, accomplished something, I suppose."

Arthur drew her closer very gently and waited to feel her arm tighten around him, too. It didn't; there was no expression of warmth at all. But that was all right. Her acceptance of the truth, finally, was reassurance enough for him. It was as though a spell had been broken. "Come on, Jo," he said. She let him lead her a few steps across the room before she stopped and pulled away from him. He waited, and when he asked, "What's wrong, Jo?" she was listening not to him but to another voice somewhere in the room.

It took her a long while to let it out—reluctantly and painfully: "He's still free, isn't he?"

She could feel his body stiffen at the question. He was silent. She repeated the words, stating them as fact this time. "He's still free."

"Joanne," Arthur said, and more than anything there was disappointment in his voice.

"You can tell me, Arthur," she said. "I'm quite up to it now. The man is still free."

She was speaking calmly and evenly now, and it was the sudden control that made it all seem unnatural and threatening to Arthur. "As far as I know," he said, just gravely enough.

The suddenness of her cry startled him. *"Why?"* She brought her face closer to his and cried out again, making it an accusation. "Why is he free?" Arthur grabbed hold of her. "Why isn't he dead?"

"Joanne!" he yelled, shaking her.

Her eyes were closed tight, as if waiting for a sudden wave of pain to pass. The look, when she opened them again, was completely different—distant and very tired.

"I'm sorry," she said. Her voice caught. She waited for the tightness in her throat to disappear. "I don't usually lose control like that. Dr. Knoedler will tell you."

Arthur shook his head. "I don't need Dr. Knoedler to tell me anything. You're telling me." He looked directly at her as he said it, gently and with conviction. He couldn't tell whether she believed him, whether she'd even heard him. The room was too distracting, bringing the terrible past back so vividly and wiping out all the healing time in between. "Look," he said, "this isn't doing either of us any good." He stepped between Joanne and the portrait of Susan.

"This is Susan's room," she reminded him defensively.

"You know what I mean, Jo."

Joanne looked up at Susan's beautiful face. "He killed her," she said. "We both know that, Arthur. We've always known it."

"No, Joanne." He made her face him and held her that way. "Accept it, will you?"

"Accept what?"

"Susan . . ." He stopped, trying to find the words.

Joanne said it for him: "Took her own life?" He made a helpless gesture that said nothing. She would have hated him if he had been able to say it—Susan's own father; if he hadn't had the decency to stop himself when he realized how absurd and monstrous the idea was. Joanne made the comforting gesture now, it was her voice that softened. "I wouldn't be sane if I accepted that, Arthur. I'd belong back at Pinehurst."

Her visits to Susan's room continued, regularly. But there were no more confrontations after that first one. Arthur made a point of not interfering—not going near the room, not entering it, even when Joanne started closing the door after her. The visits and the meticulous preservation of the room were bad ideas, as far as he was concerned. Morbid even. He was being honest and intelligent about it, he felt, and in no way unfaithful to Susan's memory. Unfortunately it would be a long time before he could be that honest and intelligent with Joanne.

But after a few days he began to find the visits less disturbing. There was something therapeutic for Joanne in that room. It seemed to be absorbing her grief. She was still a mother mourning an only child's death, but the emotion she carried out of the room was a sorrow that was less obsessive, less the driving force of her life. They might never—neither Arthur nor Joanne—come to terms with Susan's death, but there was Susan's *life* as well, and with it a flood of good memories that they were now helping each other to find.

Maybe it was being home again; or time or Arthur or Pinehurst—*something* was working. Susan's death, the ghost of it, was becoming a melancholy presence Joanne might learn to live with, was no longer what it had been for so long—a force that had come close to destroying her.

She started to take long walks, reacquainting herself with the grounds. The weather was so perfect, the activity outside so inviting, that she started working in the garden again with Stewart, and taking over the house, giving Madge orders, sometimes just to hear herself give orders.

Midway through the week Arthur held a meeting with the lawyers of the Ellis Corporation, which was a big and still growing electronics company specializing in small computer systems. Since he still wouldn't leave the house, the meeting was held in his study, and it was awkward and frustrating, with too many lawyers and papers, and too few personnel available from the company. Joanne's patience gave way—either life got back to normal or she went back to Pinehurst, she told him, only half joking. She managed to dislodge him, and the next day Arthur spent the morning at the office, which was just outside of Poughkeepsie. Every hour he called the house. One of the calls Joanne herself answered, breathlessly. "I'm chasing Madge with a meat axe," she told him. "Can I get back to you later?"

He left her alone longer the next day, and toward the end of the week trusted her for a full day.

"Do you believe it now?" she said to him Friday evening. "I can actually make it through a day without you."

"I never doubted it," Arthur said. He did though, still. The memory of those weeks just before Pinehurst hadn't faded yet. Probably they never would.

She made him call Dr. Knoedler at Pinehurst for her, to see if the medication could be eliminated, or at least reduced—the midday Elavil mainly, and the tranquilizers, which she would prefer to take "as needed." She stayed in the study with him while he made the call. He reached for her hand and told Knoedler that the transformation was really extraordinary, better than anyone had expected. He listened then, and Joanne tried to hear as well, but Arthur released her hand and moved away from her. His silences were longer, his replies monosyllabic.

He was suspiciously quiet after he hung up. "All right," Joanne said impatiently, "what awful things did he tell you?"

Arthur reached for her hand again. "How really encouraged he is."

"Arthur," she warned him.

"Really." He gave her the encouraging smile. "He'd like you to stay on the medication, though."

"Why?"

"Just a precaution. Let's not move too fast, he says."

She gave him a particularly belligerent look and told Arthur it wasn't for him, not at all; it was for Knoedler.

Despite the doctor's advice she skipped the bedtime Elavil and a few days later the midday dosage, and felt just fine. Better, as a matter of fact. Obviously she knew her own mental state at least as well as Dr. Knoedler. Without the Elavil she didn't feel the need for the afternoon nap she always found debilitating. She worked in the rose garden instead, which was a lot healthier and a lot less depressing. For the first time she was feeling really placid, in control of her own mind.

In the past Joanne had always preferred driving herself, using her own BMW. The limousine was reserved for longer trips, usually to New York City, or several-stop shopping excursions. Since the expansion of the Ellis Corporation, Arthur had been in the habit of using it on Mondays and Thursdays, on his traveling days; but with Joanne's return he began using the BMW exclusively and leaving her the limousine. As a convenience to her, he said; what he meant, Joanne knew, was that he didn't trust her to drive herself.

Monday morning Paul was waxing the limousine in front of the garage when he saw Joanne reflected in the polished surface. He continued working, his open sportshirt hanging out over water-stained khaki trousers. She said, "Good morning, Paul."

He turned halfway and said, "Good morning, Mrs. Ellis."

"Will you be finished by eleven? I want to go into Rhinebeck."

"Yes, ma'am." He paused to rub his arm across his forehead.

Joanne walked idly to the other side of the car, watching her distorted reflection. Paul rubbed more wax into the hood.

"Tell me, Paul," she said casually, without looking in his direction, "your detective friend, Mr.—?"

There was a slight break in his even back-and-forth motion. "Trevino," he said, adding, "an acquaintance, Mrs. Ellis."

"Yes, of course. He was very useful to me at one time, as I remember. I wonder—is he still available?"

Paul was repolishing the same area. "I don't know. We've been out of touch."

"I see. Would it be very hard to get back in touch?"

He hesitated, then searched the ground around the car for a clean wax cloth. "It might be," he said, "very hard."

"But you could try," she suggested. She was moving back to his side of the car.

"I don't know about that."

"Sure you could, Paul."

He shook his head uncertainly. "I don't think I want to get involved this time, Mrs. Ellis."

"Involved? I don't know what that means. I'm talking about a simple business proposition." She was closer to him. Her voice was quiet, seductive. "I'd really appreciate it, Paul—very much." She had something in her hand. She reached out and touched him, slipping it into the pocket of his shirt. Her touch startled him. "For the phone calls," she said, smiling in appreciation.

When she left he pulled two hundred-dollar bills, folded very tightly, out of his shirt pocket.

Her bed hadn't been slept in, not for several afternoons now, but Mrs. Ellis hadn't changed her instructions, so Madge continued to turn down the covers every day at three and to darken the room as well; and then at five to make up the bed again. During those two hours Madge rarely saw Mrs. Ellis anywhere in the house. She assumed she was in her bedroom, doing *something* if not napping; or she was in Susan's room where the door was usually kept shut now and where Mrs. Ellis herself had taken over the cleaning. Madge knew that for a fact, she had seen her airing the room, dusting it. It was more than strange or improper to Madge; it was pathetic, and—what was frightening—it was familiar.

There were other reminders, too, of the days before Mrs. Ellis had gone away to the hospital in Connecticut. Moods rather than actual incidents, and sudden changes in the moods. There was a tension in the house that was becoming infectious. At first Madge didn't understand the feeling or the cause of it. And then she did. She had darkened the room and was laying Mrs. Ellis's nightgown across the bed when it struck her that Mrs. Ellis hadn't been cured at all. She was still a patient. The hospital itself had merely been moved to the house and they were all, everyone up to Mr. Ellis, attendants. She, Madge, was an attendant and the white she had been forbidden to wear would have been completely appropriate.

Madge was sure she was right. When the mind *went*, after all, when the cause of the sickness still remained and was as close as the room next door. . . .

The ringing of the phone on the desk startled her, thankfully driving the morbid thoughts out of her head. It was too much for her, that kind of thinking, and it kept coming back to her too often now. She lifted the receiver and heard an unfamiliar voice ask for Joanne Ellis. Madge requested his name; the caller preferred not to give it, assuring her that his call was expected. Before Madge could tell him Mrs. Ellis wasn't available, Joanne was in the open doorway, coming from the direction of Susan's room.

"A gentleman," Madge said. "He refuses to give his name."

Joanne took the phone and covered the mouthpiece. "It's all right." She nodded in the direction of the door. "Close the door on your way out, will you?"

Joanne watched her until she did, the receiver pressed to her chest. Madge stood outside the door for a few moments, but heard nothing from the bedroom.

Later Joanne pushed open the swinging door to the kitchen and signaled Madge to switch off the electric mixer. "About that call, Madge," she said quietly. "I'd rather Mr. Ellis didn't know anything." Madge looked puzzled. "You *do* keep him posted, don't you?"

She looked indignant now, her face ruddy, and said, "No, Mrs. Ellis, I don't." Mrs. Ellis was smiling at her—a disbelieving smile that was mocking as well.

"It's all in my mind then," she said, still smiling. "You'll have to be a little more patient with me, all of you." She gave a helpless shrug and left the room, letting the door swing shut after her.

Madge glared at the door until it stopped swinging. She was certainly sensitive to Mrs. Ellis's condition, but sympathy went just so far, she felt, in the face of an accusation like that. Was she some kind of paid informer in Mrs. Ellis's opinion? She shoved a few bowls around. It was the medication probably—all those drugs in her room. Mrs. Ellis's eyes had looked glazed and she had slurred her words very noticeably. Whatever the reason, the suggestion was insulting.

She brooded until she realized that the timing of the batter she'd been working on was all off—ruined probably. She turned on the mixer again. If it was ruined, let Mr. Ellis ask her why. She'd tell him, all right; tell Mrs. Ellis too, crazy or not.

CHAPTER TWO

His name was Peter Drexler. He was thirty-five and the president of a large toy-manufacturing company called Playcraft that had been founded by his great-grandfather. Two incidents had occurred recently which were either puzzling or upsetting, depending on how much he thought about them.

The first of the incidents occurred at the Playcraft factory in Long Island City. Pam, a new receptionist, had passed a man through to Ron Biddle's office without waiting for Ron or his secretary to come out to the reception area first. Security was usually tight in the executive wing because the toy-design section was located there as well. There were red-lettered warnings, several large safes, and even official code words which were much more forbidding than the "Big Birds" and "Woody Wobblies" they represented. The man in question, a Pittsburgh department-store buyer, had seemed credible enough to Pam—amiable, with short hair, conservative clothes, an attaché case. However, he hadn't gone to Ron Biddle's or anybody else's office. Nor was he seen again, not in the show-rooms, the warehouse, or any of the huge assembly rooms.

There was an intramural investigation, a small one, but nothing at all was found missing or out of place. Only the Pittsburgh buyer. Eventually the report reached Peter Drexler, along with Biddle's suggestion that the bins of dolls' eyes be sifted carefully, and the mounds of torsos and dismembered limbs scrutinized.

That same week there was the second incident, this one at Peter's apartment on East Fifty-fourth Street.

Jackie, his maid, had carried some trash to the incinerator chute at the end of the hall. Less than two minutes later she was startled to find a man (short hair and conservative clothes) standing in the middle of the living room. She cried out and fumbled with the door, which she had locked automatically, but the man looked just as frightened; very confused and then extremely apologetic. Damned if he wasn't in the wrong apartment—10B instead of 12B. It was one hilarious coincidence, he said.

Peter didn't find it so hilarious when Jackie told him about it a few days later. The whole incident was suspect even though, like the Playcraft episode, nothing was missing or out of place. He would have contacted the people in 12B, but Jackie on further questioning could be sure only of "the twelve part." Besides, the man's explanation was too lame to pursue. What made more sense to Peter was the idea that Jackie had surprised a fast and—lucky Jackie—amiable thief.

Who had short hair and was conservatively dressed.

Peter waited for another incident, minor or otherwise. Nothing happened and within a few days he had stopped puzzling over it. Occasionally, though, something would happen to remind him. *Now,* for example—outside his building's garage as he waited for the morning traffic to move on Fifty-fourth.

His Volvo was half on the sidewalk, forcing pedestrians around it. A few times he shrugged and smiled apologies. The entrance to his building was within view and he could see the doorman out in the street, waving at a distant cab. Peter counted two, three people entering the building while the door was unattended. Tenants, no doubt, but a stranger might have made it in unchallenged as well. As a matter of fact the garage door behind him was open, the ramp accessible to anyone. Inside, the steel door at the far end of the garage, which led to the building's elevators, was always locked. Unless you happened to walk closely behind a tenant with a key. Peter had done it himself, as well as held the door open for a total stranger.

The building, in other words, was more vulnerable than he liked to think. So was Playcraft, for that matter. Fortunately he didn't think about things like that, or as he reminded himself—not anymore. The fortress mentality was a thing of his past.

Ahead of him traffic was beginning to move on Fifty-fourth. He inched the car forward and waved thanks at a sour-faced driver who was motioning him out into the street, grudgingly.

The Playcraft building was one of several factories bordering the vast railroad yards in Long Island City. It was smaller than National Casket, its neighbor, and Ideal Toy, its massive competition some distance away, but it was still a large building covering almost a city block, five oversized stories high. More than three hundred people worked inside. Outside was a shabby industrial neighborhood and the Queensboro Bridge, visible from the fifth floor executive offices. There was another Playcraft building—a small warehouse near Hunts Point in the Bronx—and a showroom on Fifth Avenue in the Twenties.

The drive from Peter's garage to his office was a short one, against the main flow of traffic in both directions. Usually he arrived at eight; this morning he had stopped at the Manhattan showroom briefly, so he pulled into his parking space after nine. He waved at Lenny, the outside security guard, and went up in the elevator with a delivery boy and Joe Frazetta's secretary, who was late and mortified.

The reception area was big and bright. Playcraft toys filled the shelves. In front of the logo on the wall was a large red desk, almost a toy itself. Pam was on duty—or more accurately on guard, with the vaguely belligerent look she had been affecting ever since the episode of the Pittsburgh buyer. Peter stopped abruptly, midway between the elevator and her desk, lifted his arms to submit to a search, and breathed hard, shifting his eyes wildly. Pam said, "Very funny," in a very bored way, and pressed the buzzer concealed in her desk. Peter passed through into the corridor.

He stepped inside one of the offices and called, "Bill?" A young man behind the cluttered desk looked up and started to rise. Peter was carrying a shoebox-shaped package. "Here," he said, "be the first kid on your block." He tossed the package gently.

"Woody Wobbly?" the young man asked, excited.

"With all the kinks out." Peter crossed his fingers and held his hand up as he walked out of the office. "Let's get the little mother in the works, chop-chop."

Marie, his overweight secretary, slammed a drawer shut as he came into her office. She wheeled around and poured him a mug of coffee. He tossed the manila envelope he was carrying into the IN basket and flipped through some of the mail on her desk. "I haven't sorted that yet," she called over her shoulder. It was the same teasingly hostile tone Pam had used with him.

Marie pushed herself toward him. The bulge around her waist billowed, stretching her blouse. Peter took the coffee without thanking her and stopped at the door to his office. "Bring me the cheese Danish you just stashed in that drawer," he said, "and Ron Biddle. In roughly that order."

She made a face and called back, "It happens to be prune."

She could hear him repeat the word hilariously as he closed the door behind him: *"Prune!"*

When Maggie Newman came into Peter's office later that morning she found him on his knees, his face almost touching the carpet. His jacket and shoes were off, his tie pulled loose. Covering a good part of the room was an elaborate network of looping tracks. Peter was checking the angle of a dip, widening a curve that had seemed too sharp. He worked the plastic track and heard the door close quietly behind him. Maggie watched him, holding a black leather portfolio in front of her with both hands. She cleared her throat. He was too absorbed to turn, and waved a quick hello at her instead.

"What kind of work is that for a grown man?" she said finally.

Peter moved on all fours for another view of the track. "Who says I'm a grown man?"

"Just an expression." She leaned the portfolio, which was large and heavy, against the couch and stepped carefully over the tracks to reach him.

"You're early," he said.

"And you're impressed."

He smiled. Her voice alone could do it to him. It had a unique husky quality, a hoarseness almost, as though she had been talking too much or, given the look of amusement Peter always seemed to find on her face, laughing too much. Maggie was twenty-seven, scrubbed looking and rosy, with beautiful eyes, brown, and very straight and long black hair. She and Peter had known each other three weeks professionally and one socially.

She knelt beside him. He looked up from the track and kissed her lightly on the tip of her nose.

"Red or blue?" he said, and held up two small cars for her to see. "Pick one."

She chose blue and asked, "What are we doing?"

He aimed her at the beginning of the track and crawled behind her. "Working, believe it or not." He showed her how to wind the surprisingly heavy little car, and then made her position it beside his. "My idea, doubling the track," he said. "Thrills *and* competition. Clever?"

"Awesome."

He explained the motor to her—a tiny, very powerful coiled spring—and then said, "Ready?" She nodded and he made the sound of a gunshot. They released the cars, which buzzed ("How do you like that son-of-a-bitch sound?") over and around the track, holding to it remarkably well. Blue won, just barely, and Maggie said, "Tough."

They ran it again, several times, with longer track and wider loops. Peter made constant mental notes. His excitement grew and, with it, Maggie's. Whether it was play or work, it was intense and absorbing and obviously fun for him.

VA-ROOM! was the name of the game, he told her in a voice that was suddenly *mach-schnell*-executive.

He wanted pictures and graphics just as vivid, a package that really *roared.* When could he expect her sketches?

He challenged Maggie to one last winner-take-all race. His car, which he wound extra tight, barely held the track while he shouted encouragement; but held it, triumphantly. Maggie smiled nobly, hoping he saw what a graceful loser was all about.

"Why, wasn't I graceful?" he asked.

"No. You're a lousy loser." She tried to rise from her knees but he was holding onto her.

"We're not finished yet," he said. His voice and the touch that went with it were suddenly very soft. He maneuvered himself into position beside her. "Winner take all, remember?"

She widened her eyes into a particularly ingenuous expression and said, "What's the all?" She let him pull her back down, liking the feel and the closeness of him, excited by it.

He moved the tracks aside without taking his eyes off her and cushioned her head on his arm. She could feel his breath on her face and his body pressing against her. Concentrating on Peter should have been easy for her, effortless, but there were distractions in the network of tracks around them and all the stuffed animals on display in the office, staring down wide eyed. Peter's face moved closer, blocking the most goofily distracting of the animals, a rabbit Maggie found irresistible.

"Losers pay penalties," Peter was saying quietly. "It's the American way."

She was afraid to speak. It would come out in her voice if she did—the laugh she could feel building. Worse than a laugh—a giggle. She looked at his face, trying as hard as she could not to think of the rabbit whose name—it came to her unbidden—was Dumb Bunny.

"This is the part for big boys and girls," Peter whispered into her ear, and it was incredibly sexy to Maggie, everything about him was. But as he moved closer to kiss her the rabbit reappeared behind him, and the laugh she was trying to contain burst out of her—into his face, literally. She rolled away, onto her side, and when she tried to apologize and saw Peter's stunned expression she laughed even harder. She pointed in the rabbit's direction and said accusingly, "That ridiculous rabbit."

Peter glared, took a piece of track, and threw it, toppling the rabbit. He waited for Maggie's fit to pass, trying not to smile himself. It passed quickly, and she lay in his arms without speaking, stroking his hand.

"I couldn't help it," she said weakly. She heard Peter make a vaguely irascible sound. She wouldn't, she fervently hoped—and told him so—see an imaginary rabbit whenever Peter became romantic—if he ever did again.

She remembered her abbreviated romance with Elliot Thorne, who was an editor at Macmillan when she'd worked in the art department there three years ago. They were in his apartment one night, making love for the first time. There was soft music on the radio in the bedroom until, at the worst possible moment, the station signed off with the "Star Spangled Banner." It killed the moment, the evening, and ultimately the relationship.

She wondered if Peter's sense of humor could take that anecdote right now. She turned to him and his expression was thoughtful and distant, his male pride obviously wounded. She passed up the anecdote and asked, cautiously, "What are you thinking about?"

"The Son of Dumb Bunny," he said, still working it out in his head. Then he announced: "Widiculous Wabbit!" He tried it out several times and finally the name clicked for him and it was all settled—a new Playcraft character had been born. He let out a moderate hoot and wrapped himself around Maggie, squeezing hard and telling her, "What *terrific* teamwork."

At eleven they went into the conference room together. Maggie would have preferred separate entrances to confound Frank Powell, the copywriter on the account, who already suspected something developing between her and Peter Drexler. Not that Frank's suspicions mattered. But sure enough, he raised his eyebrows when he saw them and, after Peter had gone to the head of the big conference table, said to Maggie, "Well, well, well." She smiled too sweetly and unzipped her portfolio. Frank raised his hand to his mouth.

"A little overtime?" He parodied a leer (Frank never did anything totally straight) and waited for Maggie's reaction.

"Ha," she replied mirthlessly. She carried her drawings to the easel that Luke, the account executive, had set up at the end of the room.

It was June and they were laying out the Christmas ad campaign. Maggie doodled during Luke's detailed presentation, and listened to Peter's challenges, all of which sounded brilliant to her. He was an extraordinary man, really. She italicized the thought with a pencil stroke on the pad. He was intelligent, absolutely on top of everything; his instincts were invariably right. It was a litany she was reciting to herself, the pencil lines getting bolder and more rapid. She let in some of the sounds from the conference room—Luke's at the moment, and boring. The more she thought about Peter Drexler, the more she had to question her objectivity, which was something she had always trusted in herself. On reflection she still trusted it: Objectively Peter *was* extraordinary.

A figure was taking shape on the paper, an astronaut from one of the Playcraft space lines. The face emerging however was not the original model's, it was Peter's. Maggie had never drawn him before. She raised her eyes and found he was looking directly at her as he listened with obvious impatience to the rambling Luke. Probably he wasn't even seeing her; she just happened to be the object in his line of vision. She copied the shape of his brow, his hairline, rubbed in the hair, and then looked up again. This time he wasn't looking through her. He even managed a slight smile which Frank caught, of course, along with her reaction to it. He started to scribble something on his pad—for her, no doubt, and sarcastic. Before he could pass it Peter startled them all into attention by groaning painfully. Maggie sensed she had missed some epic stupidity from Luke.

"Come on, you guys," Peter was pleading, "that doesn't make any sense, no sense at all."

What she was doing so obsessively on the paper, Maggie realized, didn't make much sense either. She turned the paper over and started drawing Dumb Bunny, with Frank's face.

Peter ended the meeting promptly at twelve-thirty. Marie came into the conference room with two harried-looking men, one of them holding a ragged blueprint. Peter raised himself above them and mouthed the word "eight" at Maggie, indicating, she assumed, tonight, her apartment. She nodded as he left the room, and gathered her drawings, most of which Peter had approved and genuinely liked.

Frank Powell had come to her side of the table. "Are you coming back to Manhattan, or what?" he asked, nodding, on the "what," in Peter's direction.

"Coming back," Maggie said. "Stop looking so surprised."

He gave her his truce smile and laughed out loud when she showed him the Dumb Bunny drawing. "You can draw," he said. "Thank God, you've got something going for you."

She took the drawing back before Frank could see the picture of Peter Drexler. When he offered to buy her lunch she said, "Fine."

"Let me push my luck," he continued. "How about dinner, too?" They were out in the corridor, heading slowly for the elevator while Luke and his assistant gathered papers.

Maggie shook her head. "Can't tonight."

"No? Well, you're in luck. I've got tomorrow open, too."

"I don't." At least she hoped she didn't.

"The Drexler account again?" Maggie didn't answer. "What do you see in a guy like that anyway? Brains, talent, looks? All that superficial crap?"

"For openers, anyway."

"Forget I asked," Frank said. He held the door to the reception area for her, and she touched his arm lightly and gave him an amused and affectionate look. While they were waiting for Luke, Maggie said, "Do you still want to buy me lunch?"

"Why not?" Frank shrugged. "Hell, I'm a great sport."

Peter had to drive to the Bronx warehouse that afternoon, unexpectedly, and it was almost eight when he reached his apartment. While unlocking the door, he could hear the phone inside giving a few final rings. He poured himself a short vodka and started pulling off clothes on his way to the bedroom, where he dialed Maggie's number. He got her just as she was stepping out of the shower.

"I wouldn't have been ready anyway," she said. "Blame it on this toy czar I'm working for."

She would meet him at an Italian restaurant he knew in the Fifties, rather than at her apartment on West Tenth Street.

He shaved, telling himself in the mirror that Maggie would come back with him after dinner and spend the night for the first time. They both wanted it, no question at all. Just the idea of it excited Peter. He stepped into the shower and turned on the water. At the same time he thought he heard the sound of a door closing in the apartment. He turned off the water and listened. Someone was walking slowly through the apartment—he could hear a floorboard creak.

He thought of his sister, who had a key to the apartment, and called, "Gail?" There was silence and after a moment the sound once again of a door being closed quietly. He pulled open the shower curtain and grabbed a towel to wipe his eyes.

No one was in the living room or anywhere else in the apartment; not in the tenth-floor corridor, either, when he peered out. There was no sign of entry, nothing out of place; just his own wet footprints darkening the beige rug in the living room. He stood listening to the silence, loosening the towel from around his middle.

It couldn't have been his imagination—not the Pittsburgh buyer working on him again, or Jackie's man-in-the-living-room. Someone had just been in his apartment.

He went slowly back into the bathroom and let cold water pour over him in the shower. Could it have been a sound from upstairs, from the street? A door slamming in the hall? All right, *could* it have been his imagination?

He dressed and gathered up the clothes he had left lying around the apartment. He closed drawers, smoothed the bedspread, and turned on soft lights in the living room and bedroom. At eight thirty he double-locked the door to his apartment. As he waited for the elevator he could hear his phone ringing again. Could that have anything to do with it—the movement he had heard? The movement he was almost *sure* he had heard?

The elevator arrived. The phone was still ringing as he stepped into the car and pressed the "lobby" button.

The restaurant was small and not uncomfortably formal. In the rear was a glassed-in garden room. Peter was greeted warmly and so was Maggie when she arrived a few minutes later and Peter introduced her to the owner. The greeting had been very much the same at the French restaurant three nights ago and the restaurants where they had had one business and one nonbusiness lunch. Maggie heard a "Signora McCabe" mentioned by Tito as he led them to their table in the garden room, and Peter replying, "Fine."

Over drinks they talked a little about the ad meeting and Peter's labor problems in the South Bronx, until he called a halt. He didn't want to talk about Playcraft, didn't want to be reminded of their professional relationship, not tonight and not in this setting. He did tell her about the incident in his apartment. Maggie shuddered and said, "Creepy." She told him about the two times her current apartment had been burglarized, about her mugging incident and her several close calls—all of it recounted with excitement and unfailing good humor. Peter shook his head and said, "Jesus."

None of it, she assured him, had changed her feeling for the city. She had come to New York seven years ago to attend Parsons and had never left. She loved the city, wasn't at all afraid, and wouldn't think of living anywhere else. "What you see here is a Pennsylvania transplant that's really taken," she said. "A survivor. Is that boasting?"

"Boast," Peter said, lifting his glass to touch hers. "To us survivors." They drank and Peter reached across the table for her hand. With the clasp she was reminded of another horror story—an attempted rape—hers—in the hallway of her previous building. Peter dropped her hand and called, "Stop, halt!"

Did he think she was making it up? She wasn't. If it hadn't been for some quick thinking on her part—a sharp knee to the alleged perpetrator's groin and a fast sprint down the hall. . . . "I leave the rest to your imagination." Her New York accent was flawless and when Peter started to laugh she said, looking very amused herself, "Don't laugh! It was awful."

They ordered more drinks, Maggie switching to vermouth, and something solid to absorb the martini which was already working on her. She leaned across the table and whispered, "Don't worry, I don't get rowdy. Just limp."

Peter could feel the knot inside himself loosening, and it wasn't the alcohol doing it, it was Maggie. He told her so, looking at her with such warmth that she couldn't bring herself to say anything light or self-deprecating. "I like being with you," he said. She could feel herself reacting to the words, feel the color coming into her face—unnoticed, hopefully, in the candlelight. She tried to remember the last time she had had such a schoolgirl reaction to anybody. The martini, obviously. . . .

The waiter came back and Maggie was grateful for the interruption. She reached for a slice of bread and buttered it. It was a long time since Peter had seen a woman dig in with such abandon and without any sign of guilt. He couldn't resist telling her that—with admiration of course—and Maggie repeated, dryly and with undiminished appetite, "Of course." At least she had managed to find her voice again with the change of mood.

He knew that she had never been married and she learned that he had—once, briefly, between college (Columbia) and NYU Law School. He extended his hand and said, "Here, touch a *real* native." He hadn't even come close to marrying again. "No time and no inclination. No likely prospects, either." Neither was involved even slightly with anyone at present and neither could remember who had managed to bring the subject up in the first place."

They ate pasta and veal and Peter's appetite turned out to be at least as healthy as hers. "I'll cook for you sometime," Maggie said. "I'm terrific."

He had started out at Playcraft in the legal department, representing his mother's interests in the company, which were large. His parents were dead, he told her—his mother for six years, his father for more than fifteen. He had an older sister, Gail. So had Maggie, and a younger brother. Both her parents were living. She adored her family and still missed seeing them regularly.

Up until that evening they had discussed very little personal background, concentrating instead on Playcraft and Berman and Main, Maggie's agency. Now everything seemed to be personal, and Maggie's eyes, despite Peter's warning, didn't glaze over. She heard about Uncle Paul who was retired and Uncle Martin who was dead, and Peter's rapid rise to the top. "Maybe you've gathered," he said, "I come from a long line of little old toymakers. Elves, actually. All Drexlers are elves, you know."

She didn't. He made her put down the small pastry she was eating and reached for her hands. "Here, feel." He brought them to his ears. "Elf ears, see?"

"My God," Maggie said, "you're right!"

They had several cups of espresso laced with anisette. A little after midnight Peter said, "I ought to think about getting you home." When the cab stopped in front of his apartment on Fifty-fourth Street he grinned and watched for her reaction. "Notice I didn't say whose home."

"Notice I didn't ask." She stepped out of the cab.

In the apartment Peter turned on the stereo and poured brandy for them while Maggie studied a painting in the hall that was stark and huge, filling the wall. In the living room she saw a Marin watercolor and a Rauschenberg she didn't like, and a striking portrait of Peter done by an artist named Joyce Froelich, whom Maggie didn't know.

"You've got some terrific pictures," she called out to him. He brought her the brandy and placed her hand around the snifter while she studied the pictures, totally absorbed. She moved away from him, greeting a new picture with a small sigh of pleasure. At the end of one wall she looked at him and said, "Why didn't you tell me about this?"

"You mean you would have fallen for a line like that?" He gave her an incredulous look and then raised his glass in the direction of the rear hall. "There're some dirty Picasso drawings through there. A nice Erni, too, and a Chagall in the bedroom. The Chagall's a watercolor."

She started into the hall, stopped herself, and said, seriously, "You don't mind, do you?"

"Your going into my bedroom, you mean? I'll suffer through it."

He followed her and to prove how trustworthy he was, he shattered the mood in the bedroom by switching on the overhead light. An antique hobbyhorse caught her eye, and a huge, beautifully carved soldier, both of them wood, their paint faded to pastels. Maggie ran her hand over the smooth wood and looked at the pictures until Peter turned off the light, telling her, "You really look lousy in that kind of light."

There was a small lamp on beside the bed and this light he found terribly flattering, just right for her. He came toward her. Maggie didn't move, didn't look at all uncomfortable to Peter, despite the setting and his obvious intentions.

He stopped in front of her. She looked beyond him, nodding her approval of the room. "I like your taste," she said, and it was her voice that gave her away—it was tense and dry. Peter put his glass down and took hers away, too, moving very slowly. He drew her closer, swaying to the music in the background.

"I like my taste, too," he said. He kissed her lightly. "Relaxed?"

"Mmm." It was a half-lie at this point.

"Me, too."

She touched his face and after a moment he kissed her again. He could feel her stiffen and resist him just briefly, and then let him ease her down onto the bed. She called his name in a small pleading voice and he said, "You're going to stay with me, aren't you?" He was making that a plea, too, repeating, "Aren't you?" against her mouth and her ear, softer and softer.

He was stroking her, on the outside of her clothes, and after that it was awkward only briefly—pulling each other out of their clothes, slipping the cool silk spread from under them. He had turned it into a teasing erotic game, and now there was no resistance at all in her. She moved hungrily, wrapping herself around him. And this time, thankfully, all the bright toy faces in the room were hidden in the shadows. Even if they hadn't been she wouldn't have laughed, not the way he was making love to her. Not even if the stereo were to burst out with the "Star Spangled Banner."

She moved naked through the quiet room and saw photographs she hadn't noticed before. Family pictures, from what she could make out in the dim light. There was a man dressed in fifties style—Peter's father probably, or one of his uncles—handsome, whoever he was. And a woman photographed near water, very elegant and attractive. There were pictures of two other women, one of whom—the strikingly good-looking one who seemed familiar, probably because she resembled Peter—might have been his older sister, Gail. The other woman, photographed with Peter, was younger; his arm was around her waist. The picture seemed fairly recent. Maggie wanted to lift it closer but she was afraid Peter would wake up and find her snooping. Not that she was—just idling really, trying to decide whether to stay the night or leave. It shouldn't have been a problem, but it was.

The major part of the problem was asleep on his stomach, facing away from her; uncovered and breathing very evenly. She stared at his body, wanting to touch him, wanting him to make love to her all over again.

She looked away from him—pulled herself away—back to the picture. Depressingly, it was still there, with Peter's arm still around the girl's waist. They looked comfortable with each other, happy—but who didn't in a photo? Who was the girl? More importantly, was she still in his life?

She was jealous, unreasonably jealous. And if she could feel this way so early in a relationship, then maybe it made sense to gather up her clothes and leave. Before she found herself even more involved in a situation that was several years ahead of schedule.

Her clothes were piled on the floor and so were his, some of them hanging off chairs where they had landed. The memory of that alone was dangerous and persuasive. She started picking hers out, and something metallic, a belt buckle, hit against a chair and made a small sound. Peter stirred in the bed. He turned and moved closer to where Maggie had been lying, reaching out with an arm and a leg. Maggie waited, holding her breath, and when he didn't open his eyes she continued quietly toward the bathroom with her clothes. She was feeling for the light when she heard sudden, quick movement behind her and Peter's voice calling sleepily, "What're you doing?"

She looked back at him and held up a handful of clothes. "Picking up the pieces." She found the light.

Peter propped himself up. "What for? Where're you going?"

"Home, I think. It's late."

"Home?"

She nodded as though it were a perfectly reasonable decision. Peter jumped out of bed before she could close the bathroom door. "Hey, what did I do wrong?" he said.

"Nothing," Maggie said. "Believe me, not a thing."

"So . . . ?" He moved into the opening which she was trying to narrow, and his voice became soft and seductive. "Come back to bed, then." He rubbed her shoulder, then moved his fingers very delicately to her breast. It was a struggle for Maggie to get the words out evenly. "If I let myself . . . I could get awfully involved. Awfully fast."

He kept touching her, watching her. "Would that be so bad?"

"Yes. No. I don't know. Does that make sense to anybody?"

He thought a moment. "Let me sleep on it. Let's both sleep on it." He put his hand around her wrist and started to tug at her when the phone rang, startling both of them. Peter looked in the direction of the sound. It was 3:10. He let it ring a few more times.

The girl in the picture, Maggie thought right away. Who else would call at that time? "Maybe you'd better get it," she said.

Peter said, "Wrong number."

"Find out."

The ringing continued, distracting Peter, making him angry now. He released her hand and moved back far enough for her to ease the bathroom door shut after she blew him a kiss. She heard him call out to her, "You're not getting away so easy. Jesus!"

Peter grabbed at the phone and said, "Yeah?" It was a few seconds before a woman's voice said, "Peter Drexler?" The voice, shaky and whispering, came at him like a blow. He closed his eyes. The voice moved closer to the mouthpiece. "This is Joanne Ellis. You remember me, don't you?"

He started to pace in a small circle. "Yes," he said, "of course I do."

"It's been a long time. Eight months at least."

"Yes. How are you, Mrs. Ellis?" He was speaking calmly—too calmly. She had to realize he was struggling.

There was a pause and then the whispering again, shakier, her voice catching: "I've tried you, several times now. You're a very hard man to get." And that time he heard it—the same tone, the same intense, threatening sound he had never managed to forget. Suddenly he was aware of being naked, of feeling vulnerable and ridiculous. He sat down on the edge of the bed. "How did you get this number?" he asked her.

"A friend," she said. "Who tells me you've moved as well. I have your new address. Even the apartment number."

He let it all pass. He shouldn't have mentioned the phone number at all—nothing to let her think he was intimidated. "What can I do for you, Mrs. Ellis?"

"I just wanted to tell you . . ." He could hear her draw a deep breath. ". . . I'm home. All it took was some time. And rest, lots of rest. I'm fine now, really. I can get around quite well, anywhere I want to go."

"I'm glad to hear that," Peter said.

"Not to be confined anymore . . . you don't know how therapeutic that is."

"I can understand that," Peter said, trying to let his voice warm just slightly. "If there's anything I can do, anything at all. . . ."

"No. Nothing."

"Well, let me know if there is, okay?" She was silent, breathing harder. "Mrs. Ellis?"

"I'm still here."

"It's late." He said it gently.

"'And I woke you."

"That's all right."

"No, it's not, not at all. It's very thoughtless of me. Forgive me, please."

"Don't even think about it. Just take care of—"

She didn't let him finish. "I just wanted you to know," she repeated, and then paused: "I'm home."

"That's good," Peter said quietly. There was silence at the other end. "Mrs. Ellis?"

"I'm still here," she said.

"Good night." Again there was no reply. He lowered the receiver slowly, and then listened once more before hanging up. He heard her breathing. He hung up and stared at the phone until the shower was turned off in the bathroom, calling him back.

He stood up and when Maggie came out of the bathroom, wrapped in a towel, he had pulled on a shirt and pants. "Come on," he said to her, "I'll drive you home."

He had barely looked at her. "I can take a cab," she said, watching him move around the room with sudden energy. He was picking up the rest of his clothes, which he rolled into a ball and threw on a chair.

"Like hell you can. I need some air anyway." He was still preoccupied, avoiding her.

"Who calls at three-something in the morning?" she asked him.

"Nobody. Business."

And clearly none of hers. She watched him find one shoe and then, on his knees, the other. "You look a little rattled," she said.

"Who does?" He got up and forced a smile which seemed to become more genuine as he came closer to her. He rested his arms on her shoulders.

"Put out, then," Maggie said. "By me. Maybe I should stay after all. Risk the fisheye from the doorman in the morning, the clucking of the neighbors. How's that for a will of iron?"

She was half serious–maybe a little more than half, to her own surprise. Peter touched her forehead with his, and either he'd lost interest or the call had really been upsetting enough to cancel her out (the romantic entanglement she'd guessed at? the blonde girl in the picture?).

He said it gently but he did say it: "Why don't you get dressed?" Which solved at least part of her problem.

She dressed in the bathroom, and they almost fought over his insistence on driving her home to the

Village. They rode the elevator in silence down to the basement, shadowy and sinister. In the car he kissed her—a little perfunctorily, she thought—and she brooded part of the way down Fifth Avenue until he reached for her hand and finally looked at her as though he were seeing her again.

"That wasn't a business call," he said, and it was obviously painful for him to talk about it. "It was personal, something unpleasant I thought was all over. It's on my mind right now. It won't be tomorrow, I swear. Christ, I wish you'd stayed."

She waited for more details but there weren't any and Maggie couldn't bring herself to press. They had reached her brownstone between Fifth and Sixth. It was one of Peter's favorite stretches of New York City, too, and he pointed out the small Federal house he had come close to buying a few years ago.

"How's that for coincidence?" he said.

The street was deserted, silent, with parked cars lining it solidly on both sides. He wanted to double-park and walk her all the way up to her door, but this time she was the insistent one, enunciating clearly, "Go home." She leaned toward him with one hand on the door handle. Peter kissed her, and if she needed any reassurance it was there in the way he was holding on to her—tight, almost tight enough to hurt.

A few minutes later he waited for her to unlock her inside door and, safely inside, wave him away. He drove back uptown and parked the Volvo not in his garage but outside, on Fifty-fourth Street, near his lobby and too near a hydrant. It had nothing to do with the phone call, he told himself, or the "friend" Joanne Ellis had mentioned (to intimidate him, no doubt—or was the paranoia starting already?). It certainly had nothing to do with something as childish as a dim basement, however uneasy Maggie had been. It would save time in the morning, that was all.

CHAPTER THREE

Joanne Ellis couldn't sleep—not before she had spoken to Drexler and not after. But he wouldn't be sleeping either now, she was pretty sure of that. Her call had to have come as a shock to him and however much he tried he hadn't been able to keep that out of his voice. Joanne had heard it, distinctly. She knew Drexler after all, better than anybody.

She had made the call from her bedroom, quietly, talking in a whisper, even though there was no way Arthur could have heard, asleep and with two doors closed between them. He wouldn't at all have approved if he had heard. He might even have disapproved enough to—what? Send her back to Pinehurst? Let Knoedler lock her into the main building this time rather than one of the small cottages where she had never been aware of any limit to her freedom? Would Arthur even think of putting her away while Drexler remained free?

Why not? He had accepted it all, hadn't he—all the lies, all the slander against Susan, against herself? He hadn't seen through any of it in the past and he still didn't. Incredibly.

The Valium was on Joanne's desk. She hadn't

needed it before but now she did. It might even make her sleep. She swallowed a tablet and tried to empty her mind, to let the silence and the soft light in the room work on her.

The book in front of her on the desk distracted her. It was a leather-bound diary, stuffed with papers. She had found it where she had left it, locked in her desk. Spread across the open pages were addresses for Peter Drexler—the townhouse duplex at 3 East Sixty-third Street where he had been living when he killed Susan, and his current address which Trevino had passed on to her. The phone number she had dialed a short while ago was written in below the two previous numbers he had had changed. Joanne turned the page. There were more listings—Drexler's sister, Gail McCabe, and several friends Trevino had traced him to during the supposed "harassment."

She entered a new address now, an apartment at 40 West Tenth Street, 4A, belonging to Margaret Newman, a commercial artist Drexler was seeing. It might or might not mean anything, Trevino had told her on the phone; he was just being thorough, as ordered.

Did Margaret Newman know anything about Susan Ellis, Joanne wondered.

The tranquilizer was beginning to work on her. She put the pen down and leaned back in the chair, thinking back to the phone call and realizing all of a sudden it wasn't enough. There was too much of the game in it and she wasn't playing games with Drexler. She wanted to see him, she wanted him *that* close. . . . She reached out and held the diary tightly in both hands. When she loosened her grip a newspaper clipping slid out. She had saved all the stories that had appeared—small paragraphs, most of them, buried in the middle of the New York tabloids. Curiously incomplete stories—to her at least—announcing the accidental death or suicide of a young woman named Susan Ellis who had fallen from the balcony of her twelfth-floor apartment. No mention of the names Drexler and McCabe, no reference to the suspicious nature of Susan's death.

It was *because* of the prominence of the names involved, Arthur had explained to her several times. As though that justified it, made it acceptable. Was she the only stupid one, the only one of them all—Arthur included—who couldn't make sense out of the "discreet" silence?

The clipping was blurring in front of her, but that didn't matter. She didn't have to read it to live the pain all over again, and the rage. Those were the words that came to her—pain, rage. . . . But calmly now, with her eyes closing on them, as though she had lived with them so long and so intimately they were an essential part of her.

Arthur had been having his breakfast in the dining room lately, and Joanne hers in her bedroom. He would knock on her door and, if she was awake, visit her briefly before leaving the house at eight-thirty. That morning Joanne was dressed and having breakfast on the terrace when he came down. She saw him before Madge could direct him to her, and called, "Out here, darling."

The air was sweet and cool, with dew on the planters and the surfaces of the garden furniture Madge hadn't wiped dry.

"Well, well," Arthur said, "what's this?"

"Surprise."

"It's that, all right."

Before Susan's death they would breakfast together on the terrace all the time. Morning was their favorite time of day; dusk, too, on the terrace, watching the sun set behind the Catskills. Arthur leaned on the arm of her chair and kissed her. She was dressed for something special; made up, too, heavily around the eyes to cover the dark circles that had been noticeable lately. He moved back a step, looked approving and then suddenly perplexed.

"I must have my dates mixed up. Your appointment with Dr. Knoedler—?"

"Thursday," Joanne said.

"That's what I thought." He made a small gesture, indicating her outfit. "Is that all for me?"

"Partly. I thought I'd take a trip into New York today." She made it an announcement, sounding excited and adventurous.

Madge had brought Arthur's half-grapefruit to the table. Joanne waited for them to finish the standard annoying exchange about how well Mrs. Ellis was looking today, so much improved from yesterday—as though she were an invalid or some infant on display. She didn't bother to conceal her boredom, looking in the direction of the river until Madge poured another cup of coffee for her and left.

"Already?" Arthur said to her.

Joanne turned back to him from the river. "What do you mean?"

"Isn't it rushing things a little?"

"I don't think so," she said, sounding too defensive—hostile almost. She sat back in her chair and patted her waist with both hands. "As you might have noticed, nothing fits anymore. I've become too damn sedentary. I don't intend to let go that easily."

"You've never looked better, Jo."

"So you all keep telling me. I don't believe it."

"It's the truth." He was silent briefly and looked thoughtful. "Fine," he decided, "anything you want. Consider it my welcome-home treat." He spread the napkin on his lap and reached for the serrated grapefruit spoon. "Tomorrow though," he added. "All right?"

"Tomorrow?"

"I can't get away today; not for anything, I'm afraid."

"Why should you have to get away? I'm the one going."

"Alone?"

"Of course alone."

"Jo, you can't do that."

"I can't? Why not?" And when he didn't answer immediately, she repeated, "Why not?"—strongly enough for him to qualify what he had said with a slight, fumbling laugh.

He touched her hand and said, "Come on, Jo, what fun would it be without me along, complaining?"

She was looking directly at him. "I don't need an attendant, Arthur."

"Of course you don't. That's hardly what I meant."

"It's exactly what you meant. I've been living with restrictions too long. I'm free, I don't have to live with them anymore."

"No," he said quietly, "you don't." He was rubbing her hand very lightly, thinking. If he of all people gave the impression she couldn't be trusted, what kind of setback might that be for her? "I'll tell Paul to have the car ready," he said.

"I've already told him," Joanne said. She smiled a tight smile and moved the folded *Times* closer to his plate. "Now read your paper."

He glanced at it briefly without seeing it. He was right, he was sure of that—it *was* too early to let her go off on her own. Not that he expected anything to happen; she would hardly have been released if that were a possibility. It was just too early for her to be exposed to the city, and some of the memories there. He would have to give Paul very specific instructions.

"You won't overdo it, will you?" he said to Joanne. "Promise?"

Her hand moved against his. "Only at Bergdorf's," she said. "That is a promise."

She hadn't really spoken to Paul since she had asked him to contact Trevino for her. She didn't speak now either, except to say, "The city," when he asked her for a specific destination; the route he took south was immaterial to her. She rode the rest of the way in silence, with her head back and eyes closed whenever Paul caught her in the rearview mirror. They picked up the Deegan Expressway and she opened her eyes and leaned forward, her fingers drumming on the back of his seat as they approached Manhattan.

At Eight-sixth Street and Fifth Avenue she announced they would be making a stop soon, and just before Eighty-fourth she said, "A left ahead."

It was an area that anyone connected with the Ellis family knew. Susan had lived there, between Park and Lexington. Paul could see a bit of the white, balconied building where she had killed herself. He watched Joanne behind him, and though it didn't mean that much to him one way or another, for her husband's sake at least he felt like asking her, "Are you sure about this, Mrs. Ellis?"

They crossed Park and she made him slow down and

then stop the car. A taxi honked and squeezed past them on the right. Joanne was staring up at the building, breathing as though the air in the car was getting thinner. Her hand was clutching the door handle, tightly. Paul turned and saw the strain in her pale face, her head shaking just perceptibly. Her eyes were fixed on an upper story, not seeing Paul, not even when he called twice, "Mrs. Ellis?"

Something inside her had snapped, he thought—that suddenly. What was the look of someone falling apart if not the look on her face at that moment? He would have pulled away from the building but Joanne Ellis had pushed open the door and was out of the car before he could stop her. A parked car was blocking his own door; he pulled up a few feet and got out.

Joanne had gone closer to the building, hitting against a young man who said something to her angrily and then stopped to look back at her. She was in the middle of the sidewalk, standing absolutely still; looking up at one of the terraces facing west, then letting her eyes drop slowly to a second-story setback. Paul had come beside her and was calling her name again, firmly this time, until she looked slowly away from the building, past the people who had stopped to watch her. She seemed stunned, her face bloodless. She felt the pressure of Paul's hand on her and let herself be moved a few steps toward the car before she freed herself.

"I never thought I'd be able to do this," she said, and she was speaking not to Paul, not to anyone; ". . . come back to this place. Ever."

"Let's go to the car, Mrs. Ellis," Paul said.

She let him guide her back without any resistance and sat for a long time in the rear seat with both hands covering her face. If she was crying Paul couldn't hear a sound or see even the slightest movement.

Outside a few people were still watching. The doorman had come out of the building and was talking to a man in a custodian's uniform. Both of them looked at the limousine. Paul watched them, keeping his eye on the rearview mirror, too.

Joanne lowered her hands finally. Still she said nothing.

"I can't keep the car here, Mrs. Ellis," Paul said. "What do you want me to do?"

He saw her reach down and open her bag. She pulled out a piece of paper which she touched to his shoulder. Paul looked at it and asked, "Long Island City?" He saw her nod wearily. He read the address again, a numbered street that would be easy to find. It wasn't Fifth Avenue, though, or any of the shopping areas he had discussed with Mr. Ellis. Did that, he wondered, put it out of bounds? He turned around and saw that her eyes were closed again, peacefully, as though she were sleeping.

"You mind telling me where we're going?" Paul asked her softly.

Joanne's eyes opened wide, and she all but shouted it back at him, *"Just do it!"*

The big doll-assembly line took up most of the second floor of the Playcraft building. There were long tables flanking the conveyor belts that rolled headless, naked forms past seated workers putting them together, boxing them, and sending them down to first-floor shipping. The eye, limb, and hair bins were there, too, all of the pieces human enough to be unnerving at first sight.

Peter was outside the office at one end of the room, listening to Jack Weiss, the foreman, above the noise of the belts and the large fans blowing over the heads of the workers. There had been a blunder in a shipment from the mill in Virginia, and it was Peter, characteristically, who was trying to calm the explosive Weiss. Almost succeeding, too, until a secretary tapped on the window looking out on the room. She was holding a phone against her shoulder and pointing to Peter.

He took the call in the foreman's office, which was air conditioned and frigid. It was Marie, his secretary. "I'm out in the reception area with a Mrs. Ellis," she told him. She was speaking low, as though Joanne Ellis was nearby. Something knotted inside Peter. "I told her you weren't available," Marie said, "and so did Pam."

"I'm not."

"She's insisting otherwise." Marie paused, then her voice lowered even more. "She's giving both of us a hard time. What do I do, call Danny?"

Peter stared at his reflection, ghostlike in the glass, and the huge, busy room beyond. Jack Weiss was showing a bolt of gingham to one of the designers who was shaking her head.

Marie said, "Are you still there?" and Peter turned away from the window. "I'll be right up," he said. "Stick her in the conference room."

He came out of the office, shook his head, and told Jack, "Jesus! Another goddamn mess!" He held up his hands in a time-out gesture and walked toward the fire stairs.

The steel door slammed shut behind him. He took the steps slowly, looking down at them as he climbed and trying to figure out what it was she wanted. It was just curiosity, he told himself, not fear (what did he have to be afraid of?); not even a repeat of the slight uneasiness he had felt hearing her voice on the phone. He had been unprepared for the call and the shock of it had unnerved him briefly. But at least it was cushioning her visit now.

He reached the fifth floor, winded, and went directly to the conference room, waving away Ron Biddle's secretary, who called out to him and held up a sheaf of papers. Joanne Ellis stood waiting for him, facing the open door. He met her look silently for a moment, nodded and said, politely, with even a hint of concern, "Mrs. Ellis . . ." He had thought about leaving the door open—just in case—but seeing her obviated the necessity for the precaution. She was frailer than he remembered, more vulnerable. He closed the door. She was still watching him—scrutinizing him, really—when he faced her again.

"Once more," she said, "I'm inconveniencing you."

Her voice, he could hear, was tight and carefully controlled; she was nervous herself. "Don't worry about it," Peter said. He indicated a seat to her across from him and started to pull out a chair for himself but she remained standing, deliberately, staring at him with a slight, fixed smiled. Peter stood too, behind the chair.

"It's been a long time," Joanne said.

He nodded and forced himself to say, "You're looking good." It was awkward and it was a lie, and he wanted to call it back while he was saying it.

Joanne's expression didn't soften at all. "I stopped on the way over here," she said slowly. "Eighty-fourth Street. You remember Eighty-fourth Street, don't you?"

There it was, right at the beginning. He heard it

without showing any reaction at all. "Yes," he said, and kept looking directly at her.

"Susan's building." She was giving the words time to sink in. "I forced myself to do it."

"Is that why you're here—to talk about Susan?"

"What else do we have in common?"

"Nothing, I suppose." He shook his head and said quietly, "I don't want to talk about her, Mrs. Ellis."

"Why not?"

"Because it's still pretty painful to me—whether you believe that or not."

She let her eyes travel over him—head, shoulders, his hands holding onto the back of the chair—measuring him, it seemed, weighing what he was saying. Finally she said, "You've survived it very nicely, I see."

"How do you know that?" He moved away, averting his face, trying to control the memories she was calling back. It was the emotional threat he couldn't handle right now—she hadn't provided him with a cushion against that. No one had as far as Susan was concerned—not yet.

"I've had some inquiries made since I've been back. The case remains closed. There's been no new evidence—naturally not. No reason, according to the police, to change the original verdict. It's official and it's final, and however it's worded it means that Susan took her own life."

"No, you've got it wrong. Susan fell from the balcony. It was an accident."

Her smile reappeared, slight, contemptuous. "The truth is it was neither."

"You still believe that," he said, and it was something completely beyond him.

"That you killed her. Oh, I know you did."

It wasn't shock he felt on hearing the words, but

impotence. It was useless to argue, to try to talk sense with her—as useless as it had been in the past. Nothing had changed at all. The idea—the insane, totally disproved accusation—still obsessed her. He started to say wearily, "Mrs. Ellis . . ." But she slammed her hand down on the table.

"I *know* the medical report!"

"Then you know she wasn't responsible." He lowered his voice, speaking firmly and trying to force her to hear him. "She didn't know what she was doing."

"The report is a *lie,* every last bit of it! It's a lie!" She leaned forward on the table, coming closer to him. "You had a lot of help there, we both know that."

His impulse was to walk out of the room; get Creegan, Whelan, the detectives who were familiar with the case. Somebody who could be more reasonable with her and objective. *Any*body who could ease her out of this room right now and leave some dignity to Susan's death.

"I loved Susan," he said to her. His voice broke. "I don't owe you that, but I'm telling you. Now how do you think I've lived with that?"

"I don't know," Joanne said.

There was no way she would be accessible to him. Peter went to the door and opened it. The secretary across the hall looked away guiltily. "I've got a meeting," he said to Joanne Ellis. He moved away from the door a little to let her out, but she didn't move.

"You did kill her," she said, calmer now, almost reasonable. "This time I'll manage to prove it."

Peter extended his hand out toward the open door. She started to walk around the table and stopped a few feet away from him, looking at him silently. "For both our sakes," Peter said, "don't put us all through it again."

"Oh, I'll put us through much more this time," she said in that same chillingly calm way. "You watch. I'm going to do anything to get you, anything at all. And I will, you know. So help me I will." She moved into the open doorway and gave him one long final look before she said, almost as an afterthought, "You murdering bastard."

Peter kept a gun, a .32 automatic, in his office; not in his desk but in the breakfront where he also kept liquor and some books and a large collection of beautifully molded toy soldiers. He couldn't remember even looking at the gun since he had put it there several months ago. It was there, though, if he needed it, unloaded now, a full box of ammunition next to it.

Originally, when he'd been living at the duplex on Sixty-third, he had kept the gun there, in his apartment. He had gotten it soon after Susan's death in response to a series of phone calls, most of them vaguely threatening, like the recent one from Joanne Ellis. She had made, although she'd denied it indignantly, a lot of the earlier calls, too. Not all of them; some had been made by a man and some had been silent, with no more than a voiceless presence at the other end of the line. That presence had grown more and more intrusive: someone watching him, showing him, with incidents that were usually minor, how vulnerable he could be. His apartment had been broken into as well—at least once and possibly three times. Nothing had been taken and frustratingly there was nothing that pointed conclusively to Joanne Ellis as far as the police were concerned. Peter had never pushed for an investigation. Joanne was Susan's mother after all, absolutely devastated by her death—not that that should have mattered, given what she was putting him through, but to Peter it did matter. It was something he assumed would pass, and harmlessly, he could only hope.

The whole period lasted about three months—a harassment directed by a woman whose mind had clearly snapped, who might well be homicidal. The calls stopped and the presence ended when Joanne Ellis was committed to a private sanitarium in Connecticut, for treatment of a supposedly minor breakdown.

Peter had never used the gun. There were a few times though, toward the end of the three-month period, when he was made uneasy enough to take it out of the night table and carry it through all the rooms of the apartment. Pointlessly, as it turned out each time. He didn't expect to use it now, either, but he packed it into his attaché case and took it home with him that evening. He put it back into the night table (same one, different apartment) and he planned to keep it there at least for a while. Pointlessly, in all probability, like last time.

Arthur Ellis hadn't intended to get home so late, but there was just no way he could have abbreviated the meeting with that army of accountants. (Good news, it turned out. Joanne would be forgiving even if he wasn't.) He left the BMW outside the garage, and when he didn't see Paul immediately he walked up the path to the house without looking for him.

He found Joanne in Susan's room, facing away

from the dying light outside with her eyes closed and her hands limp on the chair. On the table beside her was a tall glass on a coaster. If there was liquor in the glass, it was probably Scotch. When Joanne did drink, that was what she poured. Arthur hesitated in the doorway. There wasn't much sense in commenting again on her presence in Susan's room. The drink, though, was something else.

Joanne didn't open her eyes until he was directly in front of her; and then serenely, with no surprise at seeing him. He leaned forward and kissed her. "I'm late," he said, "I'm sorry. I've got a good excuse, though."

She closed her eyes again and smiled. Arthur looked at the glass and Joanne saw him and explained, thickly, "It's a very, very light Scotch, just a touch." She lifted the glass closer to him and then lowered it without drinking. "What you're hearing is the Elavil."

"That sounds like a pretty rotten combination, Jo. What do you suppose Knoedler would say?"

She shrugged and said, "Who cares?"

Arthur took the drink out of her hand, sipped it (it was a light one), and put it down out of reach. Joanne didn't offer any protest. It was hard for him to make out just how far gone she was. It was his fault, in any event; he could have sliced an hour off the meeting or—something. Guiltily he held her hand. "Was I right?" he asked.

"About what?"

"Going down to New York."

"New York was fine."

"Okay, then I was wrong." He waited and when she seemed about to doze again he reached into his jacket pocket and pulled out a thin blue velvet jewelry case. "This might match one of your . . . simpler selections today," he said, and pressed the case into her hand.

It took her a moment to understand and give a shake of her head. "There weren't any."

"No? Why not?"

"Nothing I wanted. Lucky you."

"I'm disappointed. What did you do all day?"

"Just wandered . . . touched things." She was rubbing her fingers lightly against the velvet.

"Well, open it anyway." He watched her fumble with the case, then turned the pearl-like clasp toward her. He would see Paul as soon as he could, although he didn't have to be told that something had happened to set her back—something besides the Scotch and the Elavil. And it was his fault for having given in to her so damned easily.

Joanne opened the box. Inside was a diamond pendant, which she looked at with only the slightest interest. Arthur tilted the box to let the stone catch light from a better angle. "It's lovely, Arthur," was all he could draw out of her.

"Allow me." He removed the pendant with its thin platinum chain and fastened it around her neck. He studied it, raising her chin so that their eyes met briefly. "Now, there's one perfect fit," he said with no less enthusiasm.

Joanne brought her hand up to the diamond and let her fingers idly trace its shape. Her eyes were duller.

Arthur held both hands out to her. "Come on, Jo, look at it in the mirror."

"I will," she said wearily, "later."

He waited for her to rise from the chair, but she wasn't moving at all now. He saw her eyes close and then her hands go limp on the chair, just the way he had found her.

CHAPTER FOUR

It had been almost a week since Peter had heard from his sister, Gail, which meant she was still in Washington—barring an unannounced excursion somewhere with Michael. Michael was her husband, Michael McCabe. A year ago he had been reelected, with a whopping sixty-eight percent of the vote this time, to his third and (they both expected) last term as congressman from the Eighteenth District in Manhattan. The McCabes, whose joint ambition was now national, divided their time between a rented house in Georgetown and a UN Plaza co-op in New York. When they were in New York Peter saw Gail regularly and spoke to her every day.

He had come home, tried to reach Maggie, who was somewhere between her office and apartment, showered, and felt a strong urge to speak to Gail. What he really wanted to do was jump on the shuttle and see her in Washington. The phone call seemed the more sensible idea though, given the McCabes' relentless social schedule. He dialed and got no answer; then tried the New York apartment on impulse and reached Louise, the maid, who told him that Mrs. McCabe was indeed in New York and was expected home just about then. Mr. McCabe was still in Washington.

"Tell her I'm on my way," Peter said, without asking anything about Gail's plans. The idea of seeing Gail, even if it was on the run, elated him and gave him a sense of relief. Hers was just the voice of reason he needed right now. He dressed, tried again without success to reach Maggie, and left his apartment.

It was a humid June evening and the streets were clogged with traffic in all directions. Peter decided to walk the seven or eight blocks. It would be faster and he could use the distraction. Like Gail and unlike everybody else, he loved the city in summer—the whole bare look of it, the warm smells. He didn't know whether Maggie felt the same way; she might prefer getting out of town, in which case there was always his house in East Hampton. His and Gail's. They would have to talk about schedules tonight; possibly drive out for the first time this weekend.

He reached the apartment before Gail. Louise let him in and complained about the New York weather and the Washington weather, which was even worse. Mrs. McCabe was due out again at eight, she told him, and the idea of it seemed to exhaust Louise. It was a dinner, a benefit. She didn't know for what exactly or where, but details would be on the desk calendar in the study. Ice was there as well, and the makings of Mrs. McCabe's martini on the cart, if that would do for him.

"That'll be just fine," he said.

The study was large and bright, with walnut paneling on three sides, most of it hidden behind bookcases and photographs. The pictures were of Michael mostly, or Michael and Gail—they made a striking couple—with an occasional photo featuring Gail. Invariably a familiar face was smiling beside the McCabes'—a politician's usually, Democrat of course, or someone in show business. All of the pictures were warmly inscribed. Peter didn't look at any of them. He used the Stolichnaya to mix a knockout martini which he carried to the wall of windows overlooking the United Nations gardens. The gardens were a rich green outlined with red and yellow border plantings. Traffic moved silently beside them. To the left light glittered on the East River.

It was six-thirty, and just as he remembered to phone Maggie he heard Gail's voice calling out to Louise, and then shouting with delight in the direction of the study, "*When? Where?*"

"In here," Peter yelled back.

She rushed into the study, a tall, strikingly beautiful blonde woman, four years older than Peter. She was wearing a bright silk dress, very full and flowing, her sleeves billowing as she opened her arms wide to embrace him. She made a sound, a long pleasurable "Mmmmmm" that she sustained all the way across the room. She fell into his arms and squeezed, saying, "Telepathy!"

He rocked her slightly from side to side, holding his drink steady, then drew away and looked disapproving. "What is this anyway, some kind of state secret?" Gail looked puzzled. "Why didn't you tell me you were back, for Chrissake?"

"I was about to do just that," Gail said. "I haven't had a minute since I got in this morning, honest." She lowered her face to the glass he was holding, breathed in the fragrance, and sighed. "Order me one of those, will you? I am beat." She kicked off her shoes and fell onto the couch. Peter went to the drinks cart and fixed her a martini a little shorter than his. She was smiling and watching him as though they had been separated a long time, which they hadn't—less than two weeks.

He dropped an olive into her glass and asked, "What've you been doing, politicking?"

The question seemed to enervate her. She yawned, distorting the word "Some," paused to compose herself, and said, "Sorry. Second wind's on the way." She shook her head and brightened. "I had to stand in for Michael."

"Why, where's he?"

"Washington still. Lots of unfinished business—half of it monkey, I'm sure. He'll be here tomorrow. *Ah,* you're an angel, thank you." He handed her the drink and sat beside her with his arm on the back of the couch, his fingers touching her shoulder. She tapped his glass with hers, took a sip, and drew one leg up under her, to face him. "A Party lunch that went on forever," she said with a shudder. "Tedious. Except for Stan Sutter. The last of the old-time bosses. I'm nuts about him. He's got this terrific idea. Why don't I run for Michael's seat next year while he runs for dot-dot-dot? We do it as an *au pair* campaign. A great gimmick, Stan says, and who should know better?"

Peter was laughing. "I agree."

"That's three of us at least. Cheap, too, when you think of all that doubling up. I'd make a great congressperson, don't you think?" She tried several thoughtful poses for him.

"You'd make a great anything."

"I know, but I want to start modestly. Hell, I know as much as most of them, and that's being very, very charitable. I photograph better, too. Which is at least three quarters of it, given the priorities of the media." The last phrase was delivered in her podium voice.

Peter shook his head and said, "Jesus, you're getting cynical."

"Practice. For the day when I become elder statesperson. The next Alice Longworth." She looked sweetly malevolent and repositioned herself on the couch, sinking in a little deeper. "Mmm, I'm unwinding already," she said. Peter held up his drink and rattled it at her as a warning. She took another sip, and pressed her bare foot against his thigh, nudging him and saying reproachfully, "I've missed you, terribly."

"I've missed you, too," Peter said.

"Well, summer's here. Playtime. We'll be seeing more of each other, won't we?"

"I don't know."

"Why's that?"

"I've got this magic kingdom to run, remember? Especially if you're going to need a fat cat of a brother, too."

They might have been joking about Gail's political aspirations (and then again maybe not), but the major backing for all Michael's campaigns had indeed come from Peter and Playcraft. The Playcraft connection, as a matter of fact, initially soft-pedaled, had turned out to be extremely beneficial—as though a vote for Michael McCabe was a vote for magic and innocence. Fortunately Michael's good looks and unmistakable sexiness kept the image from moving any closer to Peter Pan. It was a perfect union, flesh and fantasy, and it had worked every time, triumphantly.

As for Gail and Playcraft, there was very little family sentiment involved in her attitude toward the company. Playcraft paid, that was what it came down to. Playcraft had always paid, and handsomely. Michael's earnings as a lawyer and congressman certainly hadn't.

Gail was a major stockholder in the company, like Peter and three or four other relatives. She was a functioning director of the company and her advice, whenever Peter consulted her, was invariably sound (it was Gail who had encouraged Playcraft's unique line of teaching-toys for handicapped children). But Playcraft was ultimately Peter, not Gail; and if she and Michael were dependent on Playcraft they were really dependent on Peter. Which made Gail very comfortable. There was no one she would rather depend on than her brother, and the feeling, she knew, was mutual.

A clock in the room chimed seven o'clock. Gail waited for the sound to stop, and then her face brightened. "Hey—there's this benefit tonight I'd give anything to miss. I mean, I've put in my time today. Why don't I work up a migraine, and just you and I—a quiet dinner here?"

Peter looked pained and said, "I can't."

"Why not?"

"Booked."

"Irrevocably?"

"I think so." He started to get up. "Reminds me—I've got to make a call."

Gail reached out and held on to him. "Pete." She was pouting. "See her when I'm not free. We've got a couple of weeks at least to catch up on." She saw something vaguely unpleasant come into his face. He was standing motionless, thinking. "All right," Gail said, "you obviously didn't stop by for a quick drink. What's wrong?"

He looked down at her, gave her hand a reassuring squeeze, and said, "Nothing I can't handle." He moved toward the phone on the desk.

Gail called, "Pete?" She lowered her feet to the floor and repeated, more insistently, "What's wrong? Come on now." It was the voice of big sister, delivered with mock severity.

Peter kept his back to her. He was facing the windows and the buildings to the south, below the UN slab. "Joanne Ellis came to see me today," he said.

Gail's back stiffened. *"Joanne Ellis?"* She saw Peter nod. "I thought she'd been put away."

"Well, she's out."

"And?" Gail said, disturbed.

Peter moved away from the desk, toward the cart. "Nothing's changed."

"What do you mean? What did she say?"

"The same crazy stuff."

"The same threats, in other words."

He was fixing himself another martini. "None of that bothers me."

"No? Well, it bothers me. I must have a better memory than you."

He started to pace, remembered the drink in his hand, and said, "Sorry, did you want one of these?"

"I want to know what she said."

He had misjudged Gail; he had thought her reaction would be cooler, more reasoned. He hadn't intended to alarm her like this, or let her magnify his own uneasiness—he wasn't sure which was more accurate.

"She still thinks I did it," he said, sounding more concerned for Joanne Ellis than for himself. "Still thinks you and Mike buried the case."

"Then her release was a little premature," Gail said angrily. "Did you call the police?"

"Why would I do that?"

"Why? The woman's certifiable, for God's sake! She was that before they put her away; she still is, obviously." Gail got up from the couch and headed for the phone. "Who knows what someone like that's capable of? I'm not taking any chances."

Peter watched her pick up the receiver. "What're you doing?"

"Calling Michael."

"What the hell for?" She had started to dial; he brought his hand down on the cradle and broke the call. "Gail, look—I said I can handle this." It was an order, firm enough to make her release the receiver and let him hang up. Then he smiled, apologetically. Gail relaxed slightly; she shook her head and made him see how much she distrusted his instinct. Peter's hand moved up her arm and caressed her shoulder. "I didn't mean to get you all worked up," he said.

"Well, nice try." She moved away from him, found her glass, and silently carried it to the cart, shooting him a look as she dropped ice into her drink.

It was a look baleful enough to be comic, and Peter seized on it, lighting up with sudden inspiration. *"Fat Cat,"* he announced. The remark seemed to throw Gail completely. "It just hit me. We do this big fat mother of a cat—orange and black stripes, big smile with lots of teeth." He smiled widely and bent into her line of vision. "We do him as a bank. Playcraft hasn't done a bank in—hell, we've never done a bank, not that I can remember. Anyway, we give him this crazy tail." He reached for an imaginary lever and pulled it toward him, making a vivid rattling sound-effect that he repeated until Gail smiled and then finally laughed out loud. It was something he could always do—make her laugh. Always.

The laughter was a brief release for both of them and while it didn't remove the threat of Joanne Ellis, it managed to ease it somewhat. They were able to discuss it coolly and reasonably, as Peter had wanted in the first place. They would notify no one unless Mrs. Ellis reappeared—in the flesh, by phone, or through the mail (there had been a few letters in the past, typed and unsigned, coherent only in the threats they contained); or unless someone she may have hired appeared (there had been that, too, in the past—the presence that had never materialized). Whichever way it happened, they would immediately call not Michael but Lieutenants Creegan and Willets, who had been assigned to Susan's case originally; or Lieutenant Whelan, who had handled the harassment business when, Gail reminded him, Peter had finally had sense enough to bring it to the police. She remembered living through that nightmare too, vividly.

"Promise me," she said.

"What?"

"You won't let it go this time. If anything happens you'll tell me, as soon as it happens."

"I'm telling you now, aren't I?"

"I don't always trust you," Gail said. She was back on the couch, her feet buried under a cushion. Peter was in the green leather wingchair opposite her, looking at the fading light outside. Both of them were feeling the martinis now. There was a long, comfortable silence, and then Gail said, gently, "You're not doing anything to Susan, Pete, or her memory. You're protecting yourself, that's all."

He nodded and she could see him turn inward—

just briefly, because Louise appeared in the doorway, and at the same time the clock chimed eight.

"That's exactly what I was going to tell you," Louise said.

Gail looked at the clock and exclaimed, "My God, already?"

Peter remembered: "Maggie!" He started to rise but Gail waved him down again. The decision had been made for both of them, she insisted. She would call her commitment, Doris Randall at the Waldorf, and plead some migrainelike excuse, and Peter would do the same with his commitment, what's-her-name. Meanwhile Louise would do something simple but miraculous in the kitchen. Agreed? She didn't wait for Peter to answer. She sent Louise out with a decisive nod and followed her, saying to Peter, "Use Michael's phone. I'll make my call from the bedroom."

"Jesus," Peter called after her. He drained his glass and sat listening to her voice, barely audible in the bedroom. She had rearranged his evening, but he was relaxed and completely at home, as he always was with Gail when there were just the two of them. It didn't happen that often and he really didn't want to break the mood, not even for Maggie.

He went to the phone and dialed her number, feeling the buzz of the martinis even more when he stood up. Maggie picked up on the first ring. "Where are you?" she said, sounding worried.

"At my sister's apartment." There was a slight stumble over the words. He cleared his throat and stood up straighter. "I tried to get you a few times, starting at five."

"I had some shopping to do. Are you on your way?"

"I was, about an hour ago."

"And what happened?"

"Nothing. Gail and I started talking. We're still at it. Family business."

"Does that mean we don't have a date anymore?" She put quotes around the word, date; still, her disappointment came through.

"Would that mess up your evening?"

"It'll mess up yours," she said.

"Agreed."

"I was going to cook for you is what I mean." He could see the look on her face right now—tolerant amusement, good-natured and unflappable. He thought about pulling himself together and riding down to Tenth Street after all, but whispery movement behind him distracted him. Gail had come back into the room, a blue terrycloth robe wrapped around her. She was carrying a bottle of wine and an opener, which she placed on the cart, wincing at the small sound they made. She turned her back to Peter and started to open the bottle.

Peter lowered his voice. "Any chance of a raincheck on that?" he said into the phone.

There was a pause and then Maggie said brightly, "I don't mind late suppers at all. Ten, eleven, it doesn't matter."

Peter faced the wall and the pictures of Michael with the mayor, the governor, and with a group of congressmen standing behind the President. "This would probably be even later than that," he said.

"I wouldn't mind that, either." There was an awkward pause and then he heard Maggie sigh. "I guess it'll just have to keep then, all that incredible work." He was grateful she wasn't carrying it any further. "To be honest—not that I've got to be—I haven't even started. It's all last minute, whatever it turns out to be."

There was a light pop. Peter turned at the sound and saw Gail twisting the cork off the corkscrew, then sniffing it. "Tomorrow night?" he said to Maggie.

"You mean maybe or definitely?"

"Absolutely."

"Tomorrow night, then." She lowered her voice to match his, as though someone had come into her room as well. "Pete?" She hesitated. "I was really looking forward to tonight. I'm just realizing how much."

"Ditto," Peter said.

Maggie caught on and said, "It's hard for you to talk. I won't put you on the spot."

Peter said, "Good."

Gail was moving away, toward the door. She caught Peter's eye and tugged at her robe, mouthing, "Change," and holding up five fingers. She left the room.

On the phone Maggie whispered, "I miss you, a lot."

"I'll make it up to you, okay?" He kept his voice at the same quiet level.

There was a long serious silence before Maggie said, "Try, anyway." Peter didn't laugh, didn't react at all, so she added, "That's a joke."

"I'm glad you told me."

Again there was a silence, each of them enjoying the presence at the other end. "I'll let you get back to Gail," Maggie said, and before Peter could protest he heard a quick moist kiss and then a click as she hung up.

His plans had changed. That was simple enough.

An evening with Gail, his *sister* (the italics were Maggie's), made perfect sense when they hadn't seen each other in weeks. More sense than another evening with her, it appeared.

Strike that last; as soon as it came to her she realized what a dumb thought it was, how self-pitying. In a few minutes, she told herself, she would be a lot more objective about it. Right now she wasn't. She was disappointed, she was lonely, and feeling mightily rejected; and more than anything she was annoyed that she was elaborating that feeling into something completely unreasonable.

She could have been more insistent, of course. Aggressive even. And then really written Peter out of her life.

She was in the hall, which was tiny like the rest of her apartment, looking across the living room to the terrace. She had set the table for Peter and herself outside where there were potted geraniums and a great view of the Empire State Building to the north. She went into the kitchen, passing a floor-length pegboard hung with pots and implements. On top of the stove was a foil-wrapped pan of lasagna like no other he had ever tasted, ready for the oven. A salad with the first real tomatoes she had seen in a long time was on the kitchen table, along with an uncorked bottle of red wine and a small loaf of bread. It would all keep, except for the salad. That was obviously going to be her dinner for the night.

A shame, though, to waste all the preparations for what was to have been a magic evening. Why not an evening anyway, without the magic? Which brought Frank Powell to mind. He would make her laugh at least or he would make her angry enough to yell, and she felt like yelling at somebody. Who better than good old, armadillo-skinned Frank? She went to the phone. It was all last-minute and she would tell him he was a name from the bottom of the B list, subbing for Peter who—what? How to explain to Frank Powell of all people that she had been stood up by Peter Drexler for his sister?

Her original thought had been better: it would all keep.

She turned off the oven, marshaling for herself all the lessons of the evening. So much for surprises, to begin with. And for persuming that Peter would accommodate any plans she chose to make. So much, in other words, for getting too proprietary too fast, against her original time-tested instincts. And for continuing to agonize over something so simple, reasonable, and unimportant.

She turned the stereo on, humming along, maneuvered the lasagna into the refrigerator, and carried her salad out to the table on the terrace. Lighted the candle even. The setting was lovely, the view, the breeze, the soft sounds coming up from Tenth Street. She poured from a jug of cheap red wine. Peter wasn't there—she came to terms with that. She wished though he had left her with something more romantic than "Ditto" to carry her through the long evening.

"All clear?"

It was Gail, her blonde head anyway, peering into the study. She found Peter on his knees beside the coffee table, spreading on a cracker the paté Louise had brought in. He held the cracker out to her, then ate it when she shook her head and patted her stomach with a horrified expression. She moved into the doorway, posing dramatically and turning for him.

She had changed from the terrycloth robe into a lounging outfit, a floor-length, rose-colored gown. Peter widened his eyes and said, "O-kay!"

Gail swept past him, holding the gown wide and brushing its feathery material against him. She let herself flutter down to the couch. "Steak, salad, and maybe some chocolate Haagen-Dazs—okay on that, too?"

"Better than okay." He had switched to wine; he offered the glass to her. Gail shook her head and listened to the music in the background—a melody she recognized, Chopin. She watched Peter until the melody dissolved. "Mmmm," she said, stretching, "bliss."

"What is?"

"This." She gestured lazily at her body. "Complete collapse."

Peter slid back on the floor until he felt the base of the wingchair behind him. He crossed his legs. "How'd your migraine go over?"

"There were waves of genuine sympathy. How about yours?"

He nodded vaguely and listened to another étude, looking off somewhere beyond Gail until she said, "Maggie"—she paused at the name, trying it silently—"is she someone I should meet?"

"You will, I think; eventually." Gail watched him smile. "She's a terrific girl."

"Ah, another one of those."

"A really terrific girl."

"Why wait, in that case? I'm giving a dinner Thursday—positively last appearance of the season. You're invited and so's the really terrific girl."

"We'll talk about it," Peter said.

"Michael will be back, there'll be lots of other glamorous types. She'll be dazzled."

"I don't think Maggie is"—he stopped himself, realizing before he said it that the word would be a struggle—"dazzleable." He looked pleased with himself and took another sip of wine.

"Give me a chance anyway," Gail persisted. "I assume this isn't too serious—not terminal or anything—or I'd have heard."

"Could be you are hearing."

"Ah, then it's serious."

"I don't know what it is at this point."

"I will," Gail assured him. They both smiled and Gail leaned as far toward him as she could without rolling off the couch. She reached for his hand and squeezed it, letting her smile grow even warmer. "I'm glad you're seeing someone again," she said. "Really." For a long time after Susan's death he hadn't, no one at all, and the problem, Gail knew (and in pretty intimate detail), had become physical as well as emotional.

"So am I," Peter said. "Christ, so am I."

She wanted to carry it further and ask him more about Maggie, but the questions, she realized, would be all the wrong ones—the only ones in fact that really interested Gail. Was Maggie anything like Susan Ellis, for example? Anywhere near—and forgive me, darling, please—anywhere near as destructive, to him and ultimately to herself? They weren't questions at all, in other words; fears, admonishments, none of which, she supposed, Peter needed after that first experience. Something like Susan had happened only once to him, thank God. The intensity of the experience sometimes made Gail forget that. As far as she was concerned, his relationship with Susan had been the one really major mistake in her brother's life. Not Grace and that dumb marriage of several years ago.

That had been a minor blunder, a lark, harmless and easily forgotten. But Susan had been traumatic, something dark and awful that he had managed to pull through, with Gail's help—and no, she told herself, she was not being melodramatic or overly protective. Just honest. And frightened to death of it ever happening again.

The memory of it made Gail shudder; and think again of Joanne Ellis, whom she had forgotten in the music and the nice haze of the martinis. She was back in his life. Correction—back in their life. Gail turned on the lamp beside the couch and caught that look in Peter—nervous, distracted—that she hadn't seen in a long time.

"I'll have Louise make up your room," she said. The guest room, to her, was always Peter's room.

Peter squinted at the light. "What for?"

"I want you to spend the night here, that's what for."

"I live ten blocks away, for Chrissake."

"I know where you live, darling."

He played with his glass. "Is it because of Joanne Ellis?"

"It's because of me," she said, and made a face at him. "I want company."

Peter shook his head. "I knew it, I shouldn't have told you anything."

"Why?"

"You're panicking."

"I am not panicking, not at all!" Her eyes widened suddenly and she gave him the most inane smile she could. "One big blank, see?" Peter didn't find it funny. Gail let herself down to the floor and crept closer to him. "I just want you with me awhile," she explained patiently. "Is that such an odd request? A little time with my own brother?"

She waited until she had forced a surrendering smile out of him. "No," he said.

"Good." She moved closer and eased herself down beside him. "I'll take a little of that wine now."

Later, when Louise came in to announce dinner, she found them lying on the floor together. Mrs. McCabe was laughing—giggling really, like a small girl. She had that relaxed and happy look she always seemed to have with Mr. Drexler. Only with Mr. Drexler. Too bad the congressman wasn't with them right now. He could do with a little loosening up himself, in Louise's opinion.

CHAPTER FIVE

A little before eight the next morning there was a fire at the Playcraft factory. It was discovered early enough by one of the custodians to keep it confined to the storeroom outside the design area, where it had begun. There were no injuries and a lot less damage than there would have been a few minutes later, considering the paints and chemicals in the storeroom.

The fire was already out when Peter arrived at the building just as his apartment was being called for the second time by the police. He said "*Goddamn*!"—angry at himself and guilty about the phone call he hadn't been home to answer, not that it would have made a difference. He explored the damage with a fire lieutenant and a policeman; and again later with two police detectives called in at his insistence, and an insurance investigator. Was there even the slightest possibility of arson, he wanted to know, and so urgently that the detective asked Peter the reason for his conviction.

"Not conviction," Peter said, "suspicion. A hunch, that's all."

It sounded lame to Peter himself, and suspect, as though he were holding back something important.

He thought about coming right out and naming Joanne Ellis, but he wouldn't, not without some hard evidence. Instead he explained to them the elaborate security of the design area; how vulnerable models and blueprints were, how larcenous the toy business could be. Ideas were lifted all the time, projects knocked out by the competition.

"Are you talking about some kind of sabotage?" a detective asked with an amused expression.

Peter said, "It happens all the time." No, there were no names he would give them. "Just look for anything at all suspicious."

They did, with Peter joining in, until well into the afternoon. As for incriminating evidence, there was none at that point. Just the opposite. Some of the chemicals in the storeroom were volatile, given the slightest carelessness—a bottle that might have been left unstoppered, for example. No one suspicious had been seen entering or leaving the building—not by Lenny the security guard or Pat Loughlin, the night watchman. The storeroom, which was always locked, was still locked when Julio discovered the fire.

It went on like that, with the evidence against arson becoming more convincing to the police. And totally unconvincing to Peter. Rationally or not, he knew the fire had been engineered somehow by Joanne Ellis. It was too coincidental otherwise. Too much like one of her phone calls or that presence Peter was made aware of every so often—preliminary chords, all of them, just sinister and threatening enough for the moment.

When the investigators left the building, he went back to his office. The charred smell was all over the place. He closed the door and turned the air conditioner higher. His desk was piled with papers and a boxed prototype of a child's pull toy, a bright and benevolent caterpillar that managed to make him smile. He sat and turned away from it, facing the ugly bulk of Libbey Containers across the street. He rocked in the chair, a slight, quick motion, like a pulse.

He would call Joanne Ellis. Now.

It was the only sensible thing to do. Confront her immediately and this time let threats come from him. She would deny her involvement—he was going to say *of course,* but he wasn't at all sure of that. He wouldn't be surprised in fact to hear her admit to it. The whole point of her strategy was the threat, after all; knowing the source of the threat, actually seeing it smile at him. There had to be enormous satisfaction for her in that.

He shook the image, the sinister smile, out of his head and turned back to his desk. He grabbed one of the papers, the draft of a personnel memo Cal Hooper had sent in for his approval, read it through, and couldn't remember a word of it.

What if the fire actually had been accidental? That seemed to be everybody's tentative conclusion. Why couldn't he accept it, even as a dim possibility? Why? Because Joanne Ellis, god damn her, had already affected his mind to the point where he was reading threat everywhere. No, that was an exaggeration. She *could* affect him if he let her, if he didn't get his mind off her and the past and back to something positive. He picked up the memo again and at the same time the phone on his desk buzzed. He reached for it and heard Marie announce, too sweetly, Miss Newman on the line.

There was relief just in hearing her voice. He told her so and she said, "Why didn't you get back to me, then? I called you a couple of times today. Including your apartment."

"I wasn't home."

"Early this morning?"

"I stayed at my sister's."

"Oh."

He found her phone messages on his desk, apologized, and told her about the fire. "No real damage. Just something to waste a lot of my time."

"Let me waste a few minutes more," Maggie said. "The flowers were lovely. Thank you." He had sent roses to her apartment that morning and more roses to her office. "One would have said it all. What are you trying to do, overwhelm me?"

"Any way I can."

"I'm not knocking roses, understand, but I'd rather have you. Are you standing me up again tonight?"

"Not a chance," Peter said.

"Do we try for eight again?"

He was there at eight precisely, bearing a bag of fruit, raspberries included, from Balducci's. "I even found a parking space, right outside the building," he said triumphantly. He followed her the two steps into the cluttered kitchen, where she adjusted dials and timers and picked at the raspberries. When she tried to squeeze past him he held her, drew her closer, and kissed her, with the time ticking away beside them. She pulled away from him, and they were both warm and a little winded.

"It's the oven," Maggie said and fanned herself with one hand.

She had set up on the terrace again and the setting worked beautifully and so did the dinner, leftovers or not. He mentioned the fire at Playcraft just once and then forgot about it. Forgot about Joanne Ellis too and whatever else had been so troubling just awhile ago. It was a gift Maggie had, an ability to drive whatever was unpleasant out of his mind, without effort, by the mere force of her personality. One other person could do that for him—his sister, Gail.

For dessert they had whatever was left of the raspberries and then Peter moved to the chaise for coffee. He patted the few inches of space beside him, urging her over. Maggie blew out the candles and let Peter pull her down silently. The terrace wall rose above them, and above that there was a misty glow in the sky from the lights of the city. Peter lifted her on top of him and caressed her, all the more urgently when she started to protest, *"Here?"*

"Why not here?"

"We're outside."

"What's the difference?"

She became silent and felt the warm night air moving like a caress too, all over her body. They made love; made sounds, too, that she became self-conscious about when they had finished.

"The neighbors heard it all," she said.

Peter said, "Lucky neighbors."

She poured brandy for them, crouching as she moved naked around the terrace. She squeezed in beside him again, her face against his chest. He had solved one problem for her, she told him lazily.

"Which one is that?"

"My bedroom. It's tiny. I didn't know how we'd maneuver."

His hand was playing with her hair. "Give me awhile and I'll show you."

Thursday night she opened her door to him,

stepped back, and did a graceful pirouette. The dress she was wearing was her most elegant, a cool-looking jade color, cut low. It flared when she turned, filling the small open space in her living room.

"A knockout," Peter said.

"What, these old weeds?"

He refused the drink she offered him, and it might have been her own nervousness at meeting the McCabes that she was projecting onto Peter, but he seemed anxious to her, distracted and subdued, saying little in the cab uptown. She mentioned this to him.

"Business," he explained apologetically. He reached for her hand and squeezed it. "Nothing important."

In the McCabes' building, Maggie stopped in front of an elaborately framed mirror beyond the elevator to look at herself. She saw Peter, too, and no doubt about it, they made a smashing couple. It was just the boost her confidence needed. She lingered long enough for Peter to take her by the arm.

"Relax, will you?" he said to her in the mirror, and something light and affectionate was coming into his eyes. "They're just folks, after all."

A maid, Louise, opened the door and Maggie could see, from an entrance hall the size of her apartment, the most recognizable of the folks, the mayor, among a small group just inside the living room. Peter introduced Maggie, let her hear a minute of political banter, and then led her deeper into the room, holding onto her protectively. A piano was being played lightly in the background. There were several political and some show-business faces Maggie recognized, and most of them lit up when they saw Peter. One and maybe two of the women he introduced her to greeted him with something more than warmth, she thought—particularly a ballet dancer whose husband was also in the room, with the mayor.

Even with his back to them, she recognized at the far end of the room the tall figure of Michael McCabe; and Gail McCabe, who had been trying to break away from a conversation ever since she'd seen Peter and Maggie come into the room. She started toward them, lovelier than any of the photos Maggie had seen.

"I was beginning to worry about you," she said to Peter. She kissed him and put her arm through his, turning to include Maggie as well. "Then I thought, no, he wouldn't do that to me." She smiled and her eyes moved over Maggie's face, memorizing it. Habit, probably; Gail had married into politics, Maggie reminded herself.

Peter introduced them and the look became less penetrating, was softened by a smile extraordinarily like Peter's. "I'm glad to meet you finally," Gail said.

They had discussed her, Maggie knew, seriously enough for Gail to have engineered this meeting. She and her brother were obviously very close, very dependent on each other's judgment. Peter stood by silently and listened to the light chatter about himself. He put his arms around both of them, connecting them, and smiled encouragement.

Maggie seemed completely at ease now. Just as Peter had predicted to Gail, she was not at all dazzled—not by Gail, the company, or Michael when he joined them and treated Maggie to a full measure of the "McCabe charm"—it was Peter who used those words, in humorously warning Maggie against him.

"There is no McCabe charm," Michael assured her. "Another media catchphrase, that's all it is." His arm went around Gail. "Unless you're referring to this McCabe, the real vote getter."

"I just smile a lot," Gail said innocently. One hand touched her hair. "And make sure my hair doesn't blow in the wind." She laughed and passed their drink order onto a maid.

They were perfectly matched, Gail and Michael; to Maggie, the quintessential Manhattan couple. There was taste in evidence, intelligence, wit—and to provide the real magic, a sense of power under it all. Growing power, if Michael's career so far was any indication. Both of them made her feel comfortable, Michael especially. He was flattering and attentive, introducing her around the room while Gail and her brother disappeared briefly; making her feel every bit as important and interesting as the mayor. Peter laughed when she told him, and Maggie, coloring, said, "Okay, it sounds just as ingenuous to me."

"It's your choice of company," Peter said, pulling her against him. He lowered his voice to a whisper. "The mayor's a clod and a hack. Michael's even said it in print. They hate each other's what I'm saying."

She looked past him and saw them laughing together beside the bar, Michael with his arm around the mayor.

The table in the large, candlelit dining room was set for sixteen. "An intimate gathering," Peter whispered to Maggie. They were seated together, with a network news executive next to Maggie and a Swedish UN diplomat and his wife opposite.

"Stockholm's beautiful," Maggie said, feeling Peter's leg rubbing against hers. "I was there two years ago." She tried to move out of reach and touched the news executive with her knee. He glanced at her and she said, "Sorry."

"My pleasure," he said, letting the look linger.

Maggie kicked lightly at Peter, who kept talking to the mayor's wife without missing a beat. The diplomat and his wife resumed the conversation, telling Maggie how much they loved New York, particularly its squalor—at least that's the way it came across the table to her. The pressure against her leg eased as Peter got more involved in conversation. Maggie heard him telling the mayor's wife about a line of toys for handicapped children, which would go into production early next year.

The voices to her right distracted her. The newsman and a politician Maggie had met and disliked—he was on the city council—were discussing the media. She heard the politician saying, "You guys, you're all nothing but big-game hunters. All out for a few pelts. I'm a pelt, he's one, he's one. . . ." He was pointing around the table, amusing the dark-haired woman between them. Maggie followed his hand and was startled to find her eyes meeting Gail McCabe's at the foot of the table. Gail was staring at her—directly, nakedly, with that same penetrating look that had unnerved Maggie before. So intently that it was a few seconds before she was conscious of Maggie returned the look. Her head jerked slightly, as though she had been snapped out of a trance, and she covered with a smile in Maggie's direction. Maggie smiled back uncertainly. Gail widened her eyes and mimed, with a nod and a delicate movement of her hand, "Everything all right?" Maggie raised her glass in reply and at the same time felt Peter turning to face her, draping his arm over the back of her chair. He looked beyond her, at Gail, and asked, "What're those signals between you two?"

"A private joke," Maggie said. Gail had looked away from them, to the entree being served to the woman on her left.

"She's crazy about you," Peter confided. His face was close to hers, his voice soft and intimate.

"Gail?" The news seemed to surprise her. "How do you know?"

"She told me. So did Michael. It's pretty unanimous, I'd say." He played with her hand on the table until, self-conscious, she moved it to her lap. The entree, a sole in white wine, had reached the city councilman, shutting him up briefly.

"It's a little early for anybody to be crazy about me," Maggie said. "I haven't even done anything *like*able."

"You're just not aware of it, it's so natural to you. Besides, you'd know it by now if Gail didn't like you."

"Is it important that she should?" Maggie asked him. She made it sound innocent and teasing.

"Moderately," he said. "I've got great respect for Gail's taste. What's more important is that you met her. Michael, too, of course. Painless, wasn't it?"

Maggie weighed the question with a small side-to-side tilt of her head. "A little intimidating, that's all."

"Why's that?"

She thought a moment, looking in the direction of Michael. "There's got to be somebody in the family who's just a little less than gorgeous."

"Not allowed," Peter said. He found her hand again, squeezed it, and brought it up to his lips, holding it there while he said very softly, "My place or yours later?"

She felt an excitement, a physical reaction to his question that had to be evident in her face; a response to his closeness and to his look and the sound that had come into his voice. She would have loved it anywhere but here where it was making her distinctly uncomfortable. And the discomfort had nothing to do with Gail either, she told herself, or at any rate not Gail exclusively—though she was relieved to see her looking away and talking to the stage director on her right.

Maggie slipped her hand out of Peter's again. "Let's play it all by ear," she said, and waited for the maid to approach her with the elaborate silver tray. Another, slower maid was moving down the opposite side of the table.

"I don't suppose you want to commit to a weekend either," Peter said.

"Weekend?"

"East Hampton. Combination work and play. You can bring those sketches out." The house had been in his family for several years, he told her, and it was very special, right on the beach.

"Just the two of us?" she asked.

"Well, who else?"

"I don't know, you said family."

"Family means Gail and me at this point."

"Gail, then," Maggie suggested.

Peter grinned. "Not for what I've got in mind," he said.

Even when he was playing sexy he was sexy.

A little later, still at the table, it happened again—Gail watching her furtively, looking away this time with no explanatory smile or gesture. She had been scrutinizing her, or maybe it was Maggie and Peter together she was scrutinizing, trying to gauge the relationship. She wanted to mention it to Peter and ask why Gail was watching her—what was she doing wrong? But it smacked so much of insecurity and sounded so comically paranoid that she said nothing at all—long enough for Peter to ask, "Bored?"

"Not at all."

"We can leave anytime you say."

"Why? What can you think of better than this?" She brought a finger up to his mouth to quiet him and lowered it when he started nibbling. She was honestly enjoying herself, enjoying the atmosphere and the company. Her own group of friends was young for the most part and "on the verge." There were no politicians among them, no one prominent in the arts, no one as high-powered as the TV executive next to her, or Peter for that matter. Certainly no one with the style and the class of a Gail McCabe.

It was a lot more pleasant to think of Gail in those terms. She did it almost grudgingly, though, and that was revealing. What she had done, even before meeting Gail, was to put herself in competition with her. Over Peter, of course. And the looks from Gail that had unnerved her were probably nothing more than curiosity, interest. Her own furtive looks (*now*, for instance; she caught herself in the act) might be just as unnerving to Gail, and equally misinterpreted.

A tap on a glass called her back. Michael was rising to speak. He always rose after coffee, he said to his guests; automatically, a reflex action. He went around the table with a series of one-liners, mainly political putdowns that were spontaneous and usually hilariously on target. He ended by lifting his glass in a toast to the company, and especially the hostess.

Gail smiled and bowed her head. "I think," she

said, "you all just heard the Congressman's kickoff speech."

The young man who had been playing the piano during cocktails materialized again after dinner and drew a group around him in the living room. With the first note Peter was ready to leave but Maggie said, "We can't."

"Sure we can." He held out his hand to her.

"Can what?" It was Michael who grabbed hold of Peter's hand.

"You wouldn't miss us if we crept off, would you, Mike?" Peter asked.

Maggie smiled and said, "I won't apologize. He's your brother-in-law." She excused herself and had a maid point her to the nearest bathroom.

When she came out she almost collided with Nina-somebody, the dancer who had greeted Peter so warmly. They smiled at each other and while letting her pass Maggie noticed the pictures on the wall. They were old prints, some of them early nineteenth century, of the Hudson Valley, New York City. There were caricatures too, by Nast and Charles, farther down the hall, flanking the door to a warmly lit study which Maggie looked into. She heard Michael's voice behind her, coming closer.

"Ah, you found my etchings. I was going to suggest you have a look." He was carrying two liqueur glasses. He handed one to Maggie, who tried to refuse. "Go on. I managed to involve Peter in the sing-along."

"Are you kidding?" She took the glass and tried to see beyond Michael, who was urging her into the study.

"There's a lot more in there," he said.

She walked over to a full wall of photographs and

read several of the inscriptions while he watched her. "Some of these faces are vaguely familiar," she said, bending forward.

Michael shrugged and looked perplexed. "I don't know any of them myself. It's all trick photography." He moved closer to her and sat on the arm of a wingchair, letting her study the pictures quietly. He was trying to see her face, intently enough for her to notice. The piano in the living room had launched into a medley of current show tunes. Maggie tried to concentrate on the photos, an impressive mix of Michael and politicians, local and national, past and present. She tilted her head to follow the angle of the inscriptions. Michael remained silent. At one point he saw her draw back and say incredulously, "Adolf Hitler with *love*?" It was so sudden and convincing that he almost rose to see the photo her body was covering. Maggie turned to catch his expression, hoping she had put an end to the silence and the vague sense of being stalked. There was a blank moment and then Michael smiled. It was an ingratiating smile, one she had seen reproduced dozens of times, but never with such candlepower.

"Sorry," he said, "but the really incriminating stuff's all somewhere else."

"Too bad." She moved a few paces away from him.

"It's not *ter*ribly inaccessible, if you're interested," he added.

She pretended she hadn't heard, absorbing herself in a Christmas shot crammed with Michael, Peter, and several children holding stuffed animals that looked familiar to Maggie.

"This looks fairly incriminating," she said. "Playcraft?"

"Where else?" His smile had become apologetic. He

came beside her and looked at the picture thoughtfully. "Remind me to show you my campaign chest sometime. It's made completely out of Tinker Toys." He was blocking her from the rest of the photos and weaving just slightly. "I'm not knocking it, understand. Hell, what you're looking at is the house that Playcraft built." He made a sweeping gesture that took in all the pictures on the wall. "It could've been worse, I suppose. I could have married into United Pollutants or Amalgamated Nitrites. What Michael McCabe's got instead are all these fuzzy little animals in the background." He laughed and waited for Maggie to react with some kind of signal. "Think of me as one of them—this big stuffed teddy bear for little girls to hug and cuddle." He opened his arms to her comically and kept them open several beats too long.

Maggie wanted to leave, casually, with no complications. "That reminds me," she said, and looked at the open door, "there's a teddy bear I came in with somewhere."

Michael held her by the arm as she moved past him. He nodded at the glass she had put on a table. "Aren't you going to finish your drink?"

"I don't think so," Maggie said. "I've had it." She smiled and eased herself out of his grip. "Thanks for the tour."

"Just one more government service," Michael said, "no strings attached." He picked up her untouched drink and started to cross the room. "I'm way behind in family gossip. How long have you and Pete been together?"

"A few weeks," Maggie said, at the door. To her relief Michael wasn't coming any closer.

"Serious?"

"You mean, like—terminal?"

He smiled the magic smile and, sure enough, it wiped away the memory of the pass. "Dumb question," he said. "'He brought you to meet Gail. Of course it's serious."

"I thought I was meeting both of you."

"Me only incidentally." He paused. "Gail and her brother are very close, you'll find."

"I know."

Michael's smile disappeared and his fingers tapped lightly against the small glass he was holding. "If you find a little resistance there—and you probably will—take heart. That's only part of the family, after all." Slowly, he raised the glass to Maggie and drained it, watching her.

She came back into the living room, feeling self-conscious even though no one seemed to notice she had been gone; only Peter, who movd away from the piano as soon as he saw her. "Now?" he asked, and Maggie agreed, "Now."

They waved or said good night to most of the guests, and to Michael, who had reappeared. He kissed Maggie lightly on the cheek, sending out no signals at all. Just that smile.

Gail was in the hall, saying good night to the dancer and her doctor husband. Her mouth opened to protest when she saw them. "You *can't*," she said and grabbed hold of Maggie's hand. "Not when we've barely gotten acquainted."

Peter said, "You'll be seeing a lot more of her."

Maggie smiled and said, "Soon, I hope." She couldn't understand at all why Michael should have attempted a pass at her. Gail was an extraordinarily beautiful woman. It was simplistic thinking probably, but Maggie couldn't imagine herself or any woman she knew in competition with Gail.

Gail walked with them to the elevator, her arms around both. "I'll be seeing a lot more of *you,*" she said to Peter. "Michael leaves again Monday. I need somebody decorative and uncompromising, like a smallish brother. Tuesday and Thursday—benefits." She winced at the word and said to Maggie, "He's awfully handy that way. I hope you can spare him."

"I'll let you know," Peter said before Maggie could reply.

The sound of the piano was barely audible in the hall. Gail kissed them both. She was smiling warmly, as though the sight of Peter and Maggie close together genuinely pleased her. And maybe it was the smile so much like Peter's, or the unreasonable guilt Maggie was feeling about Michael, but the distracting looks Gail had given her earlier in the evening seemed less disturbing in retrospect; even when she remembered Michael's comment about "resistance."

The elevator door closed and she moved against Peter, behind the uniformed operator, and held on tightly. "Okay, how'd I do?" She cushioned herself comfortably. "Pass?"

"A-plus," Peter said, and kissed her.

Outside the building he gave her a choice, pointing north and then south. She steered him north on First Avenue, in the direction of his apartment. "One nightcap," she warned, "that's all."

"Hell, that's all you're getting."

They walked leisurely, looking in shop windows and sidewalk restaurants, glass-enclosed, still crowded at twelve-thirty. It was the New York singles scene. Maggie had tried it—"For about a week if you bunch all the nights together. It's demeaning, I hate it." She was aware of being watched from inside.

Peter hated it less—or *had,* he corrected himself.

"Maybe because I was one of the demeaners." He asked her about the present, about Gail and the evening, and Maggie was nothing but positive. "And Michael? Has he got himself a new supporter?"

She hesitated briefly. "He's everything I expected."

"And then some," Peter added. They had reached Fifty-fourth Street and were walking west. Peter was silent, not diverting his eyes from the sidewalk ahead even when he asked, "What did he do, make a pass at you?"

The question startled Maggie. "How did you know that?"

"There have been, let's say, precedents." He looked at her. "It comes with their life-style—I suppose, I don't know. They're away from each other a lot, you know."

"I didn't. I thought they were a team. Professionally, too."

"Only when they have to be." He didn't volunteer anything further and Maggie didn't press. They walked awhile without speaking. "I wish you'd told me what was going on."

"Why? I managed all right."

"I'll bet you did." He took her hand again. On Third Avenue they waited for a light to change. Maggie looked at him.

"Hey, Peter Pensive." He came back to her and smiled. "Is this going to make for family problems?" she asked him.

"No new ones," he said, adding, on the other side of Third, "the bastard."

They reached his building and the doorman was tactless enough to acknowledge "Miss" along with Mr. Drexler; to leer at her in fact, she said. She covered the side of her face with one hand and stepped quickly into the elevator. "God, my reputation."

Peter said, "What reputation?"

He pressed the button for ten, and spoke to her softly, commiserating and bringing the words closer to her face. They became just sounds then, quiet and soothing, and then light brushes against her lips with his, with the tip of his tongue. His body moved slowly against her, pressing her back until she could feel the cool wall of the car behind her.

The doors opened quietly on the tenth floor and were closing again before either of them noticed. Peter shoved them open and half-carried Maggie into the hall. It was that sudden effort, he indicated with a gesture, that had winded him so completely. Maggie was breathing as hard. "Me too," she said, while Peter felt in his pocket for the key and pressed his other hand against the front of his trousers—where it actually *hurt,* he told her.

They walked to 10B and Peter put his key in the first of the two locks. He tried turning it left but it wouldn't move. He pulled it out and was about to try the second key when he stopped himself and stood without moving, his face a few inches away from the door.

Maggie saw the change in him right away. "Pete?" she said, and when he didn't reply, "What's wrong?"

His hand went to the doorknob. He turned it, pushed, and opened the unlocked door just a crack, keeping his hand tight on the knob.

"What *is* it?" Maggie said.

Peter shook his head and opened the door wider. He reached inside the dark apartment and his face, which Maggie was watching anxiously, went white as he turned on the hall light.

"Christ." He stared ahead into the apartment, not even hearing Maggie's cry when she saw what had happened.

It had been torn apart, shattered, as far in as they could see. The walls were bare, pictures ripped off; drawers had been pulled out and emptied on the floor. An open closet, its shelf and rack picked clean, was piled with clothes which spilled out into the hall.

Peter kept shaking his head. He started to move into the apartment, and Maggie grabbed hold of his arm, saying, "Pete, *don't*!" He let her hold him briefly, then freed himself and stepped over the clothes and the scattered papers into the living room. Two overturned lamps lighted when he found the wall switch. The room had been wrecked, all of it, frighteningly, and so had his bedroom. Particularly his bedroom. The bed was pulled apart, stripped, and the floor was littered with all the framed photographs and antique toys, many of them broken. He stood in the middle of the room and looked around him helplessly, rooted by the sheer mass of the damage.

Maggie, horrified, moved from the living room into the rear hall. She called out to him and heard him say, dully, "Stay out." She didn't; she came into the doorway and saw him standing with his back to her. She called his name again, and this time he spun around and shouted at her, "Goddamnit, I told you to stay *out*!"

She had never heard him raise his voice. It shocked her and she started to leave, but then stopped herself and stared back at him. She waited before she said with deliberate calm, "We've got to call the police." Peter nodded slowly. He didn't move. "Do you want me to do it?" Maggie said. He nodded again and looked at her.

"I'm sorry I yelled like that," he said, and looked away again. He bent down and put two of the photos—one of them of Gail—on top of a bureau. "Jesus Christ. . . ."

Maggie looked all around the room. The only light was coming in from the bathroom and the overhead fixture in the hall, leaving wide, shadowy stretches. "How could anybody *do* something like this?" She shuddered. In the building across the street one of the few remaining lights went out. "I need a phone," she said, sounding exhausted all of a sudden, drained.

"Try the one in the kitchen," Peter said, piecing together fragments of the large wooden soldier. The two other phones in the apartment had been pulled out of the walls. When she'd left the room, he called out to her, "Maggie? Forget it." He stepped into the rear hall. "Let me put you in a cab instead."

"A *cab*? Are you nuts?"

He shook his head. "I don't want you involved in this."

"No?" She turned and scanned the damage all around her. "I'd say I'm right in the middle of it, wouldn't you?"

CHAPTER SIX

His gun was missing; so were some photos, and the letters and joke greeting-cards Susan had sent him. Everything connected with Susan seemed to be gone. There hadn't been that much to begin with, and little of it was especially personal or compromising or anything else that might make it even vaguely worth stealing. Maggie had called the police at twelve-thirty; it was close to two in the morning before they arrived—a detective sergeant named Rowe and a uniformed policeman, both of whom were polite but either tired or immediately bored with the case.

"It might help to mention Michael McCabe," Maggie suggested to Peter while the two men were in his bedroom. "Otherwise it's just one more New York break-in."

"That's what it is, then," Peter said, and Maggie let it drop.

The detective came back into the living room alone, writing in a small spiral notebook. Peter answered a few questions about the evening, which Maggie corroborated, describing herself as "a friend, just visiting." The name McCabe didn't come up.

"Any valuables missing?" the detective asked Peter. "Cash, jewelry?"

He didn't keep much cash around and he didn't like jewelry. The only valuable piece he owned was the Patek Philippe he was wearing. None of his paintings was missing, nor any of the antique toys—though some of them had been damaged. The Betamax was still in the apartment, so were the stereo and the color TVs.

"I had a gun that might be gone."

The detective looked up from his notebook. "Might be?"

"I haven't found it yet."

He called out to Costanza, the policeman, to search for the .32 automatic Peter described. "What else?" he asked.

"Some personal things—photos, a few letters. They're of no value to anybody but me."

Rowe was waiting for more but Peter remained silent, listening to Costanza pick through the wreckage in the bedroom. "No value, did you say?" Rowe looked around the room to appraise the damage. "Somebody sure thinks otherwise."

"Yeah," Peter said quietly. Maggie was watching him—suspiciously, like the detective. Or was that just Peter's nerves working on him? He didn't know how far to go with them, how much of the past to dredge up. It would have been a hell of a lot easier with Lieutenants Creegan or Whelan—someone from the uptown precinct who was familiar with the background of the case.

"Mr. Drexler, what you're saying doesn't make much sense," Rowe said. "You mind telling me what else 'might' be missing?"

Peter told him where to find the less than one

ounce of pot he had, and the Benzedrines and Seconals, for which he had prescriptions—if that was Rowe's implication. There was no cocaine, he assured him, or anything harder that might provide a motive.

"Easy," Rowe said. "I'm on your side, remember?"

"I'm trying to." Peter's face was flushed, his right hand was moving nervously against his side. If there had been a clear enough path in the room he would have been pacing. "Look," he said, trying to make it sound sensible and convincing, "all this is by way of a threat. It doesn't matter what was taken. Hell, she knows by now there's nothing incriminating—"

"Wait a minute," Rowe cut in. " 'She'?"

"Joanne Ellis," Peter said. The mere fact of a name, any name, took Maggie by surprise; especially the sure way he had said it.

"You know who did this?" Rowe said.

"That's what I'm telling you. Anytime she wants she can get at me—that's what this is all about."

Rowe said, "Give me that name again."

Peter gave him the name and the upstate address he still remembered; also the name of Arthur Ellis, whose electronics company had its headquarters in Poughkeepsie. While Rowe copied it all down Maggie came beside Peter and took his arm. It was a sweet and comforting gesture and it made him feel even guiltier about Maggie. He had brought her into a frightening situation, one that could be dangerous to her as well as him, with no warning, no explanation at all.

He brought her hand up to his lips. "I didn't want you involved," he said. "Why the hell didn't you run?"

"I told you—I *am* involved. Does that make sense to you?"

Rowe checked his watch and flipped to a fresh page in the notebook with enough of a snap to attract their attention. "Okay, Mr. Drexler," he said, "You want to give me something to back up that charge?"

He was giving the details of his involvement with Joanne Ellis not only to Rowe but to Maggie too, for the first time; and feeling, he told her later, pieces of himself flying in all directions.

Susan Ellis had jumped or fallen to her death from the balcony of her twelfth-floor apartment at eight-twenty in the evening on Tuesday, July ninth. There had been no sounds in the apartment or on the balcony prior to the fall, no cry when she fell. The drug screen performed during the autopsy showed a blood level of alcohol combined with Nembutal that was dangerously high, almost lethal in itself.

The investigation showed that Peter had been in her apartment up to seven in the evening. They had argued, a minor skirmish, and he had left, though he would probably have come back to spend the night (he did usually, or Susan would spend the night at his apartment).

There was no evidence anywhere of foul play; no motive, either, that anyone could discover. But there was evidence to suggest suicide. Twice before Susan had tried to kill herself. In college, before she knew Peter Drexler, she had slit her wrists. Once, early in their relationship she had taken an overdose of phenobarbital. Peter had saved her life on that occasion.

Murder, in any event, was an unlikely explanation to everyone but Joanne Ellis. According to her, jealousy was a motive, Susan's money was a motive, the violent side of Peter that supposedly terrified her daughter was a motive. She had a whole catalogue of illogical, at times insane motives to explain why Peter had killed Susan. But none of them as important as her absolute conviction that Susan *couldn't* have done something like that to herself.

Susan was dead and not only had Peter murdered her, but he had used the McCabes to cut off any investigation. Joanne Ellis was convinced of that, too, and she would prove it. So she harassed him, she hired "detectives" to find and at times manufacture evidence against him. The idea obsessed her. Eventually it had her committed to a sanitarium.

It was happening all over again. Only now it was even more violent and unreasonable. It was homicidal, Peter was sure of it.

The facts, Peter told Rowe and Costanza (who hadn't been able to find the gun anywhere in the apartment) were all on file. Creegan and Whelan, the original investigating officers, would be able to confirm them.

"Okay, you've got it all," Peter said to Maggie later. "Hell, any sensible lady would *run.*"

"Why should I run?" Maggie said. "I live here."

At Maggie's suggestion they had taken a cab down to Tenth Street for what was left of the night, once the police left his apartment. It was a good idea, Peter admitted; he was less edgy at her place, he could think.

"When was the last time you saw the sun come up?" he asked her, watching the first gray come into the sky.

Maggie came in from the kitchen, carrying two glasses of milk. "Probably my high school prom."

Peter sprawled on the couch and drew her against him. He turned off the lamp.

"What do we do about sleep?" Maggie asked.

Peter moved his hand lightly against her shoulder. "You make an attempt."

"And you?"

"Pass. I'll take something later to keep me going."

She took his hand and brought it to her face. For a long time they were both silent.

"Ask," Peter said.

She did, without any hesitation. "Were you in love with her?"

"Yes."

"Still?"

"She's dead, she doesn't exist."

"You kept her pictures, her letters."

"Not for any reason."

"I'm prying, I'm sorry."

"You're entitled, Christ knows."

"No, I'm not." She held on to him tighter. "Of all the things I could be right now that make *sense*—like afraid or upset or just exhausted—what I've got to be is jealous. What does that say about my priorities?" He snuggled closer to her without replying. Ouside, a car came down Tenth fast, rattling a manhole cover. Light was beginning to enter the room. "I'm sorry, Pete, really—about everything that happened. I just wish—"

She stopped when she realized he was asleep, and wrapped her arms around him protectively.

The following afternoon Madge called Arthur Ellis at his office and interrupted an important meeting to tell him that two New York City detectives were at the house, questioning Mrs. Ellis. No, she couldn't tell him what it was about but Mrs. Ellis seemed genuinely upset by the visit. Madge was sure Mr. Ellis would want to know that.

The detectives were Sergeant Rowe and Lieutenant John Creegan, who had been in charge of the investigation of Susan Ellis's death. Peter had spoken to him at the uptown precinct that morning and told him about the break-in and his conviction that Joanne Ellis was somehow behind it.

"You mean it's the same thing all over again," Creegan had said.

"That's the way it looks. Can you help?"

"Any way I can."

If at all possible Peter wanted the call kept private as far as Gail and Michael McCabe were concerned. They didn't know about the incident and he wanted them completely uninvolved this time, especially if there was the possibility of any press coverage.

Joanne Ellis had brought Creegan and Rowe out onto the terrace. She apologized for her appearance ("I've been gardening"), offered them coffee, and laughed when Rowe told her Peter Drexler's charge. "Is that his newest one? Incredible and ridiculous, as always." She was speaking to Rowe, avoiding Creegan except for an occasional glance. He was making her nervous, listening without comment while she answered Rowe's questions.

It took Arthur Ellis twenty minutes to drive home from the office. He hurried out to the terrace, shook hands with Creegan, whom he remembered, and nodded at Rowe, who was turning the pages of his notebook. When he was told that Sergeant Rowe was handling the case he said, "What case, what's this all about?"

"Susan's murderer," Joanne said in a shaking voice, "has brought some charges against me."

"Peter Drexler," Creegan corrected her.

Rowe took it up, reading from his notes: "His apartment was broken into between eight and twelve last night."

"What's that got to do with Mrs. Ellis?" Arthur asked angrily. "We were together here all night. There are witnesses."

"He claims I hired someone to vandalize his apartment," Joanne said and gave the same incredulous laugh. "A gun's missing, and letters—"

"The charges are absurd," Arthur said. He had come to his wife's side.

"Of course they are," Joanne said. "Who would I hire, for God's sake?"

"And very badly timed, Lieutenant," Arthur added, to Creegan. "You know what my wife's been through." He put his arm around her.

"Yes, sir, I do," Creegan said, "but the fact is"—he stopped himself and tried to express it as gently as possible—"there have been some incidents in the past involving your wife and Mr. Drexler."

"The past," Arthur said, "was a very emotional time for all of us. This isn't the past anymore." He pressed Joanne's hand. "If there are any formal charges we'd better hear them."

"There aren't," Rowe said. "This is just a preliminary investigation."

"What does that mean? More police, more questions?" He shook his head. "We've been through enough of that."

Rowe became silent and deferred to Creegan, who said, "It can all end here. Mr. Drexler doesn't have to press any charges. All he needs is some assurance from you—"

Arthur interrupted him: "Assurance of what?"

Creegan hesitated. "That there won't be anymore contact at all between Mrs. Ellis and him. None at all. You'll take full responsibility for that."

"Become my keeper, in other words," Joanne said. She moved away from them and stared at the jagged outline of the Catskills across the river.

"Is this a deal you're proposing, Lieutenant?" Arthur asked.

"Mr. Drexler's proposing it. I'm just passing it along. There's nothing wrong with it, either, Mr. Ellis. I think it's pretty generous."

"I don't see any need for a deal, do you, Jo?"

"Of course not," she said emphatically. She looked directly at Creegan. "It's amazing, isn't it—how easily these investigations of yours can be terminated. Still their little lackey, aren't you, Creegan?"

Creegan's face turned red. "Look, Mrs. Ellis—" he started to say, but Joanne kept going, raising her voice above his and Arthur's, who was trying to quiet her.

"Still protecting him. Well, I'm sure they've made this trip worth your while."

Arthur said, "Joanne!" louder.

"I don't know what that means, Mrs. Ellis," Creegan said, still red.

"It means that once again you've struck gold, Lieutenant. Congratulations. You've got yourself a nice little annuity with that family." She started to move away from them into the house and stopped in the open doorway. "No, Arthur," she said firmly, "I don't see any need for a deal, either."

Nobody called her back or followed her, and if

there was any real threat involved in what Creegan was saying she would let him take that up with Arthur. She went upstairs to her bedroom and looked down at them on the terrace. The words were muted but from the way Arthur was speaking, calmly, he was pacifying them, and they were listening, amicably. Creegan's face had lost its incriminating flush. She saw him nod. Arthur was obviously making the deal with them, confessing for her, accepting Drexler's generosity.

She hadn't been taking any strong medication lately, just an occasional tranquilizer. But looking down at them discussing her so damned conspiratorially, she needed something. The heat too was suddenly oppressive; she was beginning to sweat and it was becoming harder for her to breathe. She went into the bathroom and swallowed an Elavil, then stood watching her face in the mirror until she felt she had to lie down. Not to sleep—just to rest her eyes a minute; close them, and block out the sounds, too, on the terrace below, the voices that had risen and were still indecipherable but somehow threatening, all three of them.

She was asleep when Arthur came into her room later. He called her name twice and when she didn't answer went to her desk in the alcove, half concealed from the bed. There were flowers on it and some books and letters in neat piles.

He looked back at Joanne sleeping and noiselessly slid open a drawer. There was nothing in it but stationary. In a second drawer he discovered a manila envelope. It might have been nothing, but he opened the clasp and stuck his hand inside. There were papers, letters. He tilted the envelope and slid out a photograph. It was Susan—her face appearing so suddenly it made his throat tighten. He stared down at that face and could almost hear her voice. And all the other faces and voices came back to him—Susan through the years. If he didn't look away or distract himself with something else, he'd lose control completely.

He found another photo, of Susan and Peter Drexler. The surge of emotion passed. He could look at the picture of the two of them more calmly and see again what he had forgotten—what a handsome couple they had been, how genuinely fond of each other. Even Joanne had felt that at the time. *Before. After,* nothing was remembered happily.

There were letters in the envelope too, addressed to Drexler in that familiar handwriting (bad, childish, the only graceless thing about Susan he could remember), postmarked New York and Quebec and Santa Fe. Bound with a rubber band were birthday cards, anniversary cards, "Sorry," "Missing You," and "Had Enough?" cards.

Drexler had saved them; he had thought enough of Susan to keep the fragments. Arthur felt a sympathy for Drexler, an affection, too. He had never really believed with Joanne that Drexler was responsible for Susan's death. Not when he could be objective about it. Unfortunately to believe in Drexler's innocence was to believe in Susan's guilt; to be unfaithful to Joanne. But he had nothing against Drexler, certainly not now. The papers were his and Arthur would get them back to him.

He slipped everything into the envelope and looked in the direction of the bed. Joanne was awake, propped up on one elbow, watching him. He laid the envelope on top of the desk.

"It's true, then," he said to her.

"You never doubted it, did you?"

"Just hoped." He shrugged. "We'll work it out somehow."

"I assume you already have."

He let it pass. "How did you manage it? That . . . detective of yours?" He knew some vague details about the detective she had hired last year.

"The less you know the easier it'll be for you," Joanne said.

Arthur tapped the envelope. "You know this is a criminal—" He saw her close her eyes against the sound of his voice, and stopped speaking.

"It was too soon for me to come home," Joanne said quietly, "I'm calling Knoedler tomorrow to make arrangements to go back. I'll call tonight if you want."

"Go back?" Arthur said incredulously. "What do you mean?" He came out of the alcove and moved closer to the bed.

"Pinehurst. It makes perfect sense."

"It doesn't make sense at all. Look, Jo, this is nothing that can't be corrected."

"On *his* terms—Drexler's."

"I don't care whose terms."

"I do." She lifted herself to a sitting position, too fast—a wave of dizziness came over her. She pressed back against the headboard and closed her eyes. "I'm trying to make things easier for both of us. We don't really trust each other. That's something I don't see coming back again ever."

"Don't say that!"

"I've already said it." She reached out for his hand and drew him down beside her on the bed. "Let me go back, Arthur."

He looked lost to her and so much older than she

had ever seen him looking; vulnerable, too, and that was an Arthur she couldn't recognize. Susan's death was catching up with him finally.

The painting of Susan as a child was on the wall. Arthur saw Joanne looking at it. "I've never come to terms with it," she said to him. "She's still everywhere. I close my eyes and she's there, too. Especially there." She closed her eyes tightly, forcing the tears down her face. Arthur felt his own control going, for the first time in front of Joanne. "Everywhere. Always."

He lowered his face to hers and kept it there a long time, until he felt her breathing calmly and evenly, safely asleep. He pulled himself up and bent to kiss her forehead.

Joanne heard her door click shut. She opened her eyes and saw that he was gone. It was an effort to fight the drug and lift herself out of bed. She walked unsteadily to her desk. The manila envelope was on top. She left it there and felt for the bottom knob on the right, then fumbled inside the deep drawer. Hidden under a leather-bound diary was a .32 pistol and a box of shells. She carried them to a closet and found an old hatbox on a shelf to bury them in—someplace Arthur or Madge would never think of looking, at least not immediately. And a day was all she really needed.

Her legs were giving way. She crawled back into bed and let herself go limp, offering no resistance at all to the drug now.

Peter and Maggie had planned on driving out to East Hampton late Friday night, but the insurance adjuster was due at the apartment between four and five. Saturday they would want to spend getting the place back into shape. Maggie would, anyway; it was a job Peter would be just as happy putting off for Jackie and the phone company on Monday. Maggie and the voice of reason prevailed. Saturday was work, Friday was play, at Maggie's apartment if Peter didn't mind another night in the cubicle.

"Mind? What kind of room freak do you take me for?"

He left the office early and reached Fifty-fourth Street with about five minutes to spare, not that he expected the adjuster to be on time. Several cars double-parked outside the garage made traffic narrow to a one-lane crawl, and then the light ahead on Lexington turned red. Peter braked and waited not too far from his garage entrance. He looked idly at the car to his left, double-parked with its motor off. At first he didn't notice the man behind the wheel, then he did.

He was looking at Peter not just idly but deliberately, at least it seemed that way to Peter. The man was middle-aged with short hair, dark jacket, and tie—and all Peter could think of, and right away, was Pam's description of the mysterious Pittsburgh buyer. Crazy, of course. Peter turned away from him to check the light. When he looked back the man was still staring. It might have been the boldness of the stare that was triggering Peter's imagination, but now that man in that car seemed disturbingly familiar, even forgetting the Pittsburgh buyer. He was sure he had seen him in front of his building before, and near the Playcraft building in Queens. It was a face from the past, or damn close to one.

A horn blew behind him and Peter pulled forward slowly and turned into his garage. He left the car for the attendants and instead of walking through the garage, went up the ramp to the street. The car was still there, the driver looking straight ahead, until Peter approached. The man looked and again held the look—not as long or boldly as before but long enough to study Peter and communicate something hostile, even threatening. Peter kept going, stopped outside his building entrance, and looked back. He knew, he was *sure* he was being watched in the rearview mirror.

He went upstairs to his apartment, and seeing all the senseless damage again only intensified his suspicion of the man in the sedan. He walked through to his bedroom facing Fifty-fourth and looked down. The car had not moved.

For his own peace of mind he should have spoken to the man. There needn't have been a real confrontation scene, though all of the openings Peter framed for himself were invariably antagonistic. He could call the police instead and have them investigate. He could also go on as indecisively for the rest of the night. He forced himself away from the window. Why in hell was he letting Joanne Ellis and her war of nerves or whatever it was work on him this way?

For a long time he resisted the impulse to go down to the street and question the man. He paced, he stared down again, waiting for the car to move, willing it away. Finally, he had to give in. He left his apartment and the building and walked up to the driver's side of the car. "Something you want here?" he asked the man on the other side of the open window.

The man looked startled; he pulled away sharply and reached for a handle inside the door. He muttered, "What?"

Peter leaned down and brought his face level with the driver's. "I said is there something you want?"

"I don't know what you're talking about," the man said, and started to roll up the window. Peter laid one hand on top of the glass.

"You're some kind of detective, aren't you?"

"What? Look, you've got the wrong man, buddy." He rolled the window a little higher and Peter pressed down harder.

"I don't think I do. Who're you working for—Joanne Ellis?"

"What is this, a joke?" He looked beyond Peter at the people walking past them.

"No, no joke."

"Get your hand off the window!"

A blue-haired woman pulling a shopping cart stopped to watch.

"You broke into my apartment," Peter said. "You've been watching me, I've seen you."

"You're nuts! Get your hands off the goddamn window!"

"I want to talk to you."

"Like hell you do!" He tried to bring his hand to the door lock but Peter had already pulled the door open. It hit the rear of a parked car. More people had stopped to watch. "You son of a bitch!" the man yelled.

"Get out of the car!" Peter reached for his arm, and the man, who was heavy and sweating, jumped out of the car suddenly and lunged at Peter, slamming him against the side of a car. He tried to hold him down, shouting to the small crowd that had gathered, "Somebody, give me a hand!" There was a murmur and then somebody shouted for a cop as Peter forced himself up and threw the man off balance. A cab braked near them and blew its horn.

The man was staggering backwards toward the curb. Across the street a woman suddenly started screaming.

"Nicholas! Nicholas!"

The man recognized the voice. He raised an arm to push Peter away and called out, "It's all right, Nina, it's all right!"

Peter stopped and turned toward the woman's voice. She had come out of a street-level doctor's office in a building across the street. She and a nurse were supporting a very old woman who carried a cane. Peter saw her move away from the old woman and start to come toward them, panic on her face.

The realization that he had attacked a stranger in the street, someone completely innocent, stunned him. He looked first at the man whose arm was still raised to protect himself, and then at the middle-aged woman crossing the street and crying, "What are you doing to him?" Traffic had stopped, there were horns blowing. Peter tried to speak. He made a weak, helpless gesture to the man who was breathing heavily, his face almost purple with the effort. "I'm . . . sorry." He fumbled the words. "Christ, I don't know what happened to me."

He reached out to touch the man, who pulled back and said in a shaking voice, "You just . . . get your ass out of here, buddy . . . you just drag it out of here now, or so help me. . . ."

Peter nodded and said, lamely, over and over, "Yeah, yeah." He tried to touch the man again and backed away. The woman who had called out to Nicholas was beside him now, ashen. She turned to the clusters of people watching, and pointed at Peter.

"He attacked my brother," she cried, while Peter moved clumsily away, keeping to the street. "You're all witnesses. Stop him!"

"Let him go, Nina," her brother was saying.

Peter walked between cars onto the sidewalk. He picked up speed, aware of everyone outside his building watching him, even Stanley the old doorman. Peter didn't say anything to him; didn't even look at him as he passed inside.

In his apartment he locked the door, poured a long brandy, and carried it into the dining room, which had been relatively undisturbed. Nothing like it would happen again, he swore it to himself. He wouldn't allow himself to lose control like that. He had panicked, made a goddamn fool of himself, and for no reason at all.

Christ! He slammed his hand against the table and everything in the room rattled. *Christ!*

Shakily he poured another drink and sat staring, waiting for the brandy to work. He closed his eyes, as if that might help it along.

Just before five the insurance investigator appeared. Peter followed him through the apartment, saying as little as possible. There was more litter than damage, though there was damage enough—lamps, the phones, some of the antique toys. Clearly, though, it wasn't robbery; as far as the investigator could determine, it was vandalism. To Peter, of course, it went beyond that—it was harassment, intimidation; but he didn't go into that at all with the investigator.

The inspection was over in an hour. Peter shaved again and showered, and while he was throwing a few overnight things into a leather satchel heard his front door being unlocked and opened—the same sounds he had heard a few days ago, under almost the same circumstances. He reached for a towel and wrapped it around his middle, listening and moving quietly into the hall outside his bedroom. He stopped. There was no sound at all inside the apartment. He waited and remembered in the lingering haze of the brandy what he had been repeating to himself just awhile ago. He wasn't panicking. He moved two steps out of the hall.

It was Gail, and the relief was like a wave knocking him off his feet. She didn't see him; she was turning slowly to inspect the damage in the room. Her body was rigid, her face as it came around horrified.

"Some fun, hunh?"

Gail cried out and whirled to face the sound. Her hand pressed hard against her chest. She could barely get Peter's name out.

"I'm sorry," he said, and if he was smiling it was nerves, not amusement. "Are you okay?"

"Never mind me." She held onto the back of a chair and when she was again breathing normally she let her eyes sweep the room. "What happened here? My *God!*"

"Believe it or not it looks worse than it is." He pushed against the coffee table with his bare leg and bent to pick up some odds and ends under it. "I got hit."

"*When?*"

"Last night. Just about the time we were having dinner. What'd you do, set me up?" He pulled the towel tighter around him. Gail looked at him closely, his chest, face, searching for bruises.

"You're all right, though." She raised her hand to his face and brushed the damp hair away from his forehead.

"No damage," he assured her. He started back to the bedroom. "I was just getting dressed."

Gail peered into the other rooms and exclaimed at the state of each of them. Peter had pulled on his shorts when she came to the bedroom doorway and demanded angrily, "Why in hell didn't you *call* me?"

"Why, what were you going to do?" He threw the towel into the bathroom, found a pair of dark-brown socks, and sat on the edge of the bed. Gail moved into the room, inspecting, pacing where she could find space.

"Lucky I came by," she said.

"Why did you?"

"Passing. What should I do?"

"Nothing."

"What do you mean, nothing?"

"The police were here."

"And?"

"They're working on it."

"Working *how?*"

"Gail . . ." he warned her, and she caught herself and mouthed, "Sorry, sorry." She watched him get up and force open a drawer he had replaced in the bureau. It was stuffed with cardboarded shirts thrown in clumsily. He selected a few and tossed them onto the bed, then searched through the slacks he had tried to drape neatly over a chair.

"You told them about Joanne Ellis, of course," Gail said. Peter nodded. "There's no possible doubt, is there?"

"Not to me there isn't." He put on a pair of tan slacks. "Whatever I had left of Susan here is gone." He looked at the top of the bureau where the framed photos were lying, Gail's among them. "Nothing else." He wouldn't tell her about the gun and he hoped Creegan, whom she was sure to get in touch with, wouldn't tell her either. Nor would he tell her about the episode with the stranger downstairs. Not now, anyway. Maybe when everything was back to normal and they could both appreciate the absurd black humor of it. Right now just the thought of it sent a chill through him.

Gail lifted the dead phone receiver and listened. "The one in the kitchen works," Peter said. She slammed the receiver down. "Damn it, Pete, *tell* me things!"

"I am."

She fumed. "You're not planning on East Hampton, are you?"

"No. Not tonight, anyway." He stepped into a pair of loafers.

"You can't stay here, of course."

"I wasn't planning to." He went into the bathroom to comb his hair.

"I'll come by with Louise tomorrow," she called out to him. "We'll start to put this back together. God, I'm really *sick. . . .*"

She was searching through the leather satchel when he came back into the bedroom, adding clothes and removing some toiletries. "You don't need these," she said, and handed him the razor and toothbrush.

He watched her rearranging his things and said, playfully, "Get away from there!" He put the toothbrush and razor back into the case. "I'd better give you Maggie's number."

"Maggie?" She managed to look surprised. "What for?"

"I'll be staying at her place." He wrote down the number and address and gave them to Gail. She didn't look.

"Do you think it's a good idea, bringing her into this?"

"It's her idea." He zippered the case shut.

"I'd really feel a lot more comfortable with you closer. At least until this thing with Ellis is over."

"As far as I'm concerned it is over." He saw her looking at him queerly. "Have a little confidence in me, will you?" He threw his arms around her. Gail moved closer to him.

"I do," she said, "you know I do, all the confidence in the world. It's everybody else that worries me." She could feel him smile against her. His arms tightened around her and she breathed in the damp, fresh fragrance of him. He let go and lifted the satchel off the bed.

"I'll drop you off," Peter said.

Gail opened her bag and read the slip of paper he had given her. "The Village," she said with a shudder. "What is it, a pad?" She snapped the bag shut.

Peter said, "Snob."

"Just promise me one thing," Gail said at the door. "Don't let it turn into one of those open-ended stays, okay? However much this one pushes."

CHAPTER SEVEN

At six in the evening Joanne Ellis was in the bathroom, splashing her face and arms with cold water, when her phone rang in the bedroom. It was John Trevino's quiet, expressionless voice telling her that Peter Drexler's car was in the Brevoort garage on East Ninth Street. Drexler would be spending Friday night at least in Apartment 4A at 40 West Tenth. A bug could be installed there as well, if Mrs. Ellis wanted—tonight probably, since he expected Drexler and Maggie Newman would be going out to dinner. It wouldn't be necessary, Joanne told him—she expected to terminate all contact with Peter Drexler that evening.

She hadn't made the decision before she actually spoke it. It was inevitable, of course, and now was as good as tomorrow or the day after. Better; anything beyond the immediate present was becoming more and more uncertain. Besides, what other way *at* him was there now?

She asked Trevino for a description of the building and a means of opening the locked inner door downstairs.

"When?" he asked her.

"Tonight."

It would be open, he assured her.

An envelope with a final cash payment of two thousand dollars would be delivered to him in the morning in the usual way, terminating their association as well.

The money was in the floor safe in her closet. She sealed it into an envelope, then went back to the closet for the gun hidden in the hatbox. She loaded all the chambers, then put the gun and the money into her handbag.

She found Arthur in the study downstairs, with papers in front of him on the desk, and a bourbon and soda—a strong one which would have him groggy and dozing in an hour or so, if the pattern of the last few days held. She was having a light dinner in her room, she told him; and then an Elavil, in view of the strain she was under, and to bed. He started to say something, but there was nothing she was willing to cope with right now. No apologies or explanations from either of them, not tonight. Nothing but sleep, *please.*

"Whatever you want," he said, and when he reached out to touch her she turned away from him and left the study.

An hour later she was dressed and passing quickly and unnoticed out of the house through the living room. She walked to the garage and knocked at the door to Paul's small apartment. When he opened it she caught a glimpse of a woman in a robe moving quietly out of view.

Joanne handed him the sealed envelope. "Would you take care of this for me, Paul? It's due tomorrow morning."

Flat against the envelope was a hundred-dollar bill.

Joanne held onto both until Paul looked up at her face again. She moved closer to the door and mouthed the words slowly and emphatically: "You haven't seen me tonight." Paul nodded and she let him take the money.

She drove the BMW, pulling out of the garage and down the drive so quietly that the sound barely reached Paul's apartment, much less the main house and Arthur, who had already closed his eyes at his desk.

As far as Maggie was concerned, even if it was just a one-night stand, Peter's formal, satchel-in-hand moving-in was a lot different from the few hours he had spent in her apartment the previous evening. It was a little more than one friend helping out another, and a lot less than an emotional commitment. The Meaning of it was hovering somewhere in between, an area vast enough to keep her puzzled and absorbed most of the day.

She found herself posing ridiculous questions and coming to absurd conclusions. What if it worked? What if they found themselves inordinately compatible over a twelve-hour period? What was the next step? It had started out simple, and the more she dwelled on the possibilities the more epochal and terrifying it became. Was Peter It? That was the question in its simplest form by quitting time. And was this brief and accidental move the irreversible step?

She came home to her/their apartment, carrying a portfolio bulging with VA-ROOM! sketches (as Frank Powell put it, her life was becoming a Peter Drexler festival), and found Peter—her chief client, she had to remind herself, her boss—waiting. It was an awkward situation, and to Maggie the apartment was suddenly confining and inadequate, not charming. She was bothered and she rehearsed something apologetic in the bathroom while Peter fixed drinks for them ("Y'know, I'm beginning to feel a little old for Village *charm* . . .").

A leather case with his toiletries was in the bathroom and some of his clothes were unpacked in the bedroom. Seeing them, she felt a rush that was distinctly erotic, knocking any thought of apology out of her mind. The apartment would do very nicely, more nicely than it had ever done.

He was on the terrace, holding out a martini to her in a frosted glass. They drank a toast to "Whatever . . ." and Peter suggested dinner at Hopper's to celebrate the same thing. On their way out of the building he noticed that the inner door did not click shut after them. He tried it. The lock, which had been working when Maggie came into the building, was broken.

"Oh, God," she said, "not again." She watched him twist the knob several times to no avail, and saw his face cloud over briefly. He turned away from the door and took Maggie's arm.

"Who's paranoid?" he said, reminding himself of Rowe and Creegan and a situation that was finally under control. He held the outer door open for Maggie.

Hopper's was crowded, with music coming from the cafe. As they were walking to their table, a woman's voice called out, "Peter Drexler!" She rose behind them, a tall and good-looking blonde whose face, her forehead especially, was turning pink. Peter recognized her immediately, did a double take, and called back, "Laurie!" She held out her hand and pulled him closer. Her face pressed against his and his color rose to the same deep pink.

Maggie was introduced and so was Laurie's date, whose tanned and too chiseled face Maggie had seen often in ads. They chatted briefly and awkwardly while the maitre d' waited ahead of them. Laurie was tactile and she spoke in reprimands, all of them delivered coquettishly. It was fairly obvious that she would have preferred more time with Peter and fewer bystanders. "Call me," Maggie heard her tell him, insistently. "You still have the number, don't you?" She smiled sweetly at Maggie.

They sat at a table far enough way, Peter with his back to Laurie. Maggie was encouraged.

"An old friend," Peter volunteered with a slight undercurrent of guilt.

"The best kind," Maggie said. "If you want to call her later, the phone's next to the bed."

He gave her a below-the-belt laugh and ordered martinis for both of them, despite Maggie's protest. As warned, her inhibitions went with a few sips and she asked, "How many of those are there around town?"

"How many of what?"

"Lauries," she said with a nod in her direction. Laurie had been stealing looks at them regularly.

"Don't you have any—old friends around?"

"None that I've had to fight off recently."

"You're too busy fighting off the new ones." He gave her hand a hard squeeze on top of the table and touched his forehead to hers. *Are you looking, Laurie?* she almost said aloud.

She was needling Peter but she was genuinely curious as well. How many women had there been? There must have been a few between the early marriage and now. Susan of course, and Laurie—which had to be the two ends of the spectrum. How many others (admittedly none of her business) and what had all of them done wrong (definitely her business)? What might she be doing wrong—besides prying, martinis or not? Or was she really different? As important to him as he made her feel?

Laurie left with the chiseled one, stopping at their table to give Peter a slip of paper with her number ("In case you misplace the phone book"), and to glare at Maggie. He played absently with the paper over coffee, rolled it into a ball, and eventually left it in the ashtray.

There was a very fine rain, like a mist, when they left the restaurant and walked down Tenth Street. They passed a woman Maggie knew, walking a Corgi, and a middle-aged man in leather and keys. The lock on the inner door hadn't been repaired in the two hours they had been gone, and when Peter expressed honest surprise Maggie said, "Are you kidding?" They started up the creaking stairs, Maggie leading Peter past the Feiblemans' legendary five rooms on the second floor and Lois and Joan's huge four—which would have been perfect right now—on the third floor.

"Will you cut it out, for Chrissake!" Peter said. "We'll be fine." He grabbed at her and she hit back at him while a dog yapped in another of the third-floor apartments.

Maggie was the one to stop before the last flight of stairs. "You're out of shape," Peter taunted her, and to prove it he moved ahead of her and prepared for a sprint up to the fourth floor. He made it to the landing effortlessly (the NYAC three times a week, he told her) and grabbed the banister for the final dash.

And then stopped suddenly, looking up at the fourth floor. He was absolutely still, breathing very hard, and when Maggie saw the change she panicked.

"Pete?" she called anxiously. She started up the stairs.

Peter heard her without looking. "Stay there," he called back to her.

"Why?" She stopped and looked up to see a woman moving into view, halting at the head of the stairs. The woman's expression was tense and frightening. She was staring at Peter with a malevolence that sent a chill through Maggie. She had never seen her before, but she knew immediately that it was Joanne Ellis standing above them and holding a handbag in front of her too tightly, with both hands.

"What do you want?" Peter asked quietly. His left hand was white on the banister. In the silence Maggie climbed another step toward him, too softly for Peter to notice.

"There's no sense prolonging it," Joanne Ellis said in a voice that was dry and trembling. "You and I know you killed her. That should be enough." She was opening her handbag.

"Mrs. Ellis . . ." Peter warned her, keeping his eyes on the bag.

Maggie climbed another step and Peter hit back at the air between them, shouting, *"Get–!"* breaking off when he saw the gun, his gun, in Joanne Ellis's hand.

Maggie gasped, her hands jerking up to her face and covering her mouth.

"Think of yourself as a very lucky woman," Joanne said to her. "Much luckier than my Susan." She moved closer to the top step, holding the gun with both hands now and pointing it at Peter's head.

"Thank her for this, thank her memory." She drew a deep, painful breath.

"Mrs. Ellis!" Peter shouted. He brought his hands in front of him as if to ward off the bullets, his whole body tightening. *"Don't."* The gun was shaking in Joanne's hands, her mouth twisting under the strain. He said it one more time: *"Don't!"* and Maggie cried out as the gun blasted at him—a second and a third time, the bullets flying wildly as he threw himself against the wall, dropping down, and then in a burst lunging up at her. Maggie's eyes were covered. She fell to the steps, crying, *"No, no, God, no."*

Joanne fired again as Peter's left arm hit out at the gun, and this time a bullet struck him in his upper arm, jolting him like an electric shock. He yelled and flung himself at her, and the fifth or sixth bullet, he couldn't remember which, fired into the wall before he could knock the gun out of her hand.

It fell beside Maggie and she recoiled, as though expecting it to detonate when it hit, and then recovered enough to grab it and hold on tightly. She looked up the stairs and there was blood on Peter's sleeve, a lot of it, and the pain she saw in his face terrified her. She started up toward him and looked away quickly as he swung his right arm at Joanne Ellis and hit her in the stomach, throwing her against the banister. And then couldn't avoid seeing him strike her again, savagely this time—a blow with his fist against the side of her face. The force of it pulled her hands loose from the banister. She plunged down the steps, clawing at the air for something to break her fall, and then not struggling at all, coming to a rest with a terrible moan at the bottom of the stairs, her body sprawled hideously.

And then silence for a long moment, with the

sounds building slowly below them—doors opening and frightened voices near the stairwell.

Peter's eyes were closed, his back pressing against the blood-smeared wall. He held his hand over the wound.

"Oh, God," Maggie was saying over and over. She looked down at Joanne Ellis's still body and stopped to touch her, to see whether she was still breathing. The image was vivid in her mind—the savagery of the blow, the sound of it. Joanne was moaning, a steady, barely audible sound. Maggie moved past her, up the stairs to Peter, forcing herself to see the blood coming between his fingers, forcing herself not to panic—not again, not now.

The voices below her were louder, the sounds lost on her as she watched Peter sink slowly to the steps. Finally there was someone—a man in a red robe whose name she knew and couldn't remember—someone finally appearing, above them on her floor, moving cautiously and then bravely down the steps when Maggie couldn't hold it in anymore and cried, "Get an ambulance! Please! *Oh, God, please!*"

The ambulance from St. Vincent's Hospital came finally, and the police, and, as Peter and Maggie were leaving the building, a reporter and a TV news crew with suddenly blinding lights. Joanne Ellis had already been carried to the ambulance, unconscious. Peter, walking unaided, and Maggie were led instead to a patrol car for the short ride to St. Vincent's. His wound, the ambulance attendant had assured them, looked and felt worse than it really was—an ugly slash mark where the bullet had grazed his upper arm. Maggie had had to look away while it was being treated on the staircase, concentrating on the policemen questioning her and Peter.

Peter even managed a weak smile. "Here we go again," he said to her, and his voice was weak, too, and full of pain. In the patrol car he was all concern, for Maggie, not himself. He held her despite the pain, trying to comfort her and saying, incomprehensibly as far as Maggie was concerned, "Forgive me, will you?"

"*Forgive* you?"

He nodded and drew her closer to him.

He was taken into the emergency room at St. Vincent's. Maggie, still shaken, was asked more questions in a small bare office, and then sent out to the waiting room where a young cop brought her a container of coffee and sat with her briefly. Neither of them spoke.

It would really hit her later, she thought. The numbness would go away, and what had happened to them would come back to haunt her awake and asleep. What had happened and what miraculously *hadn't* happened. . . . The reaction was already starting, as a matter of fact: the container began to shake in her hands and coffee was spilling to the floor between her legs. She lowered it carefully onto the stained Formica table beside her.

"Maggie?"

Her name was being called. She looked past the drab and frightened figures in the waiting room to find Gail McCabe in the doorway, dazzling in a white gown and looking incongruously distraught. She was motioning Maggie out of the room. The gesture and the whiteness of the gown, with nurses moving behind her, would be another image, Maggie knew, that would surface surrealistically in her nightmares. She got up quickly, grateful to have Gail or anyone with her now. *How had she heard?* she was about to ask, and then she remembered it was she who had given the name of the McCabes to the police.

Gail put her arms around her and held her for a moment, whispering fervently, "Thank God he's all right, *thank God*!" It was a voice she couldn't associate with Gail.

Gail released her and took a deep breath. She scanned Maggie's face with concern and let her eyes travel as far down as her waist. "You're all right?" Maggie nodded and let Gail take her hand and lead her away from the waiting room.

There were police and what looked like a group of reporters near the emergency entrance. Gail turned right and brought Maggie down a quiet corridor, to the office where she had been questioned by the police. Michael McCabe, dressed formally, was speaking into the phone, clearly upset, giving Maggie only a quick nod. A man introduced by Gail as Lieutenant John Creegan was in the office as well.

"I'm not asking you to kill it," Michael was saying, "just play it down. No headlines. Hell, you can bury it somewhere." He looked at Gail and shook his head in exasperation. "Look, Putsch and DeCicco don't owe me the favors you do and they're going along with me." He listened impatiently, his hand went over the mouthpiece and he said, "Jesus!" to Gail and Creegan; then uncovered it to say, "I know you will and I appreciate it, Stan, I really do."

He hung up, looked thoughtful, and lifted the receiver again, calling out, "How are you, Maggie?" He was dialing a number before she could reply.

Gail whispered something to Lieutenant Creegan. He made a note of it. She came toward Maggie just as Michael was saying into the phone, "Joyce? What time is my flight tomorrow?" She put her arm around Maggie and ushered her out of the office. Michael's voice faded behind them: "See who's available in the DA's office, will you? *Now.*"

In the corridor Gail said to Maggie, "There's no sense in all of us waiting around."

"I don't mind," Maggie replied, and walked silently beside Gail.

A stretcher was being wheeled into the emergency room. The head of a young woman was visible, thrown back, tubes coming out of her nose. Maggie and Gail stopped abruptly and turned their backs to the woman, Maggie first, closing her eyes. They moved at the same, waiting pace in the direction of the office.

"Of course," Gail said. "I'll be taking Peter home with me tonight."

She waited, watching Maggie who said, "Of course." Maggie had the feeling Gail expected some protest from her. She had none: Gail's idea made perfect sense.

"Why don't you go home and get some sleep?"

"I'm not tired," Maggie said. She was, though—exhausted. Where she would sleep tonight was a problem. Her apartment? Walk up those stairs again and see the bloodstains, the bullet holes in the wall? And then what—lock the door on them and sleep peacefully? Right now she didn't know how she could live in that building again, with those people.

"This could go on a lot longer," Gail said with a vague gesture.

"That's all right. I'll wait." She smiled and hoped it came out more appreciative than defiant.

"I'd think you'd have had it by now." She sounded exhausted herself. She didn't look it at all.

"Not yet," Maggie said.

They had reached the small office. Michael was still on the phone, sounding calmer now, less antagonistic. Maggie stayed in the hall and heard him say, "She's been in a mental institution. I don't know if we should be thinking of any *criminal* prosecution. . . ."

She walked away from the sound and went back to the waiting room alone. There were some new arrivals. A heavy black woman with a swollen face was sitting in her chair. She found another seat next to the soda machine and rose every few minutes to check the activity out in the corridor. The third time she peered out she found herself looking into Michael's calm and inexhaustibly glamorous face. She heard the name McCabe whispered behind her two or three times. Michael turned his face away without acknowledging anyone. He put his arm around Maggie's waist and moved her in the direction of the exit.

"If you don't know what's good for you," he said with mock severity, "I know what's good for you."

"What are you doing?" She quickened her pace to keep up with him.

"Taking you home."

"I don't want to go home."

"I know you don't. That's why I've been called in." They turned into the quiet corridor, avoiding the clutter of empty stretchers and wheelchairs, and stopped. "Look, Maggie," he said, "there's nothing to do here. He'll be fine and everything will be taken care of. Help us along, hunh?"

Stay out of the way, in other words: she heard it clearly. They were right, both of them—she was an unnecessary complication at this point. Michael was waiting for her to agree, trying not to show his impatience or his discomfort in the corridor's stark light.

Maggie noticed Gail looking out at them from the office. She nodded reluctantly at Michael and started to move away, telling him, "I can get home all right."

"Like hell you can," Michael said beside her. He turned her around and led her toward another, quieter exit. She heard Gail's voice behind them, calling out, "We'll be talking to you soon."

The corridor was empty when she looked back. "It's just a few blocks," she said to Michael. "You really don't have to—"

Michael cut her off. "It's on my way."

There was no one to recognize him in the corridor. On Greenwich Avenue he hailed a cab, which Maggie insisted was ridiculous. He ordered her inside in that same commanding tone. Four blocks later, in front of her building, now eerily deserted, he followed her out and paid the cabdriver. She had been too nervous and distracted by the building to notice that the cab was pulling away. His hand on her arm as they walked to the entrance called her back suddenly.

"You let the cab go," she said, pointing at the yellow light moving toward Fifth Avenue.

Michael shrugged it off. "Friday night, there'll be plenty of cabs." He held the outside door open for her and she entered the vestibule warily, as though some terrible remnant of the evening were lying in wait.

At the inner door, its lock still broken, she turned to Michael and held out her hand. "I can make it upstairs alone. Thanks."

Michael shook his head and made an about-face

gesture with his right hand. "March," he ordered her. "I intend to tell Pete I saw you to and through the door."

Maggie made a small exasperated sound. "You're really—"

"Politicking, that's all." He smiled, parodying his poster image. "Hell, you're a vote, aren't you?"

She gave in with as much good humor as she could muster and pushed open the inner door. She paused briefly before crossing the threshold and covered her anxiety by saying lightly, "This can't be helping your image."

"Screw my image," Michael said. But he was on guard, screening the immediate area as carefully and subtly as he had done at the hospital. Michael very seldom found himself in any compromising position; his handling of the situation, when he did, was a marvel of charm and cunning.

Maggie led the way up the stairs. She was, to be honest with herself, grateful for Michael. Now that she was in the building, she couldn't imagine herself making it up those stairs alone, or, worse, facing anyone alone. The awkward scene in Michael's study inevitably came to mind and she would have preferred someone else providing the security right now; but that was hardly a major consideration after what she had been through that evening—what *they* had been through together, she and Peter.

It was Peter she missed, Peter she wanted with her. She reminded herself how reasonable it was that they be in separate places (Gail's idea, of course, all Gail's), but that didn't make the separation any easier. Her nerves were too raw for logic, everything still too much heightened. If only her feelings would translate themselves into something physical—the burst of tears finally, the scream she still felt building.

On the third floor Michael stopped behind her, held onto the banister, and panted to amuse her. She barely smiled. "I think I warned you," she said, and pulled herself up the last flight with her eyes fixed straight ahead. It was important that she look at the wall and the steps, and she would—tomorrow, definitely. But not now.

She was rattled and there was no way to conceal it. She searched through her bag for her keys too long, and when she found them it was easier for Michael to unlock the door. She started to thank him but he raised his hand to quiet her and then went into the apartment ahead of her. She saw overhead lights being turned on and off as he searched through the rooms. When he reappeared she was in the small vestibule with the door still open behind her.

"All clear," he announced from the living room. She nodded gratefully and waited for him to come toward her and leave. He wasn't moving, though. "You've been through it all and I'm the fellow that needs the drink." He indicated the small collection of liquor bottles on the table and asked, meekly for him, "One to send me on my way?"

Maggie made a wearied sound and let her chin fall to her chest. "I am about to *drop,*" she said to ease him out of the apartment.

"That's what we've been telling you." He smiled charmingly, lifting the bottle of Scotch, and found glasses in the étagère. "Here, this ought to do the job."

"Michael." She said it as though just pronouncing the name exhausted her.

He forced the glass into her hand anyway and

touched it with his own. "Neat," he said, "like my grandma taught me." She watched him drain it and waited for him to put down the glass so that she could do the same and finally show him to the door. He was attractive and thoughtful, and if he were to make another pass she could handle it easily; she wanted him out, though, as she would have wanted anybody else but Peter out.

He held onto the glass, carrying it around the room with him. Blue light colored the top of the Empire State Building, visible through the glass door of the terrace. Michael looked at it a few seconds before asking Maggie, quietly, "Does tonight change anything between you and Pete?"

"Why should it?" she asked defensively. Michael turned to see her face and then moved thoughtfully back to the Scotch bottle, as if weighing an answer to a very difficult question. Maggie was anticipating him, she was sure, by adding, "I knew all about Susan Ellis."

Michael was reaching for the bottle. "That she killed herself?"

"Yes. Peter told me."

"Ah," Michael said absently, and poured himself a stronger drink.

"It's over now, isn't it? He's not in any danger?"

"Peter?" He shook his head. "No danger."

"And Mrs. Ellis?"

"Will be put away for a long time, probably." He said it quickly, the subject apparently being distasteful to him. He held out his glass to her. "You don't mind, do you?"

"Didn't I hear you say 'one'?" She forced herself to smile.

"I don't remember. You shouldn't believe a common politician anyway."

"Since when is Michael McCabe a common politician?"

"Since—" He made a show of checking his watch. "Do you need exact dates?" He lowered his arm and paced a bit, away from her. He was taller than Peter, six two at least, and the apartment seemed even more cramped with him moving through it, his shoulders bent forward slightly. He pulled his tie loose and Maggie thought, Oh, God, he's settling in. She couldn't face even the thought of a scene.

"Okay, Congressman," she was about to say, along with something witty but firm to terminate the evening. But Michael, standing between the bedroom and bathroom, spoke first: "I noticed before . . . you're all set up for two here."

It was said casually—a simple observation with no malice in the tone and nothing suggesting a leer; but still, Maggie felt her face getting warm. "Just something we improvised," she said, and immediately regretted answering him, even testily.

"You and Peter." This time she remained silent. "Well, Peter's a good-looking man. Very attractive to women." He paused to make sure she was listening. "He's gone through a lot of them."

It was a stupid and insensitive remark and since Michael was neither stupid nor insensitive, she waited for something like a punchline. There was none; he was looking away from her pensively.

"Is there something you're trying to tell me, Michael?" It was an effort for her to keep it light at this point.

"I suppose so," he said, and made her wait again. "You're smart enough to know it wouldn't work out."

"I don't think I'm all that smart," she said, not wanting to hear more or to cut him off, either. "You sound like you're doing me a favor."

"Trying to; a big one. I've been in the family awhile, after all."

"It doesn't seem to have hurt you," she said. Did that even things up between them? His face told her plainly enough. "Sorry," she said quietly. "You managed to antagonize me."

"Why be sorry? It's the truth." He stared down at the empty glass in his hand. "It's also the reason why, deep down, I don't like them that much, either of them. One of the reasons, anyway." He lowered his voice to a whisper. "That's by way of a secret . . . from one sour son-of-a-bitch, hunh?"

"I get the feeling you've got a lot of them—secrets."

"What do I know about secrets? I'm in politics." He was carrying his glass back for a refill. "Warning, by the way—let me help myself to another one of these and it counts as an invitation." He stopped close to her and his voice sobered and softened. "To spend the night is what I'm getting at."

He held himself behind an imaginary line and gave Maggie time to lift the Scotch bottle delicately and hold it behind her back, as if she were a magician pulling off a disappearing trick.

"Poof," she said, gently, and Michael yielded, setting the glass down.

"Too bad—or just as well," he said with a shrug. "I'm not sure which." He smiled to show her there were no hard feelings; he would withdraw peacefully. He looked at his watch. "Mind if I make a phone call?"

"Through there," she said, and let out a quiet sigh of relief when he had gone into the bedroom. Her feelings toward Michael were distinctly ambiguous at the moment. The pass, as unconscionable as it was, hadn't really offended her; she didn't dislike him. She didn't trust him, either, seeing that she and his wife were for him so obviously interchangeable—twice now. What she did trust were her own instincts about Peter and her relationship with him—a lot more than Michael's vague admonitions, whatever the motive behind them may have been. If it was the past he was boozily warning Maggie about, surely she had seen the worst of it tonight.

Michael's quiet voice from the bedroom cut into her thoughts. Maggie heard him say, "Julie. . . ." His flight was at ten in the morning and he was free until then, Maggie gathered from the fragments of conversation. She moved farther away from the bedroom and noisily replaced the Scotch bottle on the table.

"Ten minutes," she heard him say, and then, "So am I." He hung up and Maggie shifted some papers on her drawing board until he came back into the room. "Anything you need before I go?" he asked her.

Maggie shook her head and said, "Thanks."

Michael took a card from his wallet, wrote on it quickly, and left it on a table. "My numbers, all of them, if ever you do." He gave her a long, unsmiling look, with something like a warning in it, unspoken, then left the apartment. Maggie bolted the door behind him and listened to his sound fade down the stairs she would have to face again in the morning.

Peter came out of the emergency room finally, with his left arm taped and in a sling. His shirt was open and draped over the one shoulder. Gail was waiting in the corridor with Lieutenant Creegan, who was off duty, and George Stahl, a Drexler family lawyer who was familiar with everything concerning the Ellises. She stopped him in mid-sentence as soon as she saw Peter, and rushed away from them. Peter's face brightened and he held out his uninjured arm to her. She looked at it anxiously.

"I'm okay," he assured her, raising the arm as far away from his body as the sling would allow. "A little numb, that's all."

"You're lying. It looks terrible."

"If that makes you any happier," he said, and drew her closer. She rested her head against him and began to weep quietly. Peter stroked her hair and said, "Hey, come on."

"I will," she nodded, "in a minute." She sniffled. "If you think this has been rough on you . . ." She pressed closer and could feel him turning to look in several directions.

"Where's Maggie?" he asked her.

"Collapsed. I sent her home."

"You sent her back there? Alone?"

"With Michael."

He looked angry. "Well, that makes me feel a hell of a lot better!"

"Stop being silly," she said, then took his hand. "Come on, Creegan's here to drive us home."

Peter held back. "Home where? I'm staying at Maggie's place."

"Not tonight you're not. Don't you think the girl's been through enough for now?"

"That's what I'm afraid of." He thought a moment. "Where's there a phone here?"

"Pete, look, you'll call her tomorrow."

He was moving past her in the direction of the

waiting room when something in the main entrance caught his eye. A policeman was holding the door open for a man in his early sixties wearing expensive sports clothes. The man, tall with a still-handsome face, followed the policeman uncertainly. It was Arthur Ellis and it was almost a year since Peter had seen him—a year that had aged him greatly. Gail recognized him too and her impulse was to look away and have Peter do the same. But Peter didn't—he walked toward Arthur Ellis, who halted abruptly when he saw him approaching.

"Mr. Ellis," Peter said, and there was pain in his voice and regret. He waited for Arthur to make the next move—away from Peter without any response, if that was what he wanted. But Arthur didn't move. He stood near Peter with an expression that wasn't hard or angry; that was, if anything, sympathetic.

At no point in the past had Arthur Ellis held him responsible for Susan's death. He had accepted the official verdict of accidental death without question when questioning it would have been unreasonable and contrary to all the available evidence. He had even once warned Peter about his wife's instability, about the threat she could become.

He seemed shaken now, drained.

"I'm sorry," Peter said, "honestly I'm sorry." Arthur nodded, just barely, and Peter could see what effort it was taking for him to hold the emotion in. "I wish there was something else I could've done, but. . ." He shook his head helplessly and reached out to touch Arthur.

Arthur looked at his hand. "I know," he said, and to Peter the words were an absolution. They were both silent, looking directly at each other, until Arthur signaled the policeman to lead him away. Peter watched them go into the admissions office. A detective joined them and then a doctor, and all of them moved deeper into the office, out of view.

Gail had come up beside Peter. "Let's go home," she said.

He had been given a painkiller which seemed to go directly to his head in the confined space of the car. He listened groggily to Creegan's summary of the police facts and to Stahl's legal advice. Gail was sitting beside him in the rear seat of the unmarked police car. Creegan was driving. "I don't think we're hearing anything at this point," she said to them in a whisper.

Peter was sleeping. He awoke when they reached UN Plaza and in the elevator told Gail that he had to call Maggie.

"In the morning," Gail said. She and Stahl were flanking Peter.

"Now," Peter insisted.

He fell asleep again, without making the call, as soon as they got him into the bedroom that was always kept ready for him.

CHAPTER EIGHT

Maggie had set her alarm for eight the following morning, not that she had expected to sleep at all. She did sleep however, soundly, waking by herself a little before eight. She dressed in jeans and a striped jersey top, her standard Saturday housecleaning outfit, and paused with her hand on the doorknob before forcing herself out of the apartment. She went down the stairs fast, watching her feet, convincing herself that it was a normal Saturday and she would buy the *Times* and the *News* as usual, and a Danish at Greenberg's. The sequence, repeated to herself several times, filled her head all the way down to the ground floor. When she reached the still-unrepaired inner door, she heard, somewhere above her, another door closing, and quickened her pace out of the building—happily without meeting anyone. There were a few pedestrians on Tenth Street, but only the janitor at Thirty-three, absorbed in hosing down the sidewalk, might have recognized her.

She headed for the newsdealer on Eighth Street, the rotten one she never used, rather than Red's, her friend on Sixth Avenue. Her name, she had convinced herself, would be in headlines and her face staring out at her from the front page of the *Daily News*.

She was wrong, at least as far as this edition was concerned. She pulled the paper open on her way back to her apartment. By page twelve she'd found nothing. She turned to the centerfold and then to the back page. Nothing at all and nothing, as expected, in the *Times* news summary. She folded both papers under her arm. Ahead of her on Tenth, which was bright with sunlight, someone was leaving her building—a man she didn't know, wearing the clothes he had probably been wearing, less rumpled, the previous evening. She saw no one else on the way upstairs.

She wondered how long she would feel compelled to creep in and out of her own building, how long the feelings of guilt and notoriety would remain this strong. Had her lease been automatically voided and would someone be knocking on her door eventually to tell her as much?

In the apartment she went through the same pages again, less frantically, and found nothing until the small headline on page twenty-two jolted her:

VILLAGE SHOOTING

> Peter Drexler, 35, of Manhattan, was shot and wounded last night in a brownstone at 40 West Tenth Street. Charged with the attack is Joanne Ellis, 58, of Rhinebeck, New York.
>
> Drexler was treated for a minor gunshot wound at St. Vincent's Hospital and released. His assailant who, police say, is a recently discharged mental patient, remains in custody.

She read it several times, and while it didn't seem inaccurate to her, clearly there had been more at some point and Michael's phone calls had carried some weight after all. There was nothing at all in the *Times*, not even a brief mention in the police blotter.

She boiled water for a cup of instant coffee and searched through her ragged address book for the McCabes' phone number. She thought she had entered it there, but apparently hadn't. In the phone book the only listing for Michael McCabe was his Lexington Avenue office. The McCabes' home number at UN Plaza, the information operator confirmed to Maggie, was unlisted, so there was nothing to do but wait for Peter's call. Of course he would call—he might even have called already, while she was out.

She carried the phone into the living room and went out onto the terrace with her coffee. It was 8:35. By nine Peter still hadn't called, which Maggie couldn't at all understand; he had to know how worried she was. She thought for the nth time of Michael's remarks the night before, this time with a sinking feeling. Was Peter in the process of "going through" her, the way he had gone through the hordes of others Michael had told her about? Maybe she shouldn't have dismissed his warnings so easily last night—or was she going in the opposite direction now and taking them much too seriously?

It was early and it was Saturday, she reminded herself. Peter hadn't called, but neither had anyone she knew who might have seen the piece in the *News*. Frank Powell, if anybody, would catch it and be in touch immediately. So would Bergen Management and a few anonymously irate neighbors, the ones the bullets had whistled past.

She walked to the edge of the terrace and pulled off a faded geranium. At nine-fifteen she called St. Vincent's. No patient named Peter Drexler was currently listed there. Maggie hung up, gave the phone a few minutes more to ring, and then dialed Frank Powell's number. He answered brightly, right away, and Maggie said, "I obviously didn't wake you."

"Are you kidding—an old farmboy like me? How'd you know I was just thinking about you, too?"

"I didn't. Listen—did you happen to read the *Daily News* this morning."

"Yeah. Ditto the *Times*. What do you want to know?"

"All of the *News*?"

"Anything fit to print, why?"

"Check page twenty two."

Frank put the phone down. Maggie could hear classical music in the background and then the sound of pages being turned. "Twenty-two," Frank said distantly, and after a brief pause Maggie heard, "*My God!*" He was back on the phone. "What the hell *happened*?"

"You just read all about it," Maggie said.

"Christ—are you okay?"

"I'm fine. I was just curious if you'd seen it."

"Must've gone right by it."

Most people would do the same, she hoped. "Thanks. That's all I wanted to know."

"Wait a minute," Frank yelled into the phone. "You're not going to leave me with that, are you?"

"That's all there is."

"Bullshit. There's got to be more. Sit tight, I'm on my way down."

"Frank?" She caught him just before he hung up. "I won't be here."

"Where will you be? I'll meet you."

"With Peter."

There was silence. "You want my reaction to that?"

Maggie could see him fuming at the other end. His concern was touching and reassuring; if she hadn't expected to hear from Peter at any moment, she would have felt very comfortable with Frank Powell close by, very secure. "I'll call you later, all right?" she said.

"Promise?"

"Promise."

"I'll be here," Frank said.

She had gone into the kitchen for a second cup of coffee when the phone rang at last. Maggie almost leaped at it. It was Peter, his voice not fully awake yet. "Talwin," he explained. "It knocked the hell out of me."

"How are you?" they asked each other at the same time.

Peter said, "Rotten, lousy."

Maggie felt her stomach sink. "What do you mean, what happened?"

"Last night," he said, sounding miserable. "Cutting out on you like that. *Jesus.*"

"Oh, for God's sake," Maggie said. "How were you supposed to help that?"

"I could've been more on top of things. I really chewed Gail out."

"Because of me?" She heard a disgruntled sound from him. "I got home fine."

"With Michael. *Smart.*"

She heard the unasked question and said, "Nothing happened."

"You're sure about that?"

"Would I lie?"

"Well, something happened somewhere. He came home to change and pick up his luggage." He had lowered his voice. "That jackass is really going to *do* it one of these days."

He had to admit, though, that Michael was handling everything pretty well, including the press. Had Maggie seen the *News* article? No headlines, nothing but the barest facts, particularly the "recently discharged mental patient" reference, which seemed to say it all. It was as much as Peter had any right to expect, he supposed, short of a piece that didn't have his name in it at all. Fortunately it was Saturday, and who read Saturday papers anyway? He was sounding more awake already; energetic and positive, too. Maggie said so.

"Why shouldn't I be?" Peter said. "It's over. Just a question of picking up the pieces now. You, y'know—you're my one real problem."

"Me?"

"Hell, yes. How do I begin to make all of this up to you?"

"Oh, come on," Maggie said.

"What's your day like anyway?"

At eleven Maggie met him at the garage entrance to his building, supposedly to start putting his apartment together again. She was protective and solicitous, and took offense when he laughed at her. He let her support him on the walk down the ramp and through the cavernous garage which was no less creepy for the bright and cloudless sky outside. At his car, the gray Volvo, he stopped her.

"Ever get the feeling you'd like to chuck it all? Just get in a car and *go*?"

"Frequently."

His keys appeared; he held them up like a bell and shook them. "Here's our chance."

"What do you mean?"

"Do you drive?"

"Sure I drive."

He threw her the keys. "Let's go."

She followed his instructions, driving (terrified by the Saturday midtown traffic) to the Queensboro Bridge.

"What about your apartment?" she asked him.

"Gail and Louise are taking care of it. They can go crazy without us."

What *about* Gail, Maggie wanted to ask him—had she given him an official release? But they had started onto the bridge and she concentrated instead on the bridge traffic. The lanes were too narrow for comfort and the grooves in the roadway grabbed at the wheels treacherously. She squeezed the steering wheel with both hands, not talking and not letting him talk either. Occasionally she would mutter "Bastard" or "Son of a bitch" as someone drove past her. At the first traffic light in Queens she let her head roll forward and her shoulders collapse. *"Whew!"* she said.

Peter reached over and squeezed her leg with his right hand. "You were terrific," he said, and directed her the rest of the way to Playcraft. "I want to take some work out with us," he explained.

"Take out where?" Maggie asked.

"Where else on a day like this? East Hampton."

"Are you crazy?"

"Could be." He pointed ahead. "A right at the corner."

"You're serious."

"Of course I'm serious."

"Look at me!" she cried in what Peter assumed was mock hysteria. She touched the old shirt she was wearing and looked down at her jeans, appalled. "I was planning to shove furniture around, I've got nothing to *wear*, for God's sake."

"I'm not dumb after all," Peter said. He listened to her fulminations as they passed through the gate and into the parking lot.

Calmer, she went with him into the building, through the single unlocked door. They stopped at the lobby desk where Lenny, the weekend guard, sat reading page four (Maggie noticed right away) of the *News*. Peter signed in for them and referred Lenny to page twenty-two to explain his injured arm. Lenny was still looking for the piece when the elevator door closed.

The fifth floor was quiet but not deserted. Peter stopped at one of the design cubicles where a man behind a George Gillan nameplate was studying blueprints. He was thin, with a mustache that reminded her of Frank Powell's—who, she remembered, was waiting for a phone call from her. She looked for an available phone, leaving Peter and Gillan bent over the blueprints.

Frank picked up on the first ring. When Maggie told him Peter's plans, he asked in a disapproving tone, "The day, the weekend—*what*?"

"I don't know, I'm just the chauffeur," Maggie told him.

"What kind of shape are you in to drive?"

"I'm in fine shape. What do you think happened, anyway?"

"You got shot at, dummo—in case you forgot."

"A good reason to get out ot town," Maggie said.

There was more disapproval in his silence. "Call me when you get back, okay?" he said.

Maggie found Peter in his office, trying to stuff papers into a manila envelope. "I need you," he called out to her helplessly. She filled the envelope and rolled up the blueprints for what seemed to be a Saturn-like planet. "It's a space station," Peter said. "Works like a gyroscope." The project was top secret and he described it to her with appropriately guarded excitement, all the way down to the lobby. At first she thought he was putting her on. He wasn't; the project thrilled him.

"Now I know what to get you for your birthday," she said. "When is it?"

"May fourteenth."

Hers was soon, August third. Neither knew whether that should make them compatible or not.

They came out of the elevator and Lenny rose to attention and held up the newspaper. "This is really something," he said to Peter, full of admiration.

Peter navigated them to the expressway and then leaned back in his seat, letting the warm air wash over him. "You're not really upset about this, are you?" he asked Maggie.

"Of course not."

He touched his left arm lightly. "It's amazing, you know? I can feel it healing already." He brought his hand up to her face. "How about you?"

Maggie nodded. Getting away from the city, even on a crazy impulse, was turning out to be exactly what she needed. Having no clothes still disturbed her and so did her uncertainty about Gail—a feeling that wouldn't go away, however much at ease she felt with Peter. Would Gail be joining them at some point? Did she know it was Maggie who was driving Peter to East Hampton? She had to ask him the first question at least, with what she tried to make him believe was mere curiosity.

"Gail?" Peter said, as though the question made no sense to him.

"She might want to get away herself," Maggie said. It seemed to her a reasonable observation.

"She's working on my apartment, didn't I tell you?"

"Oh, right," Maggie said. The questions, she decided, would stop there. Something inevitably came into her voice whenever she talked about Gail.

The house, sleek redwood and glass with two large stone chimneys, was set way back from the road, directly on the ocean. A stone wall ran the width of the four-acre property, along the road; the original wall that had survived, Peter told Maggie, the huge white wreck of a house he and Gail had had leveled after their mother's death six years ago. The new house belonged to Gail and him jointly. They used it all year round, sometimes together, sometimes separately—Gail as often as Peter, despite the time she spent in Washington.

The plantings, full and beautifully tended, hid the house from the road and from the neighboring houses, which were a good distance away. Even the ocean side was private—or private enough, the deck with its potted pines clearly visible only at certain angles.

Peter had led Maggie through the house onto the rear deck. She walked its length, taking deep breaths of the sea air.

"Didn't I tell you?" Peter said, enjoying the look of pleasure on her face. "Private, which means dress optional. *Any* kind of dress." He moved his shirt by lowering his left shoulder and slipping his right arm out of his sleeve. He threw the shirt onto a deck chair and heard Maggie saying, "Gorgeous, spectacular," to the ocean view.

He kicked off his shoes. "Come on down to the beach."

There was a flight of sturdy wooden steps from the deck to the sand. Peter waited while Maggie took off her shoes and rolled up her jeans. She said, "If they take credit cards around here, I'll invest in a swimsuit." Bent over, she looked up at him. "And don't tell me we swim raw."

"Of course we swim raw," Peter said. He undid his pants and slid them down with one hand. "Your turn." He waited. Maggie walked past him with a barely tolerant look. "You need a little more encouragement? Okay, you got it." He pulled off his shorts too and kicked them over her head to the sand.

Maggie looked up at him sarcastically. "Oh, for God's sake—" she began, but the ringing of the phone in the house cut her off.

"Just when things were warming up," Peter remarked. He listened to the ringing and hesitated.

"I'll go wet my feet," Maggie said. She was halfway down the steps, the wood smooth and hot under her feet.

"I'll be out in a minute." He went into the house and slid the doors shut behind him.

Maggie continued down and stooped to pick up Peter's shorts, which she tossed up onto the deck. The ringing stopped. She listened briefly for Peter's voice from the house and heard only the surf behind her.

"Gail," she said to herself.

"It's *worse* than thoughtless. I've been going crazy here!"

It was, as Peter had known on the first ring, Gail.

She was playing big sister again, and frantic big sister at that—which was all right in view of what he had been putting her through lately. She needed the release and Peter listened, letting his silences describe the guilt Gail couldn't see in his face.

Why had he left her apartment without waking her; why had he left at all? She'd gone to his apartment with Louise, and hadn't found him there either; nor had she found his car when she went to look for it in the garage.

"I panicked all over again."

"I'm sorry," Peter repeated.

She had called the direct line to his office and gotten nothing. What was she supposed to think after everything that had happened? Peter remained silent.

"You can't drive. How did you get out there, anyway?"

"I can drive," he said, and realized he was stalling, avoiding Maggie's name.

"Of course you can't."

"I didn't, though—which is not the same thing. Maggie drove."

There was the pause he expected before Gail said, in the hurt tone he had also expected, "I see. And she's with you now?"

"Yes, just got here."

"How long are you staying?"

"Till tomorrow or Monday morning, I don't know yet."

"But she'll stay with you. I'm asking out of concern," she added quickly. "You need someone with you."

"Maggie'll stay. Stop worrying. I'll call you when we get back to town."

"Before, if you need anything."

"We won't," he said firmly. "You're not still mad, are you?"

"Furious," Gail said.

Peter went into his room and tried to get into a bathing suit. Still half out of it, he slid open the glass doors facing the ocean and called to Maggie, who was knee deep in the surf. She couldn't hear, not until he came down to the beach and stopped at the edge of the foaming water. He called her name and she turned, laughing, wet up to her waist, and saw the suit he had managed to pull all the way up, a bit unevenly.

"I figured you were putting me on," she said.

"About what?"

Maggie nodded at his suit and at the distant figures on the beach in both directions. "There are people." She raised a hand to shield her eyes. "Including children."

"Not here there aren't." He was walking into the surf toward her. He held his left arm, taped from waist to shoulder, stiffly against him. The thin sling ran diagonally across his chest. "Jesus, this is cold!" he said, moving slowly.

"Who called?" Maggie asked.

Peter raised himself higher as a small wave rolled in, and made a chilly sound. "Gail," he answered matter-of-factly. "Checking in. She sends her best."

"Thanks. Will we be seeing her after all?"

Peter shook his head. "Just you and me, I'm afraid." He was close enough to touch her. "I needed some help in there," he said, tossing his head in the direction of the house behind them.

"What kind of help?"

He looked down at his crotch and pulled at the elastic uncomfortably. "One hand wasn't enough. I still need some help, in case you haven't noticed."

"What you really need is a cold shower," Maggie said, moving quickly out of reach. She scooped a handful of water at him, aiming below his waist. Peter pulled his stomach in and hunched his shoulders as the cold water hit. He grimaced in pain and grabbed hold of his taped arm. Maggie cried out, pulled herself a few steps toward him and framed his arm with her hands, not daring to touch him.

"I'm *sorry,*" she almost wept. "How stupid, how goddamned *dumb* of me—"

Peter held his right hand up, palm toward her in a peace gesture. He smiled broadly. "All better, Honest."

Maggie felt water and sand rushing away from her and her heels sinking slightly. "Are you sure? God, I could kick myself."

Peter kept two fingers pointing stiffly at the sky in a scout's oath and waited for the tearing sensation in his upper arm to fade. It did, rapidly, and he held out his hand to lead Maggie back to the house, saying, "Come on, prude, let's go dig up a suit for you."

On their first arrival they had passed through the house too quickly for Maggie to notice much more than the space and the light, and these impressed her again when they came back inside. "You're spoiling me," she said. "Tenth Street's become claustrophobic at this point."

"Among other things," Peter added guiltily, and Maggie said, "Will you stop worrying about that—once and for all?"

She moved through the house more leisurely now, enjoying the luxury of turning with both arms spread out if she wanted.

"You mean that's all it takes to make you happy?" Peter said. "A few spins around a room?"

He went into another part of the house and Maggie stopped in front of a portrait of Gail that immediately became the focal point of the room for her. Not that it was prominently hung or a particularly striking portrait; it was simply a good likeness of Gail, which was enough to subordinate anything else in view.

Near the painting was a corridor leading to the bedrooms—Peter's and the McCabes' facing the ocean, with a guest bedroom and study opposite. Maggie heard Peter announce, "Found one!" and saw him coming into the corridor, holding up two pieces of red cloth which turned out to be a bikini. "Found some other goodies for you, too. Come on and look."

He had placed a selection of women's clothes on the big bed in his room. There were slacks, a sweater, a size-ten dress which would or should fit Maggie perfectly, and silk jersey lounging pajamas that made her say, "Mmmm!"

"Didn't I tell you the Lord would provide?" Peter said, holding onto the red bikini. Maggie carried the peach-colored pajamas to the full-length mirror on the closet door. She looked at herself approvingly. "Gail's?" she asked, addressing Peter in the mirror.

"No," he said. Maggie became silent and examined herself from another angle. Peter said it for her: "Susan's." There was nothing at all mournful in his tone. "You don't mind, do you?"

"Not at all," Maggie said without meeting his eyes in the mirror. "She had taste."

"Yeah." Maggie heard it this time, the note of sadness, and saw it, too, in the way he was staring at the clothes on the bed. Maggie laid the pajamas down carefully, breaking Peter's stare. "She had a hell of a lot going for her . . . Susan. . . ." He shrugged helplessly, then smiled an apology and said, brightening, "You're not going to need any of them, of course. Guarantee you'll be living in this little number." He handed her the bikini. "Put it on."

"Right now?"

"Sure." He took a few steps back and leaned against a bureau, facing her while she examined the bikini—Susan's—stretching it, her hands through the openings. An image of Susan kept coming back to her, the only one she had, remembered from the dim light of Peter's apartment bedroom—the pretty blonde girl photographed with Peter, their arms around each other. (Were there pictures of her here, too, lovingly preserved, like her clothes?)

She placed the suit on the bed and tried to lose the distracting image by undressing, pulling the striped jersey top up over her head. Peter was beside her when she surfaced. He said, "Let me help."

"Help with what?"

He replied by putting his hand on her back. "I think I can manage," she said. She reached back to undo her bra and Peter slapped her hands away lightly.

"I like helping."

Maggie let her hands fall to her sides and said, "If I didn't know you were incapacitated I'd suspect your motives along about now."

The image of Susan flashed briefly into her mind again, and then Peter had her bra unfastened and was removing it slowly. He bent his head and kissed first one breast and then the other. Maggie closed her eyes and drew in her breath sharply. There was no image now, no disturbing thought of Susan or sense of her presence; nothing but the sensation of Peter's lips moving slowly over her skin. Her legs moved back against the mattress; Peter was trying to force her down. She resisted, pushing back against him to keep herself upright, remonstrating.

"Pete . . ."

It .was an automatic reaction on her part that meant nothing at all. She wanted him as badly as he did her—and she wanted him exclusively, with no references to Susan Ellis, to her wit, her beauty, the way she wore her clothes, or anything else she might have had going for her. He pushed harder and although Maggie kept saying, "We can't . . ." she was caressing Peter all the while, helping him to undress her.

"What do you mean, we can't?" He forced her down onto the bed.

"Your arm," she said to remind him.

"My *arm?*" He lay beside her on his back, pulling her over him. "What the hell has that got to do with it?"

They made love, intensely, using the "little imagination" Peter suggested to compensate for his trussed arm. Afterwards they sunned on the deck and in the sand and Maggie took a quick and shivering plunge into the ocean. They went into town for lobsters and ate them greedily on the candlelit deck after watching the sun go down.

"A good idea after all?" Peter asked her, raising his wine glass to the dark ocean.

"A passable one," Maggie said. She looked blissful.

"Stick around, then. There might be a few more."

They made love again inside, in front of a fire Maggie had helped Peter to build. And that might have been what finally did it for Maggie—exorcised the past from the evening, exorcised Gail and Joanne and Susan Ellis.

At two in the morning they picked themselves up and went to bed in Peter's room. He looked at Maggie before turning off the lamp and saw that her eyes were closing.

"Okay?" he asked her.

"Okay," Maggie said. She snuggled against him.

She had fallen asleep to the rocking sound of the surf. Now she awoke to another sound—movement somewhere in the house. For just a moment after opening her eyes she was disoriented, until she became aware of the surf again, gentler than it had been the night before, and heard the cries of gulls. Peter was sleeping pressed against her back, his breath warming her neck. Maggie listened for the dim sound in the house that had awakened her. It had stopped abruptly. She was facing the windowless wall of the room, white and bright with reflected light. Her watch on the night table read 9:40. It was Sunday, she remembered.

She lay motionless, listening and feeling Peter's deep breathing, and then she slid away from him to the edge of the bed. She pushed aside the sheet and sat up slowly, lowering her feet to the floor. A white terrycloth robe, like her own, lay on a chair draped with the selection of Susan's clothes that, except for the bikini, she had managed not to wear. She would wear her own clothes now, too, or she would wear nothing, at least in the house. She started to rise and stopped herself suddenly, aware not of a sound now but of a presence close by. She turned, sitting stiffly on the edge of the bed, and there was Gail watching her from the open doorway. The shock of it almost made Maggie cry out. Her hands jerked up to her face and then grabbed at the sheet to cover her nakedness. The movement brought a small moan from Peter. He turned his face away from Maggie and buried himself deeper into the pillow while she tried to pull the sheet up over him.

Gail's hard, trancelike stare broke. She looked away from the bed—at the floor, at something farther down the corridor, to cover what Maggie couldn't decipher in her face—anger or hurt or embarrassment. She made a vague gesture with her right hand, as if to erase what she had seen and was now looking away from, and moved wordlessly out of the doorway, in the direction of her bedroom. Maggie heard her door close, not quietly, and heard too the change in Peter's deep, regular breathing. His face was turned away from her but she could sense his eyes opening at the sound down the hall. She waited for him to look at her, the sheet still pulled tightly over her breasts.

Peter raised his head from the pillow, wide awake and alarmed when he saw Maggie's face. "What's wrong?"

"Gail," Maggie said.

Peter turned his body toward Maggie and the door, the sheet twisting around his ankles. "What about her?"

"She's here." She nodded at the empty doorway.

"Here?" Peter drew the sheet up to his stomach and let one leg hang over the side of the bed. "You're kidding." He sounded almost pleased. "Where'd she go?" Maggie gestured in the direction of the sound and Peter called, "Gail?" He waited. *"Hey!"* He was listening, staring past Maggie at the wall between the two bedrooms. There was no answer from Gail, no sound at all.

"She seemed a little . . ." Maggie left it unfinished.

Peter shrugged. He got out of bed and pulled on a pair of jogging shorts that were loose and easy for him to get into.

"She saw us together," Maggie said.

Peter thought about it briefly and said, "So what?" He went to the windows and pulled the drapes open all the way. It was another bright day, a warm one already with only the slightest breeze coming into the room. He opened the glass doors wider and drew several deep breaths. He was delaying, it seemed to Maggie; Gail's appearance was a jolt to him too.

"I feel a little funny about her seeing us like this," she said. "Embarrassed."

"You've got no reason to be. Hell, she knows we screw."

The thought of Gail's reaction made Maggie wince. "Okay, it's the prude in me again."

"Who's a prude?" He came to her side of the bed, sat beside her, and kissed her, at the same time trying to pull the sheet from around her. Maggie drew her knees up and said, "Don't."

"Why not?" Peter gave the sheet another tug. "Nothing's changed just because Gail's here."

"I said, *don't!*" She raised her voice slightly and gave him a look serious enough for him to remove his hand from the sheet.

"Okay, okay." He stood up and Maggie called him and held her hand out to him contritely. She was smiling and after a moment he smiled, too. "Get dressed while I find her," he said. He turned and made the peace sign before he left the room, then closed the door behind him.

* * *

The McCabes' bedroom (Gail's really—there was very little evidence of Michael around) was larger and more finished than Peter's, with a lot more greenery in view at the north end of the house. Peter had come into the room without knocking. Gail's overnight case was on the bed. The glass and screen doors out to the deck were open, with Gail beyond them, leaning on the railing with her back to the room. Peter stopped just inside and cleared his throat quietly.

"What're you doing here?" he asked brightly. Gail turned her head just enough to show him her profile. She heard him step out onto the deck and walk toward her.

"I was going to call," she said, looking at the ocean again, "and then I thought, why call, let me surprise them." She waited for a wave to roll in and break. "I should have called."

Peter was beside her at the railing, watching her face. "It doesn't matter."

"Maybe not to you." She tilted her head slightly in the direction of Peter's bedroom.

"Not to Maggie, either."

"I'm intruding."

"It's your own house, for Chrissake."

"You know what I mean." She looked at the exposed fingers of his hand and followed the tape up to his shoulder, avoiding his face. "How does it feel?"

"Not bad." He wiggled his fingers for her and lifted his arm as far away from his body as the sling would allow. "I'm pretty damn resilient, you know that."

"So is Joanne Ellis," Gail said. Peter's fingers stopped moving; he lowered his arm. "She came out of it last night, according to Creegan—too late for me to get in touch with you."

"She's all right?" Peter asked anxiously.

"She'll survive. A few cracked ribs, that's all—physically anyway. Creegan says there'll be a hearing."

"I don't want a hearing. All I want is for her to be put away."

"She'll be that all right. There are certain formalities I don't think we can avoid this time."

"Why not?"

"Because it went a lot beyond harassment. There are other people involved—whoever she got to wreck your apartment among them."

"I'm not pressing any charges."

"The DA probably is."

"Then let Michael move his ass! He owes us that at least." Peter paced half the length of the deck, forming a loose fist and hammering at the rail which, like the deck boards, was already warm in the sun. He turned and came back to Gail. "I just want it buried, Gail—the whole goddamn mess. Otherwise I'm gonna wind up at Shadylawn myself."

Gail touched his lips and whispered, "Relax. Relax." She traced the line of his mouth lightly, back and forth, edge to edge, until the tension no longer showed in his forehead. "Would I let something like that happen, ever? Just relax."

He closed his eyes and raised his face to the sun shining just over the roof, letting the heat soak in. There were gulls circling very close, noisily. "Still mad that I showed up?" Gail asked above their cries.

Peter kept his eyes closed. "Never mind me," he said.

"You think *I'm* mad?" she asked him defensively. Peter shook his head at the suggestion. "A little miffed maybe," Gail couldn't resist adding. "You thought coming out here was a bad idea when I suggested it."

"I didn't think I could get away."

"What changed your mind?"

"Not thinking at all, just doing it."

"Exactly what I did." She checked her watch and looked pained. "At—God!—seven in the morning. On one cup of coffee."

There was a rolling metallic sound as Maggie slid the screen open and came out onto the deck, wearing her jeans and striped jersey. Gail turned to her and raised her voice: "No wonder I've been manic." It was an apology and, judging from the light tone she used, an unembarrassed one. As though she hadn't been discovered standing in that doorway and watching them in bed with a look that to Maggie had seemed almost malevolent. She even opened her arms to Maggie and embraced her warmly. "I'm a lot more discreet usually," she said, turning it into a private joke between herself and Maggie. "Pete will tell you."

She resented doing it but Maggie found herself imitating Gail's friendly tone, which didn't seem at all forced or phony. The politician's wife again. "That's all right," she said, "I didn't expect to find me here either." She could be just as devious and convincing at it, she was happy to discover.

Gail laughed. "That's my brother for you."

"What's your brother?" Peter said. "What's going on between you two?"

Gail said, "Nothing." She drew them both together and stood between them, assuming her usual hostess pose. "I owe you dinner at least—the Club, the Town House, whatever you're in the mood for." She caught the quick look between them. "Unless you've made other plans."

Peter was waiting for Maggie to respond. She wanted to narrow her eyes at him but shrugged instead, more yes than no since she'd been put on the spot, and passed it back to him on an outstretched palm. "No plans," Peter said.

"No clothes, either," Maggie added.

"What did we improvise?" Peter reminded her.

Maggie wanted to say, "They're Susan's," but they weren't, not anymore.

"I forgot about them," Maggie said, and felt a sudden chill in the light breeze from the ocean.

CHAPTER NINE

Independence Hall, Gail called it—everybody on his own until cocktails at seven. Their dinner reservation was for eight o'clock, at the Town House since Peter would have nothing to do with Gail's club ("Boring, snooty—be social on your own time.").

Gail made a pot of coffee and drank several cups alone on the terrace, working her way through the *Times.*

"Coffee's great if anybody's interested," Maggie heard her call out. The red bikini was hanging over the curtain rod in Peter's bathroom. She pulled it down, thinking not of Susan but of sun and ocean and waves of heat rising from that vast, luxurious stretch of empty sand. When Gail disappeared from the deck, Maggie left the house, baked in the sand, got wet, and started on a long walk along the beach.

Gail, who had changed into a one-piece black swimsuit, cut very low in back, watched Maggie, watched the bright red of Susan's bikini (she remembered it) become a pinpoint of color in the distance. She piled the newspapers on the driftwood-and-glass table and weighed them down with a rock shining with mica.

The waves were breaking gently and the ocean was alive with light; the sound, soft and regular, was hypnotic enough to put her out if she didn't lift herself from the chair. She would allow Peter another fifteen minutes of work behind the closed study door, then urge him outside and onto the beach with her. It was an effort to move but she got up and entered the house through his bedroom, calling his name. There was no reply from the study across the hall.

Gail waited in the bedroom. The bed had been fixed, the rust-colored spread evenly arranged; even the throw pillows were piled neatly. Maggie, of course. Gail examined the surfaces of night tables, bureaus. She looked in the closet and saw Maggie's jeans and jersey top on a hanger next to Susan's clothes and next to Peter's smelling so distinctively of Peter, warm and fragrant.

It was an image—the closet, the clothes—that brought back the summer of three years ago when Susan and Peter had come out to the house regularly. Gail remembered Susan's clothes beside Peter's, another hanger or two of them every weekend, multiplying in his closet.

It had been the same with his apartment in town, the duplex on Sixty-third that he'd had then, where there would be more of Susan every time Gail came up from Washington. There was a drawer with Susan's underwear and the nightgown Gail knew had never even been unfolded—except once, by Gail herself. The fact that there was at least as much of Peter in Gail's Eighty-fourth Street apartment was something they had joked about at the time, all three of them. It would have been cheaper and more convenient to eliminate one of the apartments, Gail had remarked.

"Disastrous, too," Susan had said.

They never did live together regularly, never seemed to know where they would find themselves. That was the way it struck Gail anyway. She never knew who would be answering the phone or when she could find Peter alone in the apartment. A few times she had come upon them suddenly and embarrassingly, like this morning with Maggie. No—worse, she remembered: one time in particular, when they were making love. Knowing she was there and could hear them. Susan making sounds, making sure Gail heard her being plugged. Bitch.

Inevitably, of course, it passed. Susan passed.

Gail shut the closet door, snuffing the image of Susan and the sound of Susan's voice in her head. Poor Susan. She genuinely felt that. Poor Susan.

The door to the study opened without warning and Gail heard Peter crossing the corridor to the bedroom. She stepped away from the closet and again called to him before he entered the room. "I was wondering where you were holed up," she said.

"With Woody Wobbly and the guys," he said in an excited parody of a child's voice. He gave her a light tap in passing and went into the bathroom. "Have I seen you in that suit before?"

"World premier," Gail said, strolling away from the door Peter had left open.

"It's sensational."

"I thought you might like it."

She heard him struggle with his suit and mutter, "Damn!" then raise his voice to her: "Where's Maggie?"

"Out walking?"

"Alone?"

"Last I saw. How about sitting on the beach with me?"

"I'm up to my ass in work."

"Well, bring your ass and your work outside. Your arm, too. A little sun can't hurt."

She waited for him to come out of the bathroom, still adjusting his bathing suit, and followed him back into the study where a bright pasted-together dummy of the Playcraft catalogue covered the desk. "How's this for industry?" Peter asked her. She applauded soundlessly. He bent forward and brought his pen to a line of copy he had been revising. "Maggie and I were talking before," he began hesitantly; he corrected a word and then crossed out the correction.

"About what?" Gail asked, immediately suspicious.

"About heading back to town tonight. Taking you up on that dinner offer some other time."

"Whatever for? We were all set."

Peter waved his hand over the catalogue. He was saying it all with difficulty, without looking directly at her. "I've got to be in the office with this early tomorrow. Very early, as a matter of fact."

"Oh no, you don't," Gail said brightly. "Take a day, two days, all the time you need. That's a Member of the Board speaking, and a major stockholder. Savvy?" She moved so that he would have to look at her face. "You're not running out on me twice in two days," she said, not at all unpleasantly.

"Who's running out?"

"You, and your guest." She took the pen out of his hand, capped it and placed it firmly down on the desk, then reached for his hand to pull him out of the room.

"I'm sorry if she's uncomfortable around me," Gail said later on the beach. She was kneeling behind Peter, rubbing suntan oil into his back, carefully outlining the tape reaching his left shoulder.

"Who said she's uncomfortable?" Peter said defensively.

"It's pretty obvious to me." She was rubbing slowly, with strong round strokes that he leaned back against. He sat facing the sea, on the towel that Maggie had left behind in the sand. "Going back tonight was her idea, wasn't it?"

"Mine. Why're you making such a big deal of it, anyway?"

"Am I?" She rubbed lower, following the line of his spine. "I don't know—I seem to intimidate a lot of your lady friends. I honestly don't set out to do it."

"Maggie isn't intimidated."

"Well, good for Maggie." Gail could see her far away, coming back. "I like her. I told you that the first time I met her." She moved from behind him on her knees and said, "This side's done. Lie back."

"One side's all I've got time for." Peter took the oil from her and gave her a gentle push forward onto her stomach. The towel was clammy under her and gritty with sand. She could smell the suntan oil.

"Mmmm." She was digging her fingers into the sand, finding it cool and damp under the surface. "Summer."

The huge straw hat she was wearing came below her shoulder blades when she was lying flat. Peter lifted it and turned it upside down in the sand. Right away Gail felt the sun weighing down on her head, and oil, too much of it, being poured on her back and the back of her legs. Peter rubbed it in with his right hand, a few times almost losing his balance with the effort.

Gail gave a long, lazy sigh and watched Maggie in the bright red swimsuit draw closer and wave in their direction. "Wouldn't it be bliss," she said, the sand muffling her words, "just us out here? A whole summer to swim in, ride, play tennis? The way it was way, way back. No Woody Wobblies anywhere; not in New York, not in D.C. Nothing to distract us. Just us."

"Don't knock Woody Wobbly," Peter said, his voice as soothing as the long deep stroke of his hand.

Gail closed her eyes. She might have dozed a few minutes because something was now standing between her and the sun. She opened her eyes behind the dark glasses and Maggie, who had been so far off just moments ago, was standing above her and talking quietly to Peter. Gail lay still, giving no indication that she was awake. Maggie moved somewhere behind her and Gail could hear her lower herself down to the sand beside Peter and laugh softly at something he did or whispered. They were silent and then they were kissing. Gail could hear it, hear the sound of their breathing, hear their bodies moving together, even feel the movement against her own body. Maggie made a sound, a small cry, and then made the sound again, a cry that was a plea too.

There was whispering, very private, covered by the sound of the surf, and then they were getting up, both of them, Maggie first, getting up behind her and moving away from her. Back to the house, leaving her there alone. Maggie leading, she was sure, drawing Peter back to the house.

They were making love. The drapes in Peter's room were closed when Gail used the deck to get to her own room, and so was the inside door when she walked past it later. They remained closed most of the afternoon. Gail didn't see or hear either of them until around five when Maggie went back down to the beach alone.

Gail stopped her and called out, "Seven?" from the kitchen, as a reminder.

"Seven," Maggie said without hesitation—as though she hadn't really suggested to Peter that sudden, early return to New York.

Just before seven Maggie knocked on her bedroom door and announced, "Crisis." Gail tensed and waited for the manufactured excuse that surprisingly did not come. Maggie was pointing to her feet which were bare under the silk jersey lounging pajamas she was wearing. "Ten-E, if you really want complications," she stage-whispered. "*Who* but me would wear a Ten-E?" She raised her voice in the direction of Peter's room: "You're not hearing any of this, are you?"

"Hearing what" Peter called back.

"A very deep, very dark secret of mine."

Gail was studying her feet, intently enough to be embarrassing. "No crisis," she said. "We've just got to find somebody with big feet."

She made a few phone calls and came into their bedroom without knocking to say that Lee Dalton could provide a pair of white satin Ten-B's which they would pick up on their way to the Town House.

Maggie had helped Peter with his shirt, even managing to get his left arm into the sleeve. They were standing next to the bed. It had been put together again, but hurriedly, unevenly; the throw pillows were still piled on the floor. They *had* made love.

"See that, babe?" Peter said to Maggie. "Marry into politics and you learn all the angles."

Maggie smiled without looking over at Gail. She was too busy buttoning and then unbuttoning Peter's shirt–one button, then the button below it, spreading the shirt open on his chest.

They had cocktails on the deck, short ones, with Maggie wearing her old brown sandals on feet that seemed enormous now, even to her. There were more drinks at the Daltons' rambling gray barn of a house closer to town, where Gail knew everyone, even the Daltons' weekend guests.

"Peter Drexler!" cried one of them, a patrician-looking woman. "How long has it been?" She was holding his good arm and, like the woman at Hopper's in New York, was not at all interested in Maggie.

"Too long," Lee Dalton said, "for all of us." Lee was a small comic woman with hands that were, much to her own amusement, the size of her feet. She turned to Gail. "I wish you'd get him out here a little more often."

"You'll see plenty of him this summer," Gail said. "I'll make sure of it."

"Michael, too?"

"Are you kidding?" Michael almost never came out to the beach.

Lee's shoes pinched and made Maggie take small steps back out to the car, hanging onto Peter.

"Look at what we're doing to this poor kid," he said to Gail.

Gail drove, with Maggie in the middle. She pulled out of the driveway and said, "Lee didn't see the *News* article."

"How do you know?" Peter asked.

"I asked her. I figured if Lee didn't see it, nobody did. Know what really concerned her? Michael. How this was going to affect him."

Peter laughed and rubbed his leg against Maggie's. "No wonder her lousy shoes pinch."

At the restaurant Gail was as "godawful social" as Peter had predicted. She trailed behind Maggie and Peter, stopping at tables on the way to their own.

"You walked right past the Leesons," she said to Peter through a fixed smile. He was holding her chair for her.

"I didn't see them."

"Wave, at least."

She was, as usual, the perfect hostess—witty, bright, considerate, introducing Maggie to several friends who stopped by, and praising her talent and her work, neither of which she knew. Peter, despite protests, was as much at ease in the setting as Gail; as voluble, too, once the last martini hit. Maggie had never really seen them functioning together this way—so smoothly and naturally that she forgot there was a Michael McCabe until a man in a blazer and white slacks, a local politician, asked, "Where's our favorite congressman keeping himself this summer?"

Peter and Gail looked at each other, amused, and Peter said, "Washington, or maybe Korea—we're not exactly sure."

"But doing good wherever he is," Gail said with great sincerity, making a V-sign. "Right?"

"Michael? Absolutely."

Maggie noticed it several times during the evening—the way their personalities interacted and their roles reversed, with Gail bringing out a bitchiness and cynicism in Peter and Peter an artlessness and enthusiasm that were almost boyish in Gail. What she also noticed, or had confirmed, and constantly, was the fact that they might have been beautiful separately but together they were knockouts; the same features, clearly the same blood and breeding—two dazzlingly beautiful people who were quite apart from anyone else in the room, herself included.

They stayed late, among the last to leave, which certainly ruled out anyone's going back to the city that evening. It had been a dumb idea in the first place, Gail said, addressing her party-pooping, workaholic brother. On the way out Maggie went into the ladies' room, leaving Gail to support Peter in the quiet lobby.

"Pretty painless, wouldn't you say?" Gail asked him.

"What was?" Peter was weaving slightly.

"Me, the evening—as far as Maggie was concerned."

Peter made an approving sound and gave her a squeeze.

"I was amusing, I think. She smiled a lot, anyway."

"Damned amusing," Peter said. "Me too."

"But you're not the problem. I don't think I was threatening or intimidating?"

"Nope."

"I was, in other words, my usual, simple self. Little Gail Drexler."

Peter repeated the name, "Gail Drexler," and smiled.

"Well, honey," Gail said in the whiskiest voice she could find, "if you don't think that took *work*. . ."

Outside the air finished Peter off, at the same time sobering Gail for the twenty-minute drive home. He sat in the middle and insisted it wasn't the martinis, the wine, and the brandy making him so shaky and vowelly, it was still the damn Talwin the doctors had given him. "For something, I forget what. . . ." His voice faded and his head rolled against Maggie's shoulder.

"I think he's left us," she said. She had gotten high

fast earlier in the evening out of nervousness; now she was relatively sober, just tired and full. She kissed his forehead and Peter slid his left arm out of the sling and around Maggie's waist with no expression of pain at all. He made a small, cozy sound and snuggled closer, his back to Gail, who was concentrating extra hard on the narrow country road.

Gail stood outside the light spilling onto the deck from the living room. She had carried out a bottle of Courvoisier and three glasses and now poured herself a drink, swirling it in the glass and sniffing. The light was on in Peter's bedroom and the drapes were open. She saw him stagger into the bathroom, dressed, while Maggie took the spread off the bed and folded it carefully. When he came out a few minutes later his pants were off and his shirt was trailing, the sleeve caught around his left elbow. Maggie got the shirt off and resisted some very tired horseplay from Peter before he fell back on the bed. He struggled out of his shorts, aimed them at a chair, and missed. Maggie picked them up, his socks too, and went into the bathroom, reappearing with his pants over her arm.

Gail swirled the brandy in the snifter. She moved a little closer to the bedroom, still keeping out of the light.

Peter's head rose slightly; he was saying something to Maggie, who leaned forward and kissed him and then let him pull her down beside him. She laughed, fighting him, and Gail heard her say, "*No!*" too loudly, covering her mouth after she had said it. She sprang up and flipped the sheet over his head. Peter lay still and then his hand began to rise slowly under the sheet, higher and higher above his groin, tenting the bed. Maggie turned her back on him with a show of great indignation. She came toward the glass doors, which had been locked, opened them halfway, and was about to shut the drapes when Gail, just dimly visible, said, "Can you take a little time for a nightcap?"

The voice startled Maggie. She brought her face closer to the glass, raised her hands, and peered out from between them. "Gail?" she said. Behind her Peter's hand dropped under the sheet.

Gail moved into the light. "It's a lovely night. Keep me company." Maggie turned to look at the bed and Gail said, "Why don't we let him sleep it off?"

"I'm really beat," Maggie said.

"So am I. We'll make it a short one."

Gail moved away, back to the table outside the living-room windows, and poured brandy into another snifter. She saw the bedroom drapes slide shut and Maggie shadowy behind them, turning to say something to Peter before she opened the screen door and came out onto the deck. Gail held the brandy out to her, touched glasses, and drank, watching her all the time.

Maggie swallowed, then opened her mouth to draw in some air. "God, this should really do it."

"Well, you don't have that far to go," Gail said. She looked away from the soft orange glow of Peter's room and walked to the far end of the deck. When she spoke it was quietly, to bring Maggie nearer: "Glad you stayed after all?"

"It was a marvelous evening. Thank you."

"You're still planning to leave tomorrow."

"I've got to."

"Too bad."

"Blame your brother." She saw Gail's questioning

look. "Playcraft," she explained. "I've got a whole bunch of sketches due this week."

"Ah," Gail said, "I forgot all about the professional relationship."

"You can bet Peter hasn't." She played with the drink she really hadn't wanted, aware of that hostile look Gail seemed to wear whenever they were alone together. She was trying not to meet her eyes, looking beyond her at the bedroom, longingly. There was a long silence and finally Maggie said, "We-ell . . ." to start a graceful exit.

Gail chose not to hear. "It's amazing," she said, and left it hanging.

"What is?"

"How much you look like Susan right now."

Maggie could hear neither compliment nor complaint in the casual way she said it. What was unsettling was the fact that she'd said it at all. "It's the clothes," she replied, and looked down at her bare feet. She started to mention Lee Dalton's pinchy shoes, but Gail shook her head and said, "No, not just the clothes." She looked thoughtful, as though trying to zero in on the exact point of resemblance.

"I'll get them back to her tomorrow," Maggie said, breaking Gail's disturbing concentration.

"No, I'll take care of it." She finished her drink and Maggie looked for a place to put her own glass down, but Gail was uncorking the bottle and pouring herself another one. She would just say good night, Maggie decided; why was it any more complicated than that? Gail didn't give her a chance, though. She asked, "Is Peter going with you?"

"As far as I know."

"He shouldn't. He could use a lot more time out here."

Maggie reacted minimally, with a could-be look.

"It's not only his arm I'm worried about," Gail went on, "it's his nerves. He doesn't show it of course, Pete never does, but he's a wreck at the moment."

"I hope he stays, then," Maggie said. It was really terrible, she thought—this prejudice she had built up against Gail. Everything Gail said concerning Peter was automatically suspect in Maggie's mind. It was a problem that would have to be resolved eventually—as soon, that is, as Gail accepted her and her relationship with Peter.

"Please tell him that," Gail said.

"You don't tell Peter things. I don't, anyway."

"You underestimate your influence." Maggie looked at her skeptically. "I've had his apartment put back together, by the way. It's habitable again."

"Good."

"Which means he won't be needing your place anymore."

"No," Maggie said, "I don't suppose he will."

"It might help if you were to make it . . ." She paused and her hand described small, vague circles in the air. ". . . I don't know, less available to him."

For the first time Maggie met her look directly. "It might help what, Gail?"

"Peter, of course. Help him to get his life back together again."

"I have a feeling he will, whatever we do. I happen to have enormous confidence in your brother." She seemed suddenly aware of the drink she was carrying and looked down at it distastefully. "You know, I don't need this at all." She carried the glass to the table and put it down. "Sorry, but I'm about ready to collapse."

"Hey!" Gail held out her hand and managed to

look confused and apologetic. "I've said something wrong, haven't I?'"

Maggie halted, her back to Gail. "You might have. Frankly, I don't think it's worth pursuing."

"I'm sorry–honestly." She had come behind Maggie, moving very quietly. "I'm overly protective of him, I know that. I like to think he needs it." She waited for Maggie to turn a little toward her. "It's just that Pete does things on impulse sometimes. Gets himself involved so easily–physically, emotionally–usually the first. And when someone has as much to offer as Pete does . . . there're always people to take advantage . . . always."

"Do you want me to defend myself, Gail?"

Gail touched her arm. "Of course not. I'm not saying you're Susan. There won't *be* any more Susans in his life, nothing that destructive ever again." Gail shuddered; she drew her arms around herself. "Not if I can help it. I'm the one who got him through that, you know–Susan's death. Not only her death, but the waste of all those years with her. I got him through, like always." She took a deep breath and then her voice became a whisper, closer to Maggie's ear. "I know my brother, I know just where he's vulnerable, just when to protect him." Again, the deep breath. "I don't think he needs you right now, Maggie. I don't think he needs any distractions at all."

Her voice, coming from the darkness behind Maggie and blending with the sound of the waves, had become almost hypnotic. It stopped and Maggie listened to the surf for a while without speaking, without raising her voice when she did.

"I think of myself as more than a distraction, Gail. Maybe you should try coming to terms with that."

"Poor Maggie," Gail said. "Don't you know it yet?

You're all brief distractions. Every last, faceless one of you."

"Good night, Gail," was all Maggie would let herself say before she walked away, toward the soft orange light of the bedroom.

The alarm had been set for seven Monday morning to get them back to the city by eleven. At seven forty-five Peter, who usually relied on his body's inner alarm, stirred at the sound of a car door closing and was then jolted awake by the light coming into the room. He looked at the clock and felt for the alarm button. It had been pushed in. Panicked, he got out of bed and ran into the kitchen for a view of the driveway. A cab was pulling away, with Maggie, to his disbelief, in the back seat. He wanted to call out to her; instead he pulled open the kitchen door and went outside, naked. The cab at the end of the long drive turned onto the road and disappeared behind the heavy shrubbery.

He was struggling into his pants in the bedroom when he noticed the note that must have blown off the night table:

Pete darling,
Didn't have the heart to wake you. Stop fuming and go back to sleep. I'll call later.

Love you,
MAGGIE

Gail hadn't heard anything; her bedroom door was still closed. The keys to her Ford, which was parked in the driveway and blocking his own car in the garage, were on a kitchen counter. Peter tried his arm, flexing his fingers. He could move it fairly well and there was strength enough in his hand, as long as he didn't stretch or move suddenly. Certainly he could drive the short distance to the railroad station where Maggie, for some incomprehensible reason, was catching—he checked the schedule tacked to the corkboard—the eight-fifteen to New York.

At eight-ten he reached the station and saw her waiting on the platform. He called out to her and saw shock come into her face and guilt when he stormed onto the platform, all but shaking his fist at her, and yelling, "What the hell's going on?"

"You can't drive," Maggie said. She looked back at Gail's car. "How'd you get here?"

"Never mind that. What're you pulling, anyway?"

There were several Monday-morning commuters on the platform, and more arriving. Peter's questions, delivered at the same indignant pitch, convinced Maggie to sit in the car with him and explain, "You could use a little more R and R. I didn't want to drag you back into town."

"Who said you'd be dragging *me*, for Chrissake?"

He let her recite all the altruistic reasons she had for leaving him and when she had finished said, "Bullshit!" Maggie looked for a sign of amusement somewhere in his face but his eyes were an icy blue boring into her and his mouth remained set, even when she tried a smile. The train was pulling sluggishly into the station. It drew her attention. "Forget about that," Peter said. He reached for her face and made her look at him. "Now, come on, what went on between you two?"

"What two?"

"Look, don't play dumb with me, goddamnit!"

It was as close as she had ever heard him come to

real anger, and while it wasn't thundering anger it was strong enough to cut through any more pretense. She stared at her lap a few seconds, aware of Peter waiting and aware of the train too that would be pulling out of the station soon. Let it, she decided: Now was as good a time as any to discuss the problem of Gail.

"I'm obviously in the way," she said.

"Whose way?"

"Gail's, yours."

"Gail told you that?"

"More or less. Let's say she made her point." Judging from the intense way he was listening, what Maggie was describing wasn't improbable or, she got the feeling, totally new to Peter. She sat sideways and touched his knee. "Look, Pete, it's not working between Gail and me, I have a feeling it never will."

"Jesus! What's Gail got to do with you and me, anyway?"

"That's what I'm trying to figure out. What am I doing that's making me a threat all of a sudden?"

They were silent while a bell rang on the now almost deserted platform.

"You're sure a lot of this isn't just your imagination?" Peter asked.

"You know it's not." She expected him to protest or pursue it somehow, but he didn't. "She doesn't like me, doesn't like what's going on between us." No more than she had liked Susan, she wanted to add, or any of the other faceless women that had passed in and out of his life. She resisted the impulse: Susan Ellis's name was something she didn't want to call up—not in connection with Gail and that hostile, almost threatening side of her Maggie was seeing right now.

It was there though, a suspicion she couldn't help. She wouldn't voice it, not to anyone, she'd make every effort to put it out of her mind. The idea of Gail having had anything to do with Susan's death was absurd, ridiculous, clearly built on Maggie's prejudice against her.

"You missed your train," Peter said, calling her back. Maggie shrugged and watched it pull out of the station. His voice became gentler, pleading: "You've got to try to understand her, Maggie."

"I'm trying, believe me. What is it, some kind of pattern with her? Does she give up finally? Accept me?"

"She will."

"*When?*"

"Whenever I tell her to." His ease in saying it, his confidence, threw her. She felt for a moment like a pawn in one of his games, learning the rules only as she moved around the board. "She hangs on," Peter said, his voice a little less steady, "because there's nobody else to hang onto, nobody but me. There's nothing between her and Michael, hasn't been for years. He uses her and she's sucker enough to hang around. Hell, he's screwed everything from here to . . . Zambia. Probably screwing it right now, the son of a bitch." He turned inward, looking helpless, distraught. "So I go along with her. I let her take over sometimes, probably too much. I just don't want to hurt her. Christ, I have, plenty of times . . . but only when I've really had to." He took a deep breath and cleared his throat, looking away from her, out the driver's window. The last car was leaving the waiting area. "Don't pull out on me, hunh, Mag? Give me a little more time."

There was a long silence and then he felt Maggie pressing against him, kissing his shoulder. "I love you," she said. She buried her face. "There—secret's out."

He turned and raised her face, searching it with a tenderness she found herself getting lost in. And even if he didn't say it, that look and the closeness of him would have been enough, but he did say it, simply and easily, as though it were something he had been living with a long time: "I love you."

Peter did the driving back to the house, despite Maggie's objections, which were, he told her, invalid anyway. "Hell, you were ready to let me drive into New York alone."

"I expected you to stay out here," she said, her eyes riveted to the road.

"And let all those little elves do the work, hunh?"

"I thought they did it anyway."

"Not without someone to kick their little asses around."

At the house Maggie backed the Volvo out of the garage and waited behind the wheel while Peter went inside. She felt awkward but not as awkward as she would have felt trying to make a hurried peace with Gail. Peter had sensed it and said, "She's probably still asleep. Let me leave her a note."

He was in the house a long time, even allowing for his change of clothes. His mood had changed, too. "Let's go," he said when he got into the car. He threw his papers behind him, and remained silent until Maggie nearly missed a turn and he had to call out, a little too sharply, *"Left!"*

"Sorry," Maggie said. She felt his hand on her

thigh, his fingers moving lightly. "Was Gail awake?" she asked.

There was a pause before Peter looked in her direction and said, "No. Still asleep."

CHAPTER TEN

As soon as they reached Manhattan they started bickering over who was dropping whom and where. Maggie prevailed and left the car and Peter in his garage, making him swear he would cab out to Long Island City and back.

"Tonight?" Peter called as she started up the ramp.

"Let's talk later." She waved back at him.

It was one o'clock before Peter got to his office and found a stack of phone memos on his desk, among them a call from Michael in Washington. He returned the call several times before they were finally able to connect. Michael said—matter-of-factly, like an insurance adjuster—"How's your arm?" He then went immediately to the reason for his call, Joanne Ellis. Her condition was stable, he said, and proceeded to read from the medical report he'd gotten hold of, rattling off "contusions" and "costal cartilages" at Peter. "Her problems, Christ knows, aren't physical at this point," he said. She would be moved from St. Vincent's sometime that afternoon probably.

"Moved where?" Peter asked.

"Ordinarily a state facility," Michael started to say, and Peter jumped in.

"Why state? I'm not pressing charges. I told Gail to—"

"Let me finish, will you?" He waited for Peter to calm down. "Ordinarily, I said. I've talked to the DA, among others—Arthur Ellis, too. What we're doing, quietly, is moving her to a private facility upstate, near Hudson. Not quite the country club Pinehurst is."

"Ellis agrees?"

"Ellis is a sensible man. All this is in lieu of a hearing or any criminal charges. Certain details still have to be worked out; there are assurances we'll want."

He went through it all without pause, making it plain that this was something disagreeable to him, to be done and put out of mind as quickly as possible. There was a slight complication, he said: Paul, the Ellis's chauffeur, might somehow be involved. This according to Lieutenant Creegan, who was working on the possibility—unofficially, as a favor to Michael. The same as last time.

"I'll be in New York this week, tomorrow if I can get away," Michael said. "Christ . . . a bloody mess all over again."

"I know," Peter said, "I'm sorry. I hate like hell putting you through this again, both of you."

"I hate it, too," Michael said wearily, "a lot." There was an unaccustomed silence at his end. "That's all I've got for you."

"Mike, listen, I really appreciate this."

"What for? I'm thinking a lot about my own ass. I'll keep in touch." He almost had the receiver down when he heard Peter call his name. "Yeah?"

"Have you spoken to Gail?"

"This morning; trying to trace you."

"Not since?"

"No. Why?"

"We had this—dumb argument before I left."

"So what's that got to do with me?"

"I just thought she might've mentioned it."

"She didn't," Michael said. "Is that it?"

"That's it."

Peter kept the phone to his ear a long time after Michael had hung up, thinking. Then brought his hand down on the cradle and got a dial tone. He listened and began dialing the East Hampton number, stopping just before the last digit. He forced himself to turn it—three—and waited. The phone rang and rang, at least ten times without being answered. Relieved, Peter hung up.

At six an unscheduled design conference was still going on, which meant Peter wouldn't be leaving the office for hours. During a break he called Maggie at her apartment and asked, "Everything okay there?"

She hadn't been evicted yet, if that was what he meant; there had been no threats phoned, mailed, or personally delivered by her super or her landlord. "Some excitement" was the only comment on the "shootout" (her word) she had heard from the only neighbor she had run into since Friday night.

"In other words I'm coping just fine," Maggie said. "Working on the VA-ROOM! package, you'll be happy to know. Just in case it's still due on Thursday."

"Damn right it's still due," Peter said. His official voice softened: "Think you can cope your way through the night?"

"Why?"

"I'm up to my ass out here, as predicted. I hate doing this to you, babe."

"Stop apologizing. I can use a little breather."

"I don't blame you," Peter said, sounding guilty.

"Pete, I'm *kid*ding."

"You shouldn't be." He heard her exasperated sigh. "Okay, I'll talk to you later. Be there."

Maggie's heels clicked together. She said, "Check."

Peter tried Gail again, and again there was no answer. She was there or, it wouldn't surprise him, back at her apartment. He wasn't concerned; when she was through brooding she would call, as she had done so many times in the past.

Fleetingly, on the way back to the conference room, the thought of Maggie being alone did concern him. The concern had nothing to do with Gail—her inaccessibility, her mood that morning. It was just the expression of a protective sense Peter hadn't felt in himself in a long time. Gail was incidental to it. The concern disappeared; it was the warmth of the feeling he carried back into the conference room.

Roses came for Maggie the next morning. Frank Powell brought them into her office, holding the box behind his back and making an elaborately bashful presentation. There was no card, not until Maggie demanded it from Frank who then said, "I'm my own card." Finally, he gave it to her and Maggie said, "You're unconscionable."

"It's entirely possibly they *were* from me," Frank protested, "even though I don't have a guilty conscience about anything."

Maggie concentrated on the note from Peter:

> Why do I miss you so much?
> Tell you later.
>
> P with L

She read it over several times while Frank watched her face. Looking up suddenly, she happened to catch him off guard, his eyes soft and loving. He covered immediately and pointed to the box of roses.

"Remember how close you came to a whole roomful of those."

"Thanks for reminding me," Maggie said. She picked up a vase of faded carnations and started out of the office.

Frank called, "Maggie?" She stopped and he came beside her. "I never did claim to have much taste, did I?"

"God, no."

"Maybe you ought to make that one of your projects."

He asked her out to dinner that evening and the invitation was delivered surprisingly straight, without any Powellisms. He even sounded a bit nervous.

"Frank." It was a gentle reproach, sympathetic, affectionate. "You know how involved I am."

"I don't know what that means. That he pinned you or something? I don't have to go along with it. Or give up if I want to be thickskinned about it."

"No," Maggie agreed quietly.

"You realize that's the most encouraging thing you've said to me since what's-his-name came on the scene?"

"Peter's his name and it wasn't meant to be encouraging."

Frank shrugged. "That's *my* problem, then. Don't you start getting weepy about it."

Maggie gave him a look that said, Hopeless, incorrigible. She also touched his hand before starting out of the office again with the vase.

"Mag?" Frank called. "Just for the record—I'm not

talking about a commitment. Just a quiet . . . achingly platonic dinner somewhere. Sometime."

Maggie halted in the doorway, mulled it over, and said, "Why not? Sometime."

While she was out of the office Frank flipped through the drawings on the table and the fresh sketch tacked to her board. The VA-ROOM! series he found very effective indeed, and surprisingly virile. Not at all Maggie, needless to say, but strong and beautifully drawn—which meant Maggie after all. Some of the muscle-bound cars were pictured with drivers, square-jawed types. The most lovingly detailed one of them was unmistakably Peter Drexler. Frank started to phrase the line he would use on Maggie when she returned—something about keeping her fantasy life and her work separate—when her phone rang. Frank picked it up for her and heard—surprise—Peter Drexler's voice.

"You're saving me a call," Peter said and kept Frank on the phone to talk about his ad copy. The copy needed, he felt, more balls. Don't we all, Frank wanted to say, but he listened quietly, looking down at Maggie's drawings. What you need is our balls lady, he also kept himself from saying . . .

Maggie came back while Frank was still listening, and had arranged the roses in the vase before she realized Peter was on the other end.

"Here's Maggie now," Frank said. "See you Thursday." He passed her the phone, mouthing, "Thank him for the roses." He winked conspiratorially and surprised her by leaving the room, unasked.

She did thank Peter and right away heard disappointment in his voice. The card was wrong: "Tell you later" should read "Tell you tomorrow."

"Another breather?" Maggie said.

"I'm really pissed about this one. I just heard from Mike. He's coming into town to straighten out all that Ellis business. It's important, babe."

"Of course it's important."

Peter continued, sounding harried. "I've got the doctor at six, I've got—Jesus, I don't know what else."

"Relax, will you?" Maggie said. "It's no big deal."

"For me it is." He paused and his voice lightened. "For you, too, if you're honest about it. What the hell are you gonna *do*? Climb the walls another night?"

"It might surprise you to learn I've got a private life independent of you," Maggie said.

"You mean girlfriends, pajama parties?"

"When the devil's in me. . . ."

"They're nothing like our pajama parties, are they?"

"We'll talk about that tomorrow, too."

"Your place. I'll bring the steaks. Maggie?" His voice changed again, became urgent. "Christ, I miss you."

"Fight it," Maggie said, "like me."

So the dinner she and Frank had been talking about for "sometime" was that evening, at Alfredo's in the Village. She warned him it was nothing more than dinner on the rebound, to which Frank replied, "You are one cautious lady, you know that?"

It was platonic, as promised, and comfortable; lovely, all of it—the food, the summer evening out in the Village, and Frank. He suggested coffee outdoors at the Peacock and she surprised both of them by suggesting coffee outdoors on her terrace.

They took the least direct route to Tenth Street, ambling. In front of her building two old ladies (one of them Rose the 3B Frog) lowered their voices when she passed and eyed her disapprovingly.

Frank asked, "Have you been getting a lot of that?"

"No, none." She unlocked the inner door, which had finally been repaired. At the door to her apartment she froze. Having just passed the pockmarks in the stairwell, Frank's reaction was to tense and ask anxiously, "What's wrong?"

Her door, which she had double-locked, wasn't locked at all now. Music was coming from the apartment. She opened the door and at the same moment she stepped cautiously into her vestibule, Peter entered the living room from the bedroom.

"I figured this is cheaper than another bunch of—" His words died when Frank appeared behind Maggie. Peter grimaced as though something large and fragile were about to hit the floor, and said, "Oh, my God."

There was a heavy silence, all three of them still. Frank spoke first: "We have here what is called a situation, I believe."

Peter began to move on tiptoe into the vestibule. He said, "My mistake," squeezing past them. "Sorry. Honest," he said and walked out of the apartment.

Maggie called after him and heard him say, "The neighbors . . ." warningly as he disappeared down the stairwell. She was waiting to hear him laugh and bound up the stairs again; instead she heard the downstairs door closing.

"I don't believe this," she said aloud to herself, and the amusement she had begun to feel evaporated. Frank saw something like anguish come into her face.

He drew her closer, kissed her, and said, "You owe me a cup of coffee sometime."

It took Maggie a few seconds to react. "Where're you going?"

He was following Peter down the stairs. "I made it over the wall at least. That's all that'll fit under my pillow tonight." His hand waving was the last thing she saw.

Maggie stopped herself from calling after him. She closed her door, locked it, and went out onto the terrace. Someone who might have been Frank moved out of the pool of lamplight in front of her building and vanished beneath one of the thick plane trees on Tenth. She leaned farther over the wall. The line of bay windows in the brownstone next door jutted out and concealed the sidewalk closer to Fifth Avenue.

It was farce, she told herself, but whether it was funny or infuriating at that moment she couldn't be sure. She came back inside and stood in the middle of the living room with her hands on her hips, finally on the verge of a laugh, when there was a quiet knock on the door. She found Peter behind it, looking sheepish.

"Frank sent me back," he said, with his hand over his heart. "Insisted. I didn't fight it."

Maggie let him in, elated and a little guilty too, in view of the evening she had been enjoying with Frank. He had been warned though, she reminded herself.

"I thought I was on my own tonight," she said.

Michael hadn't been able to get away from Washington after all, which left Peter free after his doctor's appointment. She interrupted to look at his arm. It had been retaped and he was wearing a looser sling which he barely needed. He demonstrated, extending his arm almost straight out.

"I called to tell you," Peter said. "You were working on your private life at the time."

"And you decided to wait. What if—?"

"Not wait," he corrected. "Pick up my things."

He moved away from her into the bedroom. Maggie followed right behind him, relieved to see the leather satchel still empty on the floor where he had left it, and his toothbrush and razor still on the bathroom ledge. Gail's words Sunday about making her apartment and herself "less available" came back to her. They still rankled, though she was hardly reacting to Gail when she said to Peter, "They're not in my way, if that's what's bothering you."

"It's not bothering me. It might bother Frank, however."

Maggie looked indignant. "What do you think I'm running up here, anyway?"

Peter fell onto the bed. "A haven for the weary traveler, I hope. Uptown's a long way away."

He stayed and the fact that she was instantly and anxiously available wasn't at all wounding to her pride. All right, she told herself, she *didn't* have a private life independent of him anymore, not one she would insist on maintaining. Frank Powell understood, other friends would understand. Reason and responsibility were temporarily suspended; they would come back eventually. Right now she was hopeless and she loved showing Peter just how hopeless.

They had Frank's coffee, but as a penance they didn't drink it on the terrace. Then they made love, with no concessions at all—not to Peter's arm, not to Maggie's three-quarter bed.

At one-fifteen, when Peter was already asleep, the phone rang, jolting Maggie out of the dozing stage. One hand went out for it, the other for the lamp.

"Yes?" she whispered anxiously, thinking long distance and family.

"Let me speak to my brother, please."

Briefly there was relief, and then a different kind of

anxiety. The voice was ice, with an assurance in the command that made Maggie feel Gail was looking directly at them. She hesitated, just to get her bearings, and Gail said, "I know he's there."

"Yes, he is," Maggie said. Peter was awake beside her—wide awake when she faced him. He didn't have to be told it was Gail. "Just a minute." Maggie held the receiver against herself a few seconds, as though Peter weren't lying in the same bed. She found her own impulse humiliating and it came through in her voice. "Do you want to be alone?" she asked Peter.

He shrugged, too casually to be unconcerned, and took the phone. Maggie got out of bed and put on her short silk wrapper, listening.

"Gail?"

"Since you won't call me, I'm calling you."

"I did try you, a few times. Where are you?"

"Right where you left me." The reproach came through clearly.

Maggie caught Peter's eye and her look said, Will you be all right? He nodded and she went out of the room.

Peter turned his back to the open door and lowered his voice. "You're not still mad, are you?"

"Mad? Who was mad?" Gail asked.

"You were."

"Uh-uh, you misread me. I was a little disappointed. I was looking forward to our spending some time together."

"Well . . . we've got all summer."

"The three of us." Gail waited and Peter let it pass, hoping his silence would force her to the point. In the kitchen a light went on and the refrigerator door was opened. Gail continued and the strain under the chatty tone was beginning to tell. "How did the apartment look to you? I thought Louise and I did a pretty good job."

"You did. I appreciate it."

Gail corrected him right away. "'You don't appreciate *me*, darling. You appreciate Louise or Maggie, but not me. Know what I mean?"

"Yeah," Peter said. He lowered his feet to the floor and sat on the edge of the bed, tensely.

"What are you doing back there?" Gail asked abruptly. Her voice had changed, darkened.

"It just happened," Peter said.

"How could you bring yourself back to that place?"

"We don't have to go into that now, do we, Gail?"

"Why? Am I disturbing Maggie?"

"It's late," he said, trying to ease out of it, "we were asleep."

"Lucky you. I haven't been able to sleep."

"Why don't we talk tomorrow?"

"We're talking now." There was a beat in which she caught herself and added pleasantly, reasonably, "Aren't we?"

Peter closed his eyes and pressed a point in the middle of his forehead. He had awakened with the pain or it had just come, he couldn't remember. "Drive in tomorrow," he said, "or I'll come out there, whatever's easier. Okay?" She didn't answer, "Gail?"

And then she did answer, tensely, the emotion barely held in check: "Why are you doing it, Pete? Why are you putting me through this?"

"Gail?" It was as though he hadn't heard, or understood.

"The same goddamn thing all over again—why are you doing it?"

He looked at the light coming from the kitchen and heard a drawer sliding shut. "Jesus, Gail, *don't.*"

"That girl is nothing, she doesn't mean a thing to you!"

"I'm not going to talk about this now."

"You *know* what'll happen! Why are you inviting it? Putting us through it all over again?"

"Gail!" It burst out of him, covering her last words. Alarmed, Maggie appeared in the open doorway, watching Peter until he shook his head and waved her away, back into the kitchen. Gail's breathing at the other end was rapid, shaky. Peter waited. There were more sounds from the kitchen, controlled enough to tell him that Maggie was listening.

"I'm sorry," Gail said finally, "I didn't call for this." She was holding the phone farther away from her mouth. "That's not true. . . . Of course I did."

"Get some sleep, will you?" Peter said gently.

"I want to. God, I'm so tired." In the silence he could hear the surf, and then the weariness in Gail's voice when she spoke again: "Pete? I'd hate her to take advantage of this. Just tell her . . . family business, okay?"

He couldn't find the energy to argue. "Okay," he said.

"Good night, darling."

"Good night, Gail."

As soon as he hung up, Maggie came back into the bedroom, holding a half-empty glass of milk. She looked anxious and Peter tried to smile, which didn't seem to work. "Sorry about that," he said with a nod at the phone. He got up and kissed Maggie as he walked past her.

"Where are you going?" she asked.

"Some air." He stopped halfway to the terrace door

and remembered he was naked. "I forget—have you got nosy neighbors?"

"It's the Village," she said.

"Right," he said, as if that made a big difference. "Go to bed. I'll be in soon."

Maggie watched him go out, wanting and not wanting to hear what it was Gail had subjected him to. She wouldn't press.

Peter went to the edge of the dark terrace and watched the few lighted windows, most of them distant. One window kept itself lit stubbornly, outlasting Peter. He came back inside and found Maggie asleep in bed, still wearing the silk wrapper. He turned off the light and held her, whispering against her shoulder, "Do yourself a favor. . . . Get me out of your life." He said it again when she stirred, but the words were just garbled sounds against her that would have been lost, even if she was awake.

The State, it turned out, had no interest in prosecuting Joanne Ellis. It would also waive any demand for a sanity hearing and any short- or long-term confinement of Mrs. Ellis in a state institution. Provided, of course, Arthur Ellis signed the papers committing his wife to the mutually acceptable Hudson View Hospital.

Arthur Ellis agreed, in writing, to sign the papers as soon as they became available.

A former Westchester County policeman now working as a private detective, John Trevino, had been hired by Mrs. Ellis to follow Peter Drexler and to conduct searches of his office, apartment, car. On one occasion he had been given explicit orders by Mrs. Ellis to vandalize the apartment, by way of a threat. Trevino had, incidentally, provided Mrs. Ellis with the weapon she had used in the attack, Peter's own .32 automatic. Paul Liddell, the Ellis's chauffeur, had arranged the hiring of the detective and had passed cash payments onto him—as he had done a year previously. The State would waive prosecution of Trevino and Liddell if Mr. McCabe so wished.

"Mr. Drexler is what they meant," Michael said. "I corrected them."

Peter nodded.

Michael was reporting it all to Peter at Michael's Lexington Avenue office in the late afternoon, when he had come back from seeing Arthur Ellis and his attorney in Poughkeepsie. He rattled off each of the numbered details tonelessly, as though they were clauses in a statute, reading from a lined yellow pad filled with his illegible handwriting (no typescript or duplicates, no secretaries involved, since Michael McCabe himself was not involved).

At the end he looked across his desk at Peter and said, "In other words, everything we wanted. Okay?"

Satisfied?—that was what he really meant and what Peter heard. He said, "Okay," and watched Michael gather all his documents and pile them neatly. "It's almost six. Can I buy you a drink?"

"Why, what are we celebrating?"

"No celebration," Peter said resentfully.

"No time, either," Michael said without amending anything. "I've got to get back to the DA and Creegan. Creegan's going to want some money eventually."

"Just let me know when." He started to get up, relieved that Michael had refused the drink. "I owe you something for all this."

Michael leaned back in his chair and flashed the poster smile. "Don't worry. You'll pay."

"Don't I always," Peter said, returning the smile with as much warmth.

Gail drove in from East Hampton that same day. She took the last exit before the Midtown Tunnel and fought the Long Island City traffic to the Playcraft building. She reached Peter's office just before five only to find he had already left. Marie couldn't tell her where, but given the hour it had to have something to do with business. Her uncharacteristic vagueness embarrassed her, especially with Mrs. McCabe. She phoned the Bronx warehouse, where he was due sometime that week, but no, Mr. Drexler wasn't there or expected.

Gail used Peter's phone to call his apartment and then her own and found him at neither. After some hesitation she dialed Maggie Newman's number. There was no answer.

"Sorry," Marie said to her as she was leaving. "This never happens." To herself she couldn't help adding, "But neither does Mr. Drexler get shot at that often."

Marie knew of the incident and so did all the other secretaries, each of them embroidering with misinformation what was already becoming a legendary adventure. Peter Drexler had never seemed a more mysterious or romantic figure.

Gail left the building. Traffic into Manhattan was impossible and it was after six when she finally reached her apartment. Louise was there, just in from some marketing, and surprised to see her. Mrs. McCabe told her to please go on with whatever plans she had made.

Up until eight o'clock she tried to reach Peter several times. At one point (well into her second martini) she was convinced he was there and not answering his or (twice) Maggie's phone, because of Gail's blundering call the night before.

Louise had gone; she was alone in the apartment, in the living room. The stereo was playing quietly. She faced the view, with her legs drawn up under her; the windows in the buildings facing west were a fiery orange which dimmed gradually and went out. It was Tuesday and she tried to remember what, if anything, Peter had told her about Tuesday, June nineteenth—doctor, theater, dinner?

Maggie Newman, of course—whatever the plans.

One more try, she thought, and she would write him off for the evening. It was her fault, after all; she should have given him warning and not acted so impulsively. So much for surprises.

She dialed his apartment again and the phone, hallelujah, was picked up, only it was the wrong phone; she had dialed the wrong number. She broke the connection and was about to switch on the lamp when she heard a key in the lock and the door opening, and then Michael's voice calling, "Louise?" He turned on the hall light.

"She's out for the night," Gail called back. "Can I help?" She raised her glass in his direction.

Michael came into the room, carrying a thin attaché case and turning on lamps as he moved toward her. "What are you doing here?"

"Helping the sun go down. Shouldn't you be somewhere else?"

"Shouldn't *you?*" He stopped on the opposite side of the large glass-and-ebony coffee table. Neither of them made a move to come any closer.

"I had a change of plans."

"So did I," Michael said. Still standing, he told her about the meetings and the phone calls and what he hoped was finally the resolution of, in his usual words, the whole goddamn mess.

"I've been trying to get Peter for hours," Gail said, and it was only the degree of her disappointment that suggested a few previous martinis. "It never occurred to me to call you."

Michael smiled. "That's something in a nutshell, isn't it?"

Gail smiled back at him and rattled the ice in her glass. "Why don't you help yourself to one of these?"

"Can't." He moved away from her. "This is just in and out for me."

"Are you leaving tonight?" She watched his reflection in the window and saw him leave the room.

"Tomorrow morning."

"Then what's the rush?"

She couldn't hear his reply if he made one. She pulled herself up and stood for a moment without moving, trying not to weave. Did she want to follow him and could she? She filled her lungs several times to steel herself and walked with surprising steadiness across the room. The cloud gathering somewhere in back of her eyes wasn't all that thick yet.

Michael was in the study with his case open on the desk. Gail watched him from the doorway. She had forgotten to bring along her drink, so she crossed her hands behind her back and leaned against the doorjamb while Michael unpacked papers.

"I thought you'd still be out on the island," he said. "As far as Peter knew, you were. What are your plans, anyway?"

"Tonight?"

"Whenever."

"Fluid."

"Are you coming back to Washington?"

"Why? Am I needed?"

"Not immediately."

"In that case maybe I'll play on the beach awhile, I don't know. That'll give you some time to do a little playing, too."

Michael didn't react. He went to the bookcase beside his desk, opened the lower cabinet where there was a safe built into the wall, and worked the combination.

Gail watched him. He was almost concealed behind the desk. "Have you had dinner?" she asked.

"No." He was transferring papers from case to safe.

"Louise has laid something in, I'm sure." She moved to where she could see him, on his knees and flipping through papers.

Michael said, "I've made other plans."

"I see," Gail said. She wished she had brought her drink in, though there were the makings of another martini on the cart in the study. She found a paperweight and played with it instead. "Where are you spending the night?" she asked him.

"In town."

"But not here."

"No."

The sofa in the study opened into a bed which he used whenever he stayed in the apartment. His dressing room and bath were through the door beside the bookcase.

"May I know where, just in case?" Gail asked.

"I'm not expecting any emergencies."

"You never know—one of us might drop dead."

"Well, if it's me, I'll make sure I do it discreetly." He locked the safe and stood up, checking his watch. "I'm late." He pulled off his tie and went into his dressing room.

Gail raised her voice. "Might I have entertained her recently, your latest?" She tried to sound amused, disinterested.

Michael reappeared in the doorway, taking off his shirt and displaying a tee shirt underneath. "Do you really want to play Twenty Questions?"

"No. It's a very boring subject."

"Always has been," Michael agreed. "Excuse me." He closed the door to his dressing room.

Gail found her drink, added a splash of vodka and lots of ice, and carried it into the bedroom. She heard distant movement and, later, the closing of the front door. The apartment remained silent until a phone rang in another room, the study probably, and then rang again a few minutes later.

Gail didn't move right away. She lay on her side, facing away from the lamp, her eyes closed. When she opened them she did it slowly, letting the light in by drops. The throbbing moved from her chest to her head, and her stomach, now that she was awake, felt like something very delicately balanced. She slid to the edge of the bed and eased herself into a sitting position. It was after midnight. That jolted her—but no more than the room did that she found herself in. The guest room, Peter's room. She had no memory at all of coming in there. She remembered leaving Michael in the study while he was taking his shirt off, and coming into her own bedroom. The phone too—she remembered it ringing twice within minutes; in her bedroom, possibly, and then in the study, which could have meant Peter was finally trying to reach her.

The last martini she had made (three? four?) was in a small pool on the night table, the glass full and warm. The thought of it repelled her. She blotted the table with a tissue and emptied the glass into the bathroom sink. Her mouth was dry, with a metallic taste. It would make her feel more sodden, she knew, and probably drunker, but she filled the glass with water and drained it.

In her own bedroom she sat beside the phone with her hands pressed together between her knees, trying to will her mind clear and her voice and hands steady. It had been Peter calling, she was certain. He had probably called East Hampton, too. By this time he would by worrying. *She* certainly would be, under the same circumstances–frantic. She reached for the phone and dialed his number, aiming her finger at the buttons very precisely. On the third ring he picked up the receiver and a few seconds later spoke into the phone groggily. Even when he realized it was Gail calling, nothing in his voice quickened.

"You called me, didn't you?" she asked.

"A few hours ago. This afternoon, too."

"I was on my way in, I guess."

"Someday we just might connect." He sounded a little less annoyed.

"Is it too late now?"

"For what?"

"To connect, to see you." Asking him was the mistake. She could hear it in the silence, in the sound of his breathing, almost see the signals being passed between them–Peter and Maggie: *What do I tell her? Tell her no.* She tried to block out the images. "I wouldn't ask if I wasn't feeling so down, Pete, so lonely." Wait; nothing from Peter. "I've had too much to drink," she confessed. "I'm sure you can hear it."

"Yeah," Peter said dully.

"Michael was here. We had this awful blowup, just

awful. I don't know what to do anymore, Pete. I can't bring it off, not anymore."

"Is he still there?"

"No, gone." Her voice softened, became caressing: "Come over? Please?"

"Gail, look"—he paused, struggling to find the gentler words—"nothing's going to make much sense right now."

"Why not? I need you. If you needed me I'd be there. I *have* been there."

She could see Maggie lying beside him, her head on his shoulder, hearing everything they were saying. Shaking her head again—*No, don't go.*

"She's with you, isn't she?" Gail demanded. "She's in bed with you."

Peter said, "No, Gail," calmly, patiently.

"Don't lie to me! That bitch is in bed with you!" It was out before she could stop it, a shrill, ugly shout. She would have understood him slamming the phone down on it. But he didn't; he waited and he knew the precise moment the silence had become insupportable to her. He said, "Give me some time."

"You'll come?"

And from the way that he said it it might have been a game, and a very nasty one, all along. "Of course I'll come."

At the agency the next day Frank Powell asked Maggie to check his revised Playcraft copy "for balls." She read it fast, said they were there all right, and went back to her drawing, a space creature she had spent half the day trying to get right. It still wasn't right, too earthbound, and time was getting short, she told Frank; so if he wouldn't mind fooling around with the receptionist instead. . .

"You're really in a rotten mood today," Frank said, resisting the impulse to add, What's the matter, couldn't Drexler deliver the goods last night? He left her office without a real exit line.

Her mood wasn't so much rotten as apprehensive. She had been with Peter when the call came from Gail. (Had he told Gail that? She suspected not.) Maggie had even urged him to see her, given the state he said his sister was in. He did see her, leaving Maggie to spend the night alone in his apartment. More than that, leaving her with time to ask herself too many questions, among them the question she had asked Peter once before: *Does* Gail give up finally and accept her? Or do the calls and pleas and the nightly emergencies go on indefinitely? And had—two-thirty in the morning and she was still wide awake—Susan Ellis gone through the same thing with Gail? There it was again, unbidden, that same awful suspicion that wouldn't go away. Gail and Susan. Ridiculous, no matter how many times it came back to her.

At four that afternoon Maggie was seeing Gail, at Gail's request. The meeting was urgent and it was confidential; absolutely confidential, Gail had emphasized on the phone. It was also at least half of what had been distracting Maggie all day and souring her mood.

The attempts at the space creature, something she must have done dozens of times in the past, were getting cruder and less inspired. She tossed the last one aside at three-fifty (which meant a wasted afternoon and a long night ahead of her) and walked to the Mandarin on Second Avenue. She remembered it unfavorably, from a mediocre but expensive lunch she'd had there with Frank a few months ago. It was the same, dim and large, but almost empty now, except for two well-dressed Chinese men at the bar, in a rear booth, Gail, who waved at her, unsmiling, as though summoning a waiter.

Maggie said, "Hello, Gail," and slid in beside her.

Gail smiled a mechanical campaign smile and gave Maggie's hand a perfunctory touch by way of greeting. Her eyes stayed on the waiter who had come to the table. She ordered a spritzer for Maggie, overruling the club soda she said she wanted, and another one, a refill, for herself. The waiter left and she looked directly at Maggie for the first time. "Thanks for coming," she said.

"You said it was important."

Gail said, "Very," and then looked meditative. Her finger traced the rim of the glass, moving in slow circles. "You don't mind this, do you?" She glanced at the art deco lamps and the stylized Chinese figures posted on the walls. "It seemed convenient. Besides, who goes to Chinese restaurants at four in the afternoon?"

"It's fine," Maggie shrugged, wanting her to get on with it.

There was another long, awkward silence which neither of them made any attempt to fill with small talk. Finally the waiter came back with their drinks, set them down, and went away. Then Gail said it, for both of them: "We're not very comfortable together, are we?"

"Not very," Maggie agreed, without any embarrassment. She resigned herself to the honest afternoon she had expected all along.

"Why do you think that is?"

"Why?"

"Yes."

"I guess we don't like each other."

Gail looked surprised. She thought about it briefly and decided, "You're wrong. I do like you."

Maggie couldn't help a slight smile. "Well, that hasn't come across too clearly."

"I'm a politician's wife. I try not to show honest feelings."

Some of her feelings had been honest enough, Maggie wanted to say. She said it differently: "Let's say you don't like me for your brother, then."

"Let's say," Gail agreed, "I don't like you for my brother."

"That's been a pretty open secret."

"It wasn't meant to be any kind of secret." She moved her watery first drink aside and sipped the fresh one, watching Maggie over the glass. Maggie wasn't drinking at all; just playing with the swizzle stick.

"Is that what we're here to talk about—Peter and me?"

"What else do we have to talk about? Weekends in East Hampton?"

Maggie tried to keep any hostility out of her voice. "I'm sorry, Gail, but you've got nothing to say about us. If it doesn't work out—"

"It won't," Gail interrupted her, quietly insistent. "I'm trying to tell you that."

"Why don't you let Peter and me find that out for ourselves?"

"Because my way is a lot faster."

"You know, I don't think this meeting's really that urgent. We've been through it all." She reached into her bag and pulled out a five-dollar bill, which she put beside her untouched drink.

Gail took hold of her hand on the table and leaned

closer to her. "Don't you understand yet?" she whispered with sudden intensity. "I'm trying to protect you."

Maggie was still. "Protect me from what?" she asked, and when she saw Gail searching her face for some kind of understanding she repeated it more urgently: "From what?"

"Peter." It was just a soundless movement of her lips but it was enough to stun Maggie. Gail moved closer. "He did kill her, you know . . . Susan Ellis."

"What?" Maggie pulled her hand from under Gail's, as if by reflex, almost knocking over her drink. She grabbed and steadied it, holding on and trying to steady herself with it. The wine had spilled over her hands, over the five-dollar bill, darkening it. For a moment, maybe longer, she blocked out Gail's voice, or perhaps Gail had stopped speaking, but now the words jolted her again.

"She didn't jump," Gail was saying, "didn't fall. And it wasn't the drugs she was on or what she'd been drinking, even though there was all that, too. She was pushed off that balcony. Peter killed her." She repeated the terrible words slowly, drumming them into Maggie, who shook her head in disbelief.

She looked at Gail, horrified, demanding, "What are you saying? My *God,* what are you saying?"

"The truth," Gail said, still without raising her voice. "One of us owes you that." She gave Maggie time to absorb it, a lot of time, before she said, with a kind of grim, desperate amusement: "Her mother's been right about Peter all along. Isn't that something? She's not mad at all."

"I don't believe you," Maggie said. Her fists were clenched and her arms pressed tightly against her

stomach, holding down the feeling of nausea. "I don't believe anything you're saying."

"No?"

"*No*! I *know* Peter!"

"Dear Maggie," Gail said tolerantly, "you don't know him at all." She was more relaxed now, more in control. She took her napkin and, still watching Maggie's reaction, pressed it down on the wine that had been spilled. Abruptly Maggie rose, mumbled something, and followed the sign to the lounges.

The two well-dressed men were getting up from the bar and speaking to the bartender in Chinese, laughing. One of them called out to the waiter, who was reading a *Post* at the opposite end of the bar, his back to Gail. He waved and said something in Chinese. The men left.

Ten minutes later Maggie came back and Gail could see she had been crying. There was a stain on her right thigh where some of the wine had spilled. "Are you all right?" Gail asked.

"No," Maggie said. She leaned over and lifted her bag. "I will be, though, once I put all this out of my mind."

"Nobody believed Joanne Ellis, either," Gail said with that same grim amusement. "Give him up, Maggie. Believe me, it's the only thing you can do."

Maggie closed her eyes. "I don't want to *hear* any more!" For the first time one of their voices reached the front of the bar and the waiter turned to look briefly. "I need some air."

Again Gail reached out and held her. "Do you think this has been any easier for me to face? How do you think I've lived with it all this time? Knowing that about my own brother? For God's sake, *let him go*! You've got no choice anymore."

Maggie looked at Gail's hand on her and said, "I want to go, Gail."

"That's all right, I finished what I had to say." She released her. "Not that I've said anything, not that I've even seen you today. Do you understand what I'm saying, Maggie?"

Maggie looked at her blankly and had started to walk away from the table when Gail called out to her. She picked up the wet five-dollar bill, fanned it, and held it out to Maggie.

"This was on me," Gail said.

CHAPTER ELEVEN

Joanne Ellis was taken by ambulance from St. Vincent's to Hudson View Hospital. A sedative made her slightly groggy; there was a patch of bandage over her left temple and some discoloration around her left eye; her lower chest was taped and there may or may not have been pain—she gave no indication.

Arthur rode beside her, and a nurse who had been sent down from Hudson View. At the request of Michael McCabe and as a favor to the Ellises, Lieutenant John Creegan replaced the armed police officer originally sent to ride beside the driver. Arthur didn't know what Joanne's reaction to Creegan would be. His concern turned out to be needless. Joanne either did not see Creegan, or didn't recognize him, or simply didn't care at this point.

She was admitted and given preliminary examinations while Arthur signed some papers (also preliminary) and consulted privately with a Dr. Rifkin who wasn't Dr. Knoedler any more than Hudson View was Pinehurst. Later he was taken to Joanne's room on the first floor, next to a nurse's station. It seemed pleasant and perfectly normal, except for the bright window overlooking a stretch of manicured lawn. Its glass was extremely thick and it was sealed shut.

Joanne had been given another, even stronger sedative which, Arthur was told, might make her somewhat unresponsive. She was exactly that, sitting in front of the window in robe and slippers. Was she comfortable? She nodded after a moment. Was there anything she wanted? She shook her head. He told her that Dr. Knoedler would be coming in from Pinehurst the following day to see her and consult with Dr. Rifkin. She nodded again, with no change of expression.

He watched her, trying to find some sign of recognition in her face. "Jo?" His voice changed, broke on her name. She hadn't heard. He leaned closer and took her hand, remaining silent until he could trust his voice. "This is all we can do right now. It's just until you're feeling better. That hasn't been for a while, Jo, we both know that. Well, here's our chance now. That's what this is all about. You know that, don't you, Jo?"

He still couldn't reach beyond the sedative—at least that's what he hoped it was. If he were honest, though, he'd admit there had been no real response to him, not since the attack on Drexler. He could go back even beyond that—to the day she came home from Pinehurst, and beyond that, too. To the day Susan died. Nothing had been the same after that. But nothing had been this bad, either. Joanne had attacked Drexler, she had fully intended to kill him. And if she were free now there would be another attempt, he was sure of it, and this time it would succeed. He was sure of that, too.

This *was* all they could do right now. If only he could hear that from his wife.

There was a sound behind him, the door opening, and a nurse's voice saying, "Mr. Ellis?"

"In a minute," Arthur said.

The nurse was waiting with the door open. Creegan stood behind her in the corridor.

Arthur touched Joanne's face. "Our lives aren't over, you know," he said quietly. "Just . . ."

He let his voice trail off. She knew what he meant after all.

Maggie was at the drawing board in her apartment and the phone was ringing again. It had to be Peter and if she didn't answer this time she was sure he would come down to the apartment to check. He had a key; there would be no way of keeping him out. And no way she could handle seeing him right now. She got up and went to the phone, lining up all the possible excuses, just in case, and settling on the truth—she was working. It was a part of the truth, anyway.

She picked up and it was Peter, frantic. "Where the hell've you *been?*"

"When?"

"All night."

"At the office."

"I called your office, I've been calling all over. *Jesus,* Mag."

"I've been working. I haven't paid much attention to the phone."

"You knew it had to be me."

"All the more reason not to answer. I don't need any distractions if you want those sketches."

"Stop making me the villain. You could've called at least."

"I know, I'm sorry. I'm crazy when I'm up against a deadline."

He gave a long-suffering sigh and made her hear grudging forgiveness in it. "Don't do that to me, okay?" She didn't reply, didn't make any sounds at all. "Hey, are you there?" Peter asked.

Maggie said, "Yes."

"Anything wrong?"

"No. Just tired. In the middle of one bitch of a sketch I want to finish so I can go to sleep."

"Can you use a little inspiration?"

"I've got all the inspiration I need. It's the energy I'm looking for."

"How about a couple of elves then? I'll take some of the guys off the night shift."

"Good night, Pete," she said, and at least there was a laugh in her voice that seemed genuine and affectionate, even if she was cutting him off for the night.

He hid any disappointment and said, agreeably, "Good night, baby. And put out that goddamn light, will you?"

"I will."

She almost had the phone down and she heard, "Maggie?"

"Yes?"

"You're sure you're all right."

"Yes."

He was still on the line when she hung up.

Gail was wrong about Peter—that had been Maggie's immediate reaction and she still, hours later, believed it. It was a deliberate, desperate lie aimed at getting Maggie out of Peter's life finally. Actually *scaring* her out of it. A lie that was so transparent; pathetic really, and, yes, frightening—but because of Gail, not Peter. Gail was more unstable than Maggie had imagined, and if Susan Ellis had really been murdered, then Gail was a much likelier suspect than Peter.

But lie or not, there was something in it that was proving to be insidiously effective—a voice added to Joanne Ellis's and bringing back, among other things, that image of Peter on the staircase, striking out at Joanne Ellis with a savagery that had stunned Maggie.

Maggie resisted but some part of her was responding to Gail. Why, otherwise, had she gone into hiding from Peter, why had she felt so uneasy speaking to him on the phone just now? And later, why had that same nightmare image jolted her awake at six, just one hour after she had finally fallen asleep?

Bleary-eyed the next morning (according to Frank, it didn't show), she cabbed out to Long Island City with Frank and Luke. Peter did notice it however, despite all the preconference bustle.

"You had me worried last night," he said, sotto voce. "You still have me worried."

"Why?"

"I don't know, just a feeling. Right or wrong?"

"Wrong. As far as I know."

"Why didn't you come in a little earlier? I had this terrific board game all set up for us." He parodied a nudge and a wink.

She pointed to the easel and the drawings she was stacking on it. "This went right down to the wire, believe me."

Peter stole a look at the two top drawings, one of them the recalcitrant space creature. "I like them," he said, a little preoccupied as a fresh knot of Playcraft executives came into the room.

"God, I hope so," Maggie said, and meant it. It was

nerves she was starting to feel, professional jitters that were suddenly blocking, at least for the moment, anything personal between her and Peter. The feeling, as harrowing as it was, was terrific.

Marie brought him a pile of mimeographed copy and smiled coolly at Maggie. "Let's talk later," he said to Maggie and walked back to the head of the table, leafing through the pages.

The meeting was long and heated, and several of Maggie's drawings were a big success, especially her design for the VAROOM! package. Interestingly, it was Peter who offered the most relentless criticism, and the most incisive. For him too their relationship was now strictly professional, with no stolen looks, no signals at all.

At the end of the meeting he relented and smiled at her across the room. When he came over he touched her arm and managed a quick, nonprofessional squeeze. "You did a hell of a job," he said, and started to move away. "Stick around. We'll have lunch in."

Maggie looked pained. "Can't. I've got a lunch date in town."

"Who, Powell?" He mock-glowered at Frank, who was leaning over a sheet of copy on the other side of the table. "I'll fire the son of a bitch."

"Not Frank. An old friend, female." She couldn't remember lying to him before, and maybe she was only imagining incredulity in his look. Fortunately there was too much activity in the room for him to pursue it.

"I'll call you," was all he said.

She watched him squeeze past a cluster of men and thought, My God, this is Peter, remember? *Peter.* Why in the hell was she letting it build like this?

He called her later at the office and got her on the second try, telling her again how proud he was of her, how she had really come through for him.

"Tonight's something special. Whatever you want you've got. Four Seasons, something Frog. . . ."

"What I'd really like is to go home and collapse," she said, trying not to make it sound like an out-and-out turndown.

"You can collapse after," Peter said. It might have been her own state of mind, but she heard more than a playful command; there was something close to a warning in his voice. "Where do I pick you up?"

Maggie didn't go home after work. She stayed in the office an extra hour, reworking some sketches, and at six-thirty called Peter's apartment. She let the phone ring long enough to bring him out of the shower but there was no answer. He was to pick her up at her apartment at eight; she was assuming he would give himself some time at home first—she was counting on it. She couldn't bring herself to go home and change into something festive and wait for him, as though everything between them was normal. Now, before there could be any more damage, she wanted the suspicions resolved, and all the fears Gail had started working inside her. It was a confrontation she absolutely dreaded, but there was no way out of it, not if she valued her sanity.

She switched off the light over her drawing board and left the office at six-forty. The sun had fallen behind the buildings but the air outside the lobby was heavy and steamy—New York summer at its worst. She hated it and Peter loved it, and that was probably the only incompatibility they had discovered in each other up until now. She walked toward Lexington and turned uptown, dodging commuters who were still rushing toward Grand Central.

For the next few blocks she tried to concentrate on something trivial—the heat, her discomfort; tried to make her mind a blank, forgetting all the lines she had been agonizing over. She would rely on her instincts, find the words when she was face to face with him.

Not *him*, she told herself—*Peter*. Say the name and stop turning him into an abstract threat. The Peter who had become such an important part of her life—the important part. The Peter she loved, still, right now.

At Forty-ninth Street she waited for the light to change. Think colors, she told herself, think numbers—not how important the same Peter might have been to Susan Ellis, not how much she might have loved him too.

There was a doorman she didn't recognize on duty at his building. He hadn't seen Mr. Drexler come in but he rang 10B anyway and got no reply. Maggie was uncomfortable waiting in the lobby. She went outside and the heat became immediately oppressive. There was a bar close by, on Lexington, and as much as she hated sitting at a bar, especially alone and especially on the East Side, she needed something cool and strong right now. At the corner she turned to look back—luckily, because Peter was getting out of a cab in front of his building. She walked back quickly and surprised him in the lobby collecting his mail.

"I thought I'd save you a trip," she said, and kissed him while the doorman handed him a manila envelope he didn't look at.

"Are we changing plans or something?" he asked her uneasily.

Maggie said no and took the mail from him and tried to take his attaché case too. He held on, lifting the case with his left arm and saying, "What're you doing, I'm in great shape." He let her go into the elevator first. "As a matter of fact I start driving again tomorrow."

"You think that's such a good idea?"

"Best one I've had in a long time." He pulled her closer and narrowed his eyes to scrutinize her face with comic thoroughness. The voice was playful, too: "You're not getting tired of me or anything, are you?" They had reached the tenth floor and the doors opened on his question. Maggie smiled at him and started to walk out. Peter held her back and asked again, this time seriously, "Hey . . . are you?"

"Of course not," Maggie said, and gave a slight cry as the doors started to close again. She jumped out, pulling him with her.

In the apartment foyer he cornered her and said, "Prove it." He lowered his arm when she tried to duck under it, repeating, "Come on, prove it."

She felt her heartbeat accelerate and a pulse start to throb in her ears. The heat outside and the walk had winded her, and all the sleep she had lost the night before. And yes, the anxiety that had been building—she wasn't minimizing that; although how much of it was sheer exhaustion? And imagination? She leaned back against the wall with her eyes closed and let him kiss her, and even felt herself responding after a few moments; pulling him closer and trying to reassure herself with the familiar feel of his body against hers, his touch, his smell.

His body relaxed and he lifted his face from hers, and after a long silence said, still breathless, "I'm convinced."

Maggie didn't understand immediately and then she remembered his question in the elevator and said, "Good."

Peter kissed her again, lightly, picked up his mail, and took it to the living-room desk. Gail had moved it to a new position during her clean-up operation. Several other pieces had been rearranged, improving, in Peter's view, the look of the room; in Maggie's silent opinion, making it cold and formal.

"How about a drink?" he called back to her. She agreed, and went into the kitchen to make them herself. He had turned away from her to open the manila envelope.

She searched through the refrigerator. It was stocked as usual with a huge selection of pickles, peppers, and relishes; wine, too, and champagne, and little else. She found a stoppered bottle of tonic, half a lemon, and a jar with three olives floating in it. "Tonic or martini?" she called out, and waited for a reply from the living room. "Peter?"

He didn't hear her call or come into the room, or acknowledge her until she was standing beside him, and then with only a glance. He was holding a photograph, one that Maggie had seen before in his bedroom—Peter and Susan Ellis. There were others scattered on the desk, snapshots she hadn't seen, of Susan, Susan and Peter, smiling in most of them, their arms around each other.

"These were mine," he said quietly. He looked pale, shaken. Letters slid out of the manila envelope onto the desk, postcards and different-sized greeting card evelopes, all addressed to Peter Drexler in the same bold, childish hand. Under the large photograph he was holding was a note from Arthur Ellis which he let Maggie read.

I'm returning these to you. They were found among my wife's things. I'm sorry. Please try to forgive her.

ARTHUR ELLIS

Peter placed the photo on the desk, almost reverently. "'I don't know why I kept all this stuff anyway. It's a part of my life I'd give anything to forget. I wish he hadn't sent them back."

Maggie watched him gather the pictures and put them back into the envelope. She gave him the note from Arthur Ellis. *I'm sorry. Please try to forgive her.* How guilty could Peter be in Arthur Ellis's eyes? He held the envelope tightly for a moment, then let it slip from his hands into the wastebasket. He stood looking down at it, his head bowed.

"If it was just that easy, hunh?" He shrugged. "Well, why the hell not?" He reached out for Maggie and drew her closer. "Help me forget it. Don't pull out on me now . . . not without giving me a chance."

She had to fight to hold herself back from him, to keep a little distance, physical as well as emotional. She could feel the strain in her body; the strain of her silence, too—until she broke it, quietly, timidly. "How did Susan die?"

From the uncertain way he was looking at her, she didn't think he had heard. She was wrong, though. "You know how she died," Peter said.

She kept her eyes fixed on his face. "Do I know everything?"

"What do you mean, everything?" His hand was sliding from around her waist.

"When she fell from that balcony"—she paused to steady her voice—"where were you?"

"Where was I?" The question caught him by surprise.

Maggie nodded.

Peter laughed, or made a sound like a laugh, that was quick, mirthless. "What's this you're trying on me, some kind of game?" He waited for her to reply. "It's a rotten idea. Take it to some of the competition—Ideal or . . ." His voice died. He made a vague sweeping-away gesture and then let his hand fall slowly. "With Gail and Michael," he said dully. "What are you looking for, some kind of alibi?"

"Don't be mad."

"I'm trying not to be. Maybe if you told me what you're after, hunh?"

"The truth."

"What kind of truth?"

"You and Susan . . . what really happened to her."

There was a pause. "What are you suggesting?"

"I don't know."

Another pause. "That I killed her?"

"I don't *know*! All I can think is, My God, what if she's telling me the truth! What if it's been true all along and nobody believed it. . . ."

"Are you telling me you *do*? You believe a woman who's out of her fucking mind?"

Maggie kept shaking her head. "No, you don't understand."

She raised her hand to stop him but he went on: "She tried to kill me, are you forgetting that? Christ, she could've killed you! You're going to believe a woman like that?"

"No, not her, not Joanne Ellis. *Gail!* It's *Gail* I'm talking about!"

"What?" He was absolutely still.

"Gail *told* me you killed her, you pushed her off that balcony. Kept saying it to me, saying how she wanted to protect me." She had to stop to catch her breath. Peter's face was white; even his eyes looked colorless to her, blank, turned deeply inward. It was a look she had never brought into another face before and it appalled and terrified her, and if there were just some way to call back her words. . . . "Pete? I don't believe her, of course I don't." She didn't know whether it was the truth or what she wanted to be the truth, but Peter wasn't lisening anyway. She took a step toward him but he waved her away and moved out of reach.

"I figured something was going on," he said dully, and then looked directly at her. "I didn't kill her, Maggie." He shrugged as if it didn't really matter. "But then again, what would you expect me to say, right?"

"Pete . . . ?"

Again he held her away from him. He picked up his jacket and headed for the door. "I'm going to get some air. Hang around if you want." He opened the door, then remembered something and half-turned toward her. "You know, I thought you were a hell of a lot smarter than this."

He traced Gail to Carl Stern's apartment on Central Park West. Carl was a publisher in his mid-fifties, a bachelor and Gail's back-up escort whenever Michael and Peter were both unavailable. There were other guests, too, all on their way into the dining room, when Carl came out to meet Peter.

Peter offered an apology for the interruption. Carl waved it away. "It's strictly informal. A few of us working stiffs, and Gail for some tone. Come on in."

Peter held back and said, I'll crash again sometime. Can I see her?"

"Nothing wrong, is there?"

"Family business. I'll send her right back to you."

Carl showed him into an airy library overlooking the park, offered him a drink which Peter refused, and left him. There was laughter from a distant room, and then Gail in the doorway, looking lovely and alarmed. "What happened?" she asked without any greeting.

Peter said, "Close the door." That made her look more anxious. "What did you say to Maggie?" She was halfway across the room and she stopped abruptly when he said it.

"Say to Maggie? What do you mean."

"What did you tell her about me and Susan?"

Gail shook her head. "I don't remember discussing you and Susan with Maggie. What am I supposed to have told her?"

He let her wait—two, three beats. "That I killed Susan."

Just briefly Gail looked startled and then she recovered, widening her eyes almost comically to show Peter the absurdity of what he had said. She cleared her throat. "*I* told her that?" she said, a little out of breath. Peter nodded. "I think she's got me confused with Joanne Ellis, don't you?"

"You're saying it's not true?"

"Pete!" she said indignantly. "Of course I am." She walked to the window. Lights were on in the park and the East Side buildings, blurred by the misty air. Gail faced him and leaned back, holding onto the sill with both hands.

"She's lying, then," Peter said.

"Yes!"

"Why?'"

"Why? That should be pretty obvious."

"It's not, not to me."

"Well, maybe you're a little blinded by the radiance right now."

"I'm not blinded by anything, Gail." It came out as a warning and it made her trace of a smile disappear. "What is it that's so obvious?"

Gail started to walk around the room, touching things. "She'll say anything, do anything to come between us. I thought you knew that. She resents me—has, right from the beginning. And what frightens me is it's working, she's got us going at each other. I mean, *look*. To have to defend myself to my own brother?" She stopped across the room and gave him a look that challenged him to deny what she was saying. Peter remained silent. "I'm amazed, you know? Appalled, really—the way things are repeating themselves." She began to pace again. "The same problems, the same . . . contention all over again. What do we do to attract it, for God's sake?" In her hand she found a crystal paperweight which she'd unconsciously lifted from Carl's desk. She replaced it, and with her back to Peter, said, "You look as though you don't believe me."

He let out a long breath of air. "I don't know whether I do," he admitted. "Christ, Maggie can't be making it all up."

"Why the hell *not*!" Gail cried and slammed her hand down on the desk. She caught herself—closed her eyes and pressed her lips together, holding to the desk until she felt a degree of control returning. She turned to Peter and forced a smile. "I shouldn't have left my drink behind."

Peter shook his head. "I shouldn't have come here."

"No, no, I'm glad you did. I'm very grateful, Pete, really." There was only a slight mocking edge to it. "But you're right—it's hardly the best place to talk. Give me a minute to make excuses and we'll go somewhere else." She was walking toward the closed door. "Home."

"Let's forget it, Gail."

"And what—leave it at this?"

"For now."

"Oh, no, we're not going to have something like this festering. It's just what she'd want. I mean, you've *got* to see what she's up to."

A knock on the door interrupted her, and then Carl's voice, too cheery: "Sarah's a little anxious about her soufflé. How're you two doing in there?"

He had heard.

"She's on her way," Peter called back, and Gail emphatically shook her head no.

"Sorry to be pushy about it," Carl said. There was a pause and then the sound of movement away from the door.

"For Carl's sake go back in," Peter said to Gail. She was standing in his way. He tried to kiss her good-bye but she raised her hand to hold him back.

"It's her own suspicions she's voicing, believe me, Pete." Her voice was quieter but no less intense. "That night at St. Vincent's—God, she was full of questions, prying into everything. You, Susan, how she died, when she died. She cornered Creegan, too, not just Michael and me. Asked where she could find the records of the case, even the autopsy report. Creegan wouldn't give her anything, of course, neither would we. You think I'm making this us? Call Creegan, ask him."

Peter listened to her patiently and showed nothing more than that; a touch of weariness maybe, but no belief or disbelief, no anger, no sympathy—none of the contradictory things he was feeling.

"It's over, Gail," he tried to make her understand, "finally over. For Chrissake, why is it so hard for us to live with that?"

"Because she's *making* it hard!"

He reached out and touched her lips lightly, holding his fingers there until she managed a properly submissive look. He put his arms around her and held her, rocking her. "Sarah's soufflé," he reminded her.

She shook her head against his chest. "I can't carry off an evening now." It was a pout, a girlish one, with the anger and the intensity gone, eased out of her.

"Come on, Mrs. McCabe," Peter said, still rocking her gently, "you've carried off a hell of a lot more than this."

When he got home again he found that Maggie hadn't left. She was waiting for him in his living room, her legs tucked under her on the couch—doing nothing but waiting in the dim light of the foyer lamp. He stopped when he saw her, surprised and not surprised because it was exactly what he had been hoping for in the cab. Maggie disentangled herself from the couch and found her shoes.

"I'll go," she said. "I just wanted to make sure you got back all right."

She found her bag and jacket and turned on a stronger light for him. Peter didn't move, not even to let her pass into the foyer.

"I'm sorry I wrecked our evening," she said.

Peter said, "Yeah, so am I," with no emotion at all.

She found herself panicking, but it wasn't the panic of a few hours ago. He would let her leave, let her walk around him, if that's what she wanted, and out of his life.

"If I was wrong about something, so were you," she said since it was obviously up to her. "I'm *not* a hell of a lot smarter. I'm gullible, I'm one of the world's great patsies. Even the most transparent motives escape me, all the time. My one talent is I get hysterical." Her voice had been getting shakier. Suddenly she turned away from him and brought her hands up to her face. "Like now. . . ." And she burst into tears that grew uncontrollable when he touched her and made her face him and see what it was she had let slip away.

"Why don't we assess the damage at least," Peter said. He put his arm around her and slowly led her back into the living room. He gestured at the walls. "Hell, what better place?"

Thursday of that week Gail got a call from Lieutenant Creegan. Joanne Ellis had shattered the glass in a small photo of Susan that her husband had brought her, without first giving it to the nurses, and used it to slash the back of her knees and both wrists as well. She was dead—at least an hour dead when a nurse had found her on the bathroom floor early in the morning, a blood-soaked towel pillowing her head. As with Susan, there was no note, and every indication that she had taken her own life.

The news was so unexpected and shocking that Gail had to hang up on Creegan and call him back later when the Librium had begun to work on her. "Call

Michael in Washington," she told him. "I'll speak to my brother."

She wasn't able to reach Peter anywhere, so she went to his apartment and paced a lot rather than pour the stiff drink she needed desperately. At seven he came home. "Where've you *been*?" She was almost scolding him.

"Doctor." He demonstrated a reach that was now even higher and wider. He had been unwrapped and rewrapped, he told her, and rolled up his sleeve to show her the smaller bandage. "Drexlers are damn resilient, according to Weimann. Did you know that?" He saw that Gail wasn't listening. "Hey, what's wrong?"

She looked suddenly distressed and reached out, as if to support him. "Joanne Ellis," she said.

"What about her?"

Gail took a deep breath. "She's dead." Peter was absolutely still. "That's why I've been trying to get you." She told him as much as she had heard from Creegan, who was on his way up to Hudson View and would get back to them later. "It's terrible news, tragic," she said, and she was still genuinely shaken, "but it's not our fault. I don't feel guilty and I don't want you to feel guilty. Do you hear me, Pete?"

He looked at her vaguely and walked away, into his bedroom. Gail followed him and heard the bathroom door close and lock, and when she came closer, heard water running, hard. She tried the door.

"Leave me alone awhile," Peter said. His voice was weak, almost inaudible. He coughed and Gail thought she heard a gagging sound, and then the water was turned on harder.

"Pete?" She rattled the knob again. There was no

reply, no sound but the water. Gail waited. "I'll be here," she said. "Okay?"

Reluctantly she moved away from the door, still listening—and then heard, at the other end of the apartment, a door being unlocked and Maggie's voice calling, "Me!"

Gail hurried into the living room as Maggie, carrying a bag of groceries, was closing the door.

"You can't!" she called out in an urgent whisper. Maggie almost dropped the bag when she saw Gail coming at her and waving her out. "You can't come in here!"

"What—?" She looked beyond Gail, who had reached the hall, and tried to see into the apartment. "What's wrong?" She let the groceries slip from her hand onto a chair. "Something's happened to Peter!"

Gail shook her head. "He'll be all right; just leave him alone."

"What does that mean, Gail?"

"Joanne Ellis killed herself," Gail said with no attempt to soften the news.

Maggie looked blank for a moment, and then her mouth opened on a silent cry. "What *happened*?"

"I just told you." She gave her a few details, grudgingly, and went for the door. Maggie held it closed. "Where's Pete now?" she asked.

"I'm taking care of him." She tried the door again, and again Maggie put herself in the way. "Look, Maggie, let's stop playing games, huh? I'm asking you to leave."

"Are you telling me I can't see him?"

"Yes, very plainly."

Maggie stalled, listening for sounds inside the apartment.

"All right," she said, and it was an effort for her

not to push past Gail and find him. She opened the door herself and stepped out into the hall. "Do me one favor at least—tell Peter—" She stopped herself and waved the thought away. "Never mind. I'll tell him myself."

She walked toward the elevators and heard the door closed quietly behind her and locked twice.

Gail came back into Peter's bedroom. The bathroom door was still closed, the water turned off now. She brought her face closer and listened.

"Pete?" She waited. "I'm not leaving, you know."

The silence worried her. Her hand went to the knob, and just as she touched it the door was unlocked. It opened slowly and stopped, half-concealing Peter, whose face was pale, drained of expression. The front of his shirt was wet and sticking to his chest.

"Hey, are you all right?"

He tightened his lips for a few seconds, looked beyond Gail, and mumbled, "Yes." His hand was still on the inside knob. Gail reached out and touched the wet part of his shirt, tracing the shape of the stain.

"What did you do?"

He looked down and shrugged. "Threw some water on my face."

"Missed, from the looks of it." She tugged at the shirt. "Why don't you get out of it?"

"Later."

"Now." She pushed the door open all the way and took hold of his arm. "Come on."

"Stop playing big sister, will you?"

"Why should I?"

He let her lead him out into the bedroom. "I need

a little time, that's all," he said. "I wasn't ready for that bit of news." He started to unbutton the shirt.

"Nobody was." Her voice became soft, reassuring.

"Christ, I don't know why it should hit me like this."

"I don't either. The woman tried to kill you, in case you've forgotten."

"I haven't forgotten."

She watched him take off his shirt and toss it onto a chair. "Pete, look, what she did she did to herself. We're not involved."

Peter looked directly at her. "No?"

"No," she said firmly. She came closer to him and repeated it, softer this time, with some sympathy even, however puzzling his reaction seemed to her. She brought her hands up to his face and held him. "Trust me, will you?" He started to say something, but Gail covered his lips with her fingers and said, "Sshhh . . ." drawing out the sound soothingly, letting it fade. She kept her fingers on his lips, then moved them lightly over his face. Tracing the lines, she said, dot to dot. She smiled and tried to force a smile out of him. She watched it working, at least halfway, saw a softness come gradually into his eyes.

"Better . . . better. . . ." She tilted her head. "Or am I wrong?"

"You're never wrong." Eyes closed, he was rubbing his face against her hands, up and down, with a soft bristly sound.

"Magic touch," Gail said, whispering. The light in the room had begun to fade. She was silent a few moments. "I haven't made any plans," she said. "You?" She waited. "Hey."

"No," he said, with the same nodding motion. His breath was warm on her hands.

"No Maggies waiting in the wings this time?"

"None."

"Good."

She wouldn't have brought up Maggie's name at all, but she thought he might have heard their conversation in the hall. He hadn't; and hadn't expected to see her, obviously. She had just taken it upon herself to appear. Still hanging on, despite all the signs, all the warnings, imposing herself on Peter when right now even her name seemed unfamiliar to him, another ghost out of his past. Pathetic, really—a brief distraction, as Gail had said all along. Or was that just wishful thinking on her part?

She tried to stop thinking one way or another about her. Why was she bringing Maggie into the room with them now? Why was she becoming such an obsession? She had gone that route before, after all.

She looked at Peter, and if, ironically, she turned out to be the one who needed comfort and reassurance, well, it was right there—she was touching it.

"Pete. . . ."

Gail lowered her hands to his shoulders, and let them slide down his naked chest, feeling his body tighten under her. She did it again, a more lingering touch, and heard him draw in his breath sharply.

"What're you trying to do to me?" he said.

She looked up and met his eyes, and held the look—both of them did—for a long time. It was the soft light in the room and the stillness intensifying everything, exciting her as though this was happening between them for the first time. As though it were something that didn't go back as far as she could remember, back to rooms in rambling old houses; as though it hadn't survived all the Maggies and Susans in their lives.

There they were again—the ghosts.

"Hold me," she said to Peter, then said it again more urgently. *"Hold me."* She leaned against him and felt his arms go around her, pulling her so close she could feel his heartbeat as strong as her own, feel him hard against her right away and moving as though he were already in her. His hands slid under her clothes, down her back, and she didn't have to say anything now, didn't have to tell him what she wanted, and what he wanted as much, from the feel of him. He was guiding her slowly across the room until she felt something, the bed, pressing against the back of her legs. She drew him down with her, and thought: If she could just lose herself completely in the feeling and block out the idea that he had ever come this close to anyone else, ever; if he could just make her believe that one more time. . . .

As much as she wanted to, Maggie didn't try to get through to Peter later that night; nor did he call her, as she had hoped he might. She had hoped even more that he might manage to break away from his sister and appear at her apartment—for her own consolation as much as his.

Joanne Ellis's suicide, following Susan's, stunned Maggie. For the two of them, incredibly, to have taken their own lives, intentionally or otherwise, was more than Maggie could handle. And she wasn't even that involved, really. What must it be doing to Peter?

It was Peter who concerned her at this point, not Joanne Ellis. Of course her death was tragic; it was also brutal and senseless—an insane act that did nothing to make her accusations against Peter any more believable to Maggie. Gail McCabe notwithstanding. (The thought of his sister, so concerned now and so protective, made her boil. And so did Peter in a way, for accommodating her.)

Maggie kept herself awake and waiting for Peter a long time—long enough for the wildest accusations to creep back into her mind and make groggy sense one minute and no sense at all the next. One feeling managed, stubbornly, to survive every change of mood and still make perfect sense—the feeling that it was Gail, if anyone, who was somehow involved in Susan's death, Gail who was on the balcony with her that night—if anyone. She realized that her own antipathy to Gail was pushing her toward that conclusion. But it didn't make the feeling any less convincing, or Gail any less of a threat to her now.

She turned on her side, away from the light, and closed her eyes for a moment, still waiting for the phone call from Peter. When she opened them again it was daylight, seven in the morning. She pulled herself up on the couch, stiff necked, disoriented. Lights were still on in the apartment, the door to the terrace open. She opened it wider and turned off the lights on her way to the bathroom. There were crease marks in her left arm, and the left side of her face, she saw in the mirror. She turned on the cold water and rubbed hard, feeling the aches in a few more muscles.

She made instant coffee and brought it to the phone. She sat awhile before finally dialing Peter's home number, bracing herself for Gail's voice. There was no answer. Later in the day, still stiff necked, she tried him at the office several times, leaving messages with Marie that got progressively testier under the banter.

Finally at three he returned her calls, apologetic, explaining what a bitch of a day it was; more than that, what a bitch of a night it promised to be. "I don't know why but the whole place has gone bananas."

She didn't believe him, but made a point of keeping it light: It's not your turn to avoid me, is it?"

"It seems to be; not because I want to, believe me. I've been down in shipping all day, I'm trying to get out to the warehouse."

"I'd better let you go, then."

"Afraid you're gonna have to, babe." He sounded regretful and unconvincing, clearly anxious to get off the phone before Joanne Ellis could be mentioned—or anything to do with Maggie Newman for that matter.

"Everything else is all right?" Maggie asked.

"Who's got time to think?'" he said without a pause. "I'll get back to you, okay?"

He didn't, not at all that day or night. Instead he sent flowers to her office the next day, red and white carnations with a *Love, Pete* card that said nothing at all to Maggie.

"They're no substitute for the real thing," she told him when she traced him to the Bronx warehouse. "Do I see you tonight?"

Peter hesitated. "Iffy. Maybe I'd better say no."

She couldn't let it pass this time. "Why iffy?" she pressed him, and then answered herself: "You are avoiding me, stop denying it."

"Okay," Peter agreed quietly.

"Can I find out why"

There was a long silence. "Because I've got this knack you might have noticed. . . . People don't seem to . . . make out too well with me around, know what I mean?"

"That's a really dumb thing to say."

"What's so dumb about it? Hell, you need any more proof? Look, I don't want you trying your luck with me, Maggie."

"Why not if I'm willing?"

"*I'm* not up to it," Peter said, "*me.* Maybe I haven't said it to you, but this thing with Joanne Ellis has really knocked the hell out of me. It's Susan all over again and I don't know how to cope anymore. Okay, I will eventually, but, Christ, right now I am *scared.* I mean, what *is* it in me?"

Gail, she should have said. Right then. *Gail.* She couldn't even bring herself close to it, not so suddenly, not over the phone. At least that was the excuse she gave herself. "Pete—let me come over tonight," she said instead.

"No."

"Please?" She'd tell him then, she was sure she would.

"No way, Maggie."

"When then? I've got to see you."

"I don't know. Look, Mag—" He wavered, then started again, sounding surer. "Maybe all I'm saying is this thing has run its course."

"What thing, Pete?"

"Us."

"Do you believe that?"

"I don't know. I'm beginning to. Maybe it's as simple as that. It's something we ought to think about, anyway."

"I don't have to think about it."

"Well . . ." Peter said lamely, and then he gave up trying to fill the silence. "I can't talk about it now."

"Pete?" She felt he was about to hang up on her. "I don't believe any of this, not a word." He was still there, hearing her. "Don't you worry about me. I will. I'm very good at it, honest." Maggie waited.

"I'll talk to you," he said, and the pained, helpless sound in his voice managed to cancel out everything else he had tried to make her believe. He paused and then hung up quietly.

The call left her shaken, unable to concentrate on anything, especially not the complicated sketch tacked to her drawing board. She paced and then stared out of her office window at the figures moving in the building opposite. Not seeing Peter again, ever, was unthinkable, and any suggestion like it had to be a joke or a test, or the strain he was under, or some misguided concern for her well-being. Anything but an honest expression of his feelings. (She even managed, with very little effort, to put Gail in the room with him at the time, dictating the words.)

Maggie pulled herself through the rest of the day, refused dinner with Frank, and waited for Peter's call again that evening. After all, he had to be feeling the need to unburden himself as much as she, had to be missing her as much. Finally at ten Maggie called his apartment.

Gail answered his phone. She said, "Hello?" once, twice, but Maggie couldn't bring herself to reply. When Gail repeated, "Hello?" a third time, and added, "Maggie?" suspiciously, Maggie lowered the receiver without a sound.

Joanne Ellis was buried on Saturday in the Wiltwyck Cemetery outside of Rhinebeck. Maggie had read the brief obituary in the *Times* and the longer one in the *Poughkeepsie Journal* she had found at a Grand Central newsstand. At one point she had thought about borrowing Frank Powell's car and driving upstate for the funeral—to allay or maybe heighten the feeling, she wasn't sure which, that something involving the Ellises was suspiciously unfinished. That seemed to be the impulse behind her wanting to take the trip. Or possibly it was just sympathy she was feeling.

She kept vacillating over the trip and when she finally did call Frank Saturday morning it wasn't to borrow his car after all.

"How would I go about getting an autopsy report?" she asked him.

Frank asked her to repeat the question, and said, "Whose?"

The name Susan Ellis would probably suggest nothing to him, but she avoided mentioning it anyway. "Nobody you'd know."

"What do you need an autopsy report for?"

"I don't know, just morbid curiosity."

"I suppose you call the medical examiner's office," Frank said.

A few minutes after their conversation ended, and before Maggie had had time to follow his suggestion, he called her back. "I was right," he said, "as usual." He had made the call for her. "You need permission in writing from whoever did the autopsy. You also need ten bucks. Does that help?"

"A lot," Maggie said. "You're really sweet, you know that?"

"But you still won't tell me what this is all about."

"It's not about anything."

Frank wasn't convinced. He pressed a little more and circled around Peter Drexler's name until Maggie cut him off. She sounded rushed all of sudden. "Let's connect later," she said.

"Where?"

"I'll call you."

When she sat herself down and thought it through calmly, Maggie wasn't sure what it was she expected to uncover. That her own instincts were more accurate than any previous investigation into Susan's death? More specifically, that Gail McCabe had killed Susan, that evidence had been suppressed? There was always the possibility of course that she was right and everybody else was wrong, culpably or otherwise—but what a dim, dim possibility.

No, what made more sense, what she was listening to, was that other instinct in her, the instinct of self-preservation—the feeling that Gail was or could be a threat to her, and it was reasonable that she familiarize herself with the threat, investigate it. It was her own case she was working on, not Susan Ellis's.

There had to be a record of the police investigation, which would probably make more sense to her than an autopsy report. The name of the detective she had met at St. Vincent's came back to her—Lieutenant Creegan. She tried contacting him twice before she hit the right uptown precinct. He was unavailable; still unavailable when she called him from the Forty-second Street library. She left her name again, and then went upstairs and read through brief, very brief, microfilmed accounts of Susan Ellis's death in the *Daily News* and *New York Post* of July 10, 1977. She went through the *Times* twice before she found the three-line mention in the police blotter. The pieces, all three of them, were as perfunctory as the report of the shooting in her building last week. She hadn't learned anything new, but she hadn't wasted her time, either; there was an eerie fascination in seeing confirmed in a few lines of print a past that was still alive, that had become so much a part of her own life now.

The next time she tried Lieutenant Creegan she reached him. He remembered her of course, remembered that whole nightmare evening for which he sounded almost apologetic. What could he do for her?

There were sounds in the background, men talking, a phone ringing. Maggie felt pressured and uncertain now about the call. She hesitated. "I wonder if I could talk to you sometime," she said.

"Sure. What about?"

"Susan Ellis," Maggie said.

Creegan missed a beat. "Susan Ellis," he repeated; "what about her?" The voice had become tough, professional.

"I'd rather not go into it over the phone."

"You're making it sound pretty important."

"It's not," Maggie said quickly. "Just . . . a few questions I wanted to ask you."

"Questions like—?" Creegan started to ask, then stopped himself and said, "Sorry." Maggie could hear the rattle of paper close to the phone. "I expect to be tied up awhile," Creegan said. "Give me a number where I can reach you."

Maggie gave him her home number. "I don't know when I'll be home, though."

"I'll keep trying."

"It's really not that urgent, Lieutenant."

"That's not what I'm hearing, Miss Newman," Creegan said.

Mistake or not, she had called him, even though, as Creegan had sensed, she had weakened over the phone and all but withdrawn the call. Exactly what she would say to him (to the *police*) wasn't clear to her. She tried to work it out on the way downtown, walking rather than catching a bus outside the library. She stopped for coffee, walked through Altman's without really seeing anything, and by the time she reached Tenth had worked herself up again to that precall urgency. It was the thought of Peter that finally did it, Peter and the sudden dead end their conversation had hit. It was one more fatality, or could be if she let it. Her sense of proportion might be totally wrong, but it was the loss of Peter she was feeling more keenly right now than the loss of Susan or Joanne Ellis.

She would call his apartment as soon as she got upstairs; *insist* on seeing him as soon as possible. She would tell him about the call to Creegan—take her chances, as a matter of fact, and tell him everything.

The walk, in the wrong shoes, exhausted her. She dragged herself up the stairs, put her key in the lock—and froze. The door was already unlocked. She held the key steady and pulled it out slowly, soundlessly. *Don't try it alone, move away fast.* It was her immediate reaction and she started to back away toward the stairs, listening for the slightest sound. And then she stopped herself and thought, *Peter*—Peter had the other set of keys. She came back to the door, stood with her hand tight around the knob, and then opened it.

A light was on in the always-dark kitchen, and across the living room the door to the terrace had been opened. Maggie called, "Pete?" from the small vestibule. She waited and after a moment saw not Peter but Gail come into the room from the terrace, slowly, smiling at the shock on Maggie's face. She said, "Hello, Maggie," and Maggie didn't reply immediately—couldn't, not with any composure. She looked past Gail and out to the terrace for some sign of Peter as well. "I'm here alone," Gail said in that same mocking way. "Hope you don't mind."

Maggie remained in the vestibule. "How did you get in here?"

Gail held up two keys on a small ring. "With Peter's keys. I'm returning them for him." She dropped them into a small china bowl and watched Maggie's reaction.

"Why are you returning them?"

"Pete asked me to. Aren't you going to close the door?"

Maggie looked at the open door behind her, hesitated, then closed it. She walked into the living room, warily. "That doesn't sound like something Pete would do." She took the keys out of the bowl, checked them, though they were certainly hers, and held them back out to Gail. "I think he ought to be the one to bring them back."

Gail raised her hands helplessly. "I don't know what the etiquette is, I'm just following orders." She moved out of Maggie's reach and paced the short length of the room, which she made seem more cramped and uncomfortable.

Maggie put the keys down. "Where is he?"

"Pete? Out of town."

"Where out of town?"

"I'm not sure." She stopped beside the tray of liquor, scanned the bottles, and said, "Were you planning to have a drink?"

Maggie heard the question without really listening to her. "This is just in and out for me," she said absently. She checked her watch and groaned. "*God,* not already!" It sounded stupid and unconvincing.

Gail moved away from tray. "I'll pass in that case." She continued to look over the room.

"Look, Gail," Maggie said, "I don't mean to be rude, but if there's nothing else—"

"There is; my brother left some things." She looked toward the bedroom and asked, "There?"

Maggie moved to block the door. "He can pick them up anytime he wants."

"I'm trying to save him the trip." She halted. "You're right, though—I'm holding you up. You're due—?" She looked at her watch.

"Right about now."

"You'll miss your call in that case," Gail mentioned casually.

"Call?"

"From Lieutenant Creegan. Isn't he supposed to call you here?"

Maggie reacted with stunned silence.

"Isn't he?" Gail repeated.

"How do you know about that?" she said finally.

Gail had the smallest trace of a smile. The eyes, though, were cold and threatening. "We've got some acquaintances in common, I guess."

"Creegan?" Maggie said it incredulously.

Gail shrugged. "Whoever."

"Creegan." It caught Maggie completely by surprise—that Creegan would have reported directly to Gail, would have warned her. It appalled and frightened her—frightened her especially. *Why* would he have done it?

"It really doesn't matter who it was," Gail said. She had stopped moving around the room and was standing now between Maggie and the door.

"To me it does, it matters enormously."

"Why? Because a confidence was violated?" The

irony, the question itself was lost on Maggie. "What is it you have to say to him about Susan Ellis?"

Maggie looked at Gail. "I don't see where that's any of your business."

"It concerns my brother and me. It's definitely my business."

"I have nothing to say to Creegan," Maggie said, "nothing at all. You tell him that, will you?"

Gail's smile had disappeared. "You know, you're way out of your depth," she said, and if there had been the suggestion of a grim game in her voice before, it was gone now. "You have been ever since you came into Peter's life."

"I know the way you feel about me, Gail. You don't have to spell it out."

"You're still around. Obviously I do." She moved forward and the emotion she was holding down came a little closer to the surface. "I did you a favor once—I told you something about my brother, something that was strictly between us. You went to him with it."

"What you told me was a lie."

"Was it?"

"You know it was!"

"You really think I'd make up something that damaging to my own brother?"

"I don't know how far you'd go to get me out of his life. Or maybe I do, maybe that's what frightens me." They were both silent. Sounds drifted into the apartment from the street, making Maggie aware of the open terrace door behind her. She kept her eyes on Gail. "There's nobody going to come between you, is there, Gail?"

"No," Gail said quietly, "nobody."

"Is that . . ." Her voice tightened. "Is that what Susan Ellis did?"

Gail shook her head slowly. "Tried," she said. "Exactly like you're trying. A little more . . . insistently maybe . . . but then again she was around a little longer." Absently, her hand had reached out for something in the bookcase beside her—the stylized figure of a cat sculpted in crystal. She touched it, ran her fingers over the smooth, cold surface. "Like you she misjudged my brother."

"And you . . ."

"Never me. She was always very . . . guarded with me. It's amazing, isn't it—how alike you are." She smiled.

Maggie looked down at Gail's hand. It had closed around the solid figure of the cat.

"What were you going to tell Creegan? That I killed her?"

"I don't know that you killed her," Maggie said. Her mouth was dry, her voice shaky. The space past Gail to the front door, too narrow—deliberately?—was distracting her nearly as much as the almost palpable tension in Gail's body.

"You have no proof is what you mean. But it all makes sense to you, doesn't it?"

It did—now more than ever. Even when for a moment she tried to tell herself this *wasn't* happening, it was all in her mind. But it was real, this is how it was with Susan, this was exactly how it had happened. Only Susan was more vulnerable—*had* to be, had to have helped somehow. She wanted Gail to know that, wanted at least that much protection.

"Do you think . . ." she said, "do you really think it would work a second time?"

She had barely gotten the words out when suddenly, jolting her, was the sound of the door buzzer. At first she thought it was her imagination again, or a sound from the street—but Gail had heard it too; she turned slightly toward the hall. It sounded again, short, grating, unmistakable. Maggie measured the space between her and the release button in the hall, almost saying it aloud—*Wait, whoever you are, wait.*

"They know I'm here," she said, and started forward slowly.

"I wanted us to finish this," Gail said.

"It is finished, Gail. Let me pass."

She would have forced her way out if she had to, and came within a few seconds of doing just that, but Gail's hand loosened on the figure and fell to her side.

"Why would I not let you pass, Maggie?" She moved a step aside. Maggie hesitated and then walked past her, listening for the slightest movement behind her, expecting it. In the hall she hit the button with the palm of her hand and held it down, sounding an alarm on a threat that might be real or might all be in her mind, it didn't matter. She pulled the door open and called down the stairwell, *"Up here!"* Whoever it was hadn't gone; Maggie heard the downstairs door close and footsteps crossing the hall. She called down again, "Who is it?" and heard Frank Powell's voice calling back.

Frank! She leaned over the railing and saw him briefly—and then close behind her, with scarcely a sound, was Gail. Maggie spun around to face her and pushed herself out of reach, away from the railing and the deep open stairwell.

The sudden movement, the panic in Maggie's face, seemed to startle Gail. She kept the distance between them, looking puzzled, aggrieved almost, while she watched Maggie try to cover her reaction.

Frank had stopped at a landing below; out of breath, exaggerating it, he called something up that neither of them heard.

Gail moved to the staircase. She stopped and turned to Maggie. "How long do you think you can live like this, Maggie?" She reached for the banister. "How long?"

Maggie's silence was all the answer she expected. She started down the stairs. Frank's voice came up the stairwell as they passed each other just about where the bullets from Joanne Ellis's gun had hit. Two steps below the fourth floor he saw Maggie, caught his breath, and said, "You were supposed to call me, for Chrissake. What happened?"

Maggie's arms went around him as soon as he reached the landing, almost throwing him off balance. She buried her face against his chest and heard the downstairs door close. Frank said, *"Hey!"* He felt the wall press against his back, and Maggie's arms tighten. "What's wrong?"

Her words were just sounds, unintelligible.

CHAPTER TWELVE

He sat her down in the nearest seat, the step-stool in the kitchen, found some Scotch, and poured a finger of it into a tumbler. She pushed his hand away, insisting between breaths that she was all right, didn't know what had come over her—a delayed reaction probably to everything that had happened to her in the past week. Frank looked less than convinced. He put the glass down and crouched beside her, hitting a colander on the pegboard wall.

"Anything to do with the woman I passed on the stairs?" Gail's face had looked vaguely familiar to him.

"I don't know who you passed on the stairs."

He was holding her arms. He tightened his grip and said, "Come on, Maggie! This morning you were talking about an *autopsy* report, now I find you like this. What the hell are you involved in?"

"Nothing!" She took a deep breath, eyes closed, and said, "Look, Frank, I appreciate the concern, really." She gently freed herself. "I'm all right." She held one arm out straight. "Steady, see?" It was, with effort. She swung herself around, got up, and left him crouched in the kitchen. "It's stifling in here," she said.

In the living room she went to the open terrace door and heard Frank call out, "I'm not convinced. Christ, not the way your life's been going lately."

Maggie didn't reply. The heavy crystal figure of the cat, which had never seemed at all menacing to her before, gleamed in the bookcase. She stared at it until something metallic in the kitchen hit the floor, and Frank said, "No damage."

She owed him some reasonable explanation, but she couldn't bring herself to tell him the truth, however much he pressed; *wouldn't* involve him in this. What could she tell him, anyway? That Gail McCabe, whom he'd probably recognize once he heard the name, had been responsible for one woman's death already? And if it weren't for him, it might have happened all over again—this time to Maggie? And then what—go with him to the police, to God knows how many more Creegans, and admit that the evidence was all in her head at the moment?

Forget Frank—*she* wasn't up to it. Not another confrontation and more complications, not when she couldn't think straight herself.

Frank had come into the living room, looking even more determined—angry almost. Maggie stopped pacing, stared back at him silently, and made a grudging you-win gesture.

"Her name is Gail McCabe," she said dully. "Yes, *that* Gail McCabe. She's Peter's sister. She disapproves of us, wants me out of his life. We had a scene, a very upsetting one. It's that simple."

Frank didn't move, his hands stuck into his back pockets. "Sure it is," he said after a moment.

She didn't realize how fragile her control was until

he said it, how frightened and helpless she really felt, and how much she resented the fact that it was Frank and not Peter here with her now, pressing her for more, refusing to let go. She turned away from him and covered her face. Right away Frank was behind her, his arms around her, comforting—the way Frank was now always within reach and comforting. Why couldn't she uncomplicate her life and fall in love with Frank?

The tears, ironically, confirmed her explanation. He believed her, or said he did, to quiet her; believed it could be as simple as she said. He stroked her arms until the sobbing stopped.

"I'm with Gail McCabe," he said, startling Maggie and making her stiffen until he added, "I don't approve, either. I want you out of his life." He kissed the back of her head. "I don't make scenes is the difference." His hands slid down her arms. He stood behind her a moment silently and moved away, putting her out of reach.

It would be called (almost definitely) MEG-A-DEAL; it was a new board game still in development, and still too complicated and cluttered and, in Peter's view, humorless. He took all four positions and played it through several times, taking notes, until his brain started fogging over—more probably from the bottle of wine he had polished off at lunch than from any fatigue brought on by concentration. He left the coffee table littered with the oversized prototype, and walked leisurely along the beach. A few times he waved at people he knew, spaced as far apart on the beach as the big houses rising above them on the bluff; friends of Gail's, most of them.

Half an hour later he came back and walked waist-deep into the water and stood bobbing. He thought about going under, just once, a short quick plunge to really clear his head, but there was still a slight soreness just below his shoulder—something he hadn't been as much aware of in town. He washed his face and chest instead, keeping the dressing on his arm dry, and dragged himself out of the water.

He was slipping on sandals at the bottom of the deck steps when he heard the phone ringing. It was still ringing when he came into the living room. He hadn't talked to anyone all day since Gail had called early that morning to check on his arrival at the house after she had all but ordered him out of the city for the weekend. He had thought about calling Maggie, at least to tell her where he was, but Gail's advice had prevailed—a little therapeutic distance for a while.

It was Maggie now on the other end of the line; just about to give up, she told him, as breathlessly as though she had been the one to run for the phone. He threw the towel he had grabbed over his shoulder and said, "How'd you know I was here?"

"You were nowhere else," Maggie said. "Don't hang up on me yet."

"I'm not hanging up," he said, and the lift he got just hearing her voice again made their last conversation seem even more of a blunder to him. "I'm sorry I did that to you. I've been brooding about it a lot."

"You were going through a lot. Stop brooding." She still sounded out of breath, tense. "Why did you send back the keys?"

"What keys?"

"The keys to my place. Gail brought them."

"Gail was there?"

"Just a while ago."

"I don't know anything about it."

"I didn't think you did."

He turned away from the glare of the ocean and moved a few paces. Drops of water ran down his body onto the tile floor. "Everything's—all right, isn't it?" Maggie was silent. "Maggie?"

He heard her breath catch. "No," she said, "no, it's not. Pete, listen, I've got to see you."

"Why? For Chrissake, Maggie, what happened?"

"I can't talk about it like this."

He stopped moving. "It's—Gail, isn't it?"

"Yes. Pete, I don't want to be alone here. Believe me, I'm not panicking over nothing. Or maybe I am, I don't know, I need you to tell me. You know what I'm talking about, don't you?" Peter was silent, pale. "I'll come out there, I'll do it anyway you want. I've got to be *with* you. Please? Please trust me?"

Peter was waiting at the station when the train pulled in, late, at six-fifty that evening. He saw Maggie pass him in the first car, touch her hand to the dirty window, and turn to look back at him. He stayed at the end of the platform, near the parking area, and signaled to her when she stepped onto the platform. She was carrying a small tote bag and a jacket, blue like her skirt; a white kerchief tied her hair back. A few paces away she slowed and looked at him uncertainly. "Don't be angry?" she said.

"Who said I'm angry?" He held his hand out to her. "Worried, that's for damn sure."

"I'm sorry I had to do that to you."

"But you're all right?" He searched her face and drew her closer.

"Now I am."

"You're sure?"

She nodded. His arms went around her and she pressed against him, blocking out the sounds on the platform and feeling him warm and damp against her face. "This wasn't just an excuse to see you, believe me it wasn't," she said. His hand was moving on her back, gently, up and down. "Though, God, I've missed you so much. Just the thought of not seeing you again. . . ." She looked at his face. His hand stopped moving against her. "You're *sure* you're not angry?" She saw a little of that quiet, melting look from way back come into his eyes. He kissed her lightly on the mouth, and she wanted to tell him how right she'd been, how much she needed just to see him—but there were voices nearby, and then a woman in a big straw hat lugging a suitcase past them toward the parking lot.

Peter let go of her and said, "Come on, let's get out of here."

In the car it was different, or maybe it was just Maggie's nerves working on her again. Closed in with him, she sensed an uneasiness in Peter, a tension that the space and the activity outside had managed to cover. He avoided looking at her now, and all the questions that should have come at her as soon as they were alone together were being left unspoken. As though Maggie's phone call had been resolved in that brief exchange on the platform.

She sat quietly, and, when they had pulled out of the parking area, looked at him staring intently ahead, and touched his hand. She saw his eyes shift down. His hand moved and closed on hers. "Relax a little," he said. "It's a short ride."

She looked away and settled back in the seat; tried to, anyway. The sun was low and strong on her side, throwing quick, flickering shadows over her. "I remember," she said.

Occasionally he did strain to fill in the silence, but it was just that—filler, spoken to some weekend guest he was being forced to entertain; not Maggie. And then, miles beyond the distance she had remembered, there was the house. The car slowed and turned into the long driveway. The smell of the ocean blew in, and the low, steady roll of it, too, as soon as Peter turned off the ignition in front of the garage. He brought his hands back to the wheel and stared at the dashboard.

"Did you bring them?" he said.

"Bring what?"

He looked at her. "My keys."

It took her a moment to react. She couldn't remember anything else she had thrown into the bag, but she remembered his keys. "Yes," she said, and reached in and found them. "Are you sure you want them back?"

"What do you mean, am I sure?"

She handed them to him. There was another silence, and then the sound of the keys clicking together as his fingers moved on them nervously. Maggie waited. "You've got to try to understand," he said, and she could hear how painful it was for him, ". . . Gail."

"I have been trying, Pete; for a long time. I do understand her now."

"Then you know this was just . . ." The clicking stopped and he made a small, vague gesture.

"What?"

He shrugged. Again, the clicking. "A misunderstanding."

A misunderstanding! "And the rest of it—a misunderstanding too?" She moved closer to him. "Pete, look—none of this is in my *mind.*"

"Are you sure about that, Maggie?"

He wasn't looking at her; *couldn't,* she knew. "The problem is," she said, "the past keeps getting in my way. That's what it was with Gail today—the past all over again, as close as *this.*" She touched him.

"What's the past got to do with anything, for Chrissake?"

"You *know* what I'm talking about."

He breathed in hard and lifted his eyes to the roof of the car. "This place is beginning to close in on me," he said. "You?" He flipped the handle and got out of the car, calling, "Come on," to her when she didn't move.

Maggie saw him start for the house, then change direction and get on the path to the beach. She got out and followed him to the edge of the bluff. He was staring at the ocean. She leaned her head against his shoulder.

"If I let you," he said quietly, "you could do a real number on my head." He rubbed his face against her hair. "Don't do it, Maggie."

She had to force herself not to say it: *Why are you protecting her?* She pressed closer and shut her eyes, tight, trying to lose the question in the sound of the surf; concentrating so hard she didn't hear what it was he whispered before he walked away from her. She opened her eyes and saw him starting down the steps to the beach. Halfway there he looked back and said, "You know where everything is," and gestured at the house.

Maggie didn't call out or try to follow. She watched him kick off his sandals at the bottom of the steps and then drop his shirt outside the reach of the surf.

He didn't turn back to her, just kept walking along the edge of the water until the small patch of white below his shoulder vanished and Maggie had to squint to see him.

There was no way she could leave it so unfinished, no way he could make her believe it was all in her mind. The threat was *real.* As painful as it was he would eventually have to come to terms with the truth (though *eventually* might be a luxury she couldn't afford). And of course the truth was painful, intolerable even. But so was the fact of not just one but two deaths now. Peter himself had demonstrated that to her.

She was in the house. The light in the room had faded, all at once, it seemed. She checked her watch and found that it was already after eight; somehow she had lost a whole hour. Still Peter hadn't come back. She turned on a lamp and the light caught the portrait of Gail watching her from across the room. She stared back at it, the face soft and lovely, and the enormity of what she was asking Peter to do hit her all over again. To his *sister,* she didn't have to remind herself. Of course he was resisting, whether it was something new Maggie was telling him or something he had had to live with for a long time now.

He *did* know, she was convinced of it.

She turned her back to the picture and switched on another lamp in the room. The reflection in the windows covered the darkening beach. The board game on the coffee table, a jumble of miniature oil wells and gold bars and colored pawns, caught Maggie's eye. Beside it was a yellow pad filled with Peter's double-space-sized notes on the game, numbered, underlined. She scanned a few pages without concentrating and let the pad fall closed.

Ahead of her the corridor in the bedroom wing was dark. She walked toward it and found the switch. Three of the four doors were open; Gail's at the far end closed. She stood with her hand still on the switch, then moved past Peter's study and bedroom and the guest room where she remembered Susan's clothes were kept. She glanced back at the living room, called, "Pete?" and when there was no answer, opened Gail's door. She took a few steps inside and stopped. The room was dim, except for the light from the corridor. The glass doors were shut, dulling the sound of the surf.

Gail's room was the way she thought of it; even Peter called it Gail's room. The McCabes' room was what it really was, and Gail was Gail *McCabe,* if Creegan hadn't been reminder enough of that. And despite the distance Michael managed to keep between them, what happened to Gail McCabe happened to Michael McCabe as well. That was intimidating enough; what was really frightening was the thought, *Did he know?* It had never occurred to Maggie before, or never with such force. Did Michael know, too? She kept moving, as though she could put the idea behind her as easily as she could the portrait of Gail in the living room.

She found herself beside a dressing table, half of which was in the light. There were framed photos on it which Maggie stared at without seeing at first. Peter's face took shape, and Peter and Gail, and a young boy and girl unmistakably Peter and Gail, and a family group which she was about to move into the light when there was a sound behind her and a shadow moving on the wall. Her hand hung in the air, her body tightened. She whirled to face the sound and saw Peter standing against the light.

"What're you doing in here?" He sounded surprised, not angry.

Maggie caught her breath. She moved back a step, out of the light. "Wandering," she said lamely; "waiting for you. I was beginning to worry."

Peter reached down and turned on a small silk-shaded lamp. He looked from Maggie to the surface of the dressing table. He was shirtless and barefoot.

"The door was closed," Maggie said. "I thought you might've come in here." She nodded at the glass doors.

"What would I be doing in here?"

"The picture's caught my eye." She turned to the photos to distract them both and touched a frame, shakily. "You?" she asked.

Peter looked. "Me." Her hand moved to another frame and abruptly Peter switched off the lamp. She felt his arm go around her waist, drawing her away from the table. "Come out of her room," he said quietly.

In the hall he pulled the door closed and leaned back against it, tired, his eyes fixed on a point somewhere behind her. The light directly overhead caught grains of sand in his hair, on his chest and arms. Maggie waited, and the silence was even more punishing this time because she could hear in it, and see in his face, just how hard she was pushing him.

"I'm usually a hell of a lot better than this under pressure," he said haltingly. "It's when it doesn't stop . . . when it really starts to come down on me. . . ." He stopped for a deep breath, then let it out slowly. "Who wouldn't, hunh?" He half-smiled at her. Maggie reached out to touch him. He grabbed her hand and held it, squeezing. "The great thing about this place is it works for me most of the time. Once in a while, though, it needs a little help. That's where you come in." He lowered her hand and let go. "Okay?"

He was talking around it but it was an ultimatum all the same. Maggie didn't say anything, didn't let anything she was feeling come into her face. She heard and that seemed to be enough for him. He started to move away from the closed door, halted, and gave it a light rap. "Let's keep this this way," he said as an afterthought.

Maggie watched him go into his bedroom. "I want to shower," he called out to her in a voice that was different now, bright and energetic. "Who've we got to make us a couple of drinks?"

In the living room she found her bag and a tin of aspirin in the small red-leather case she had packed. She took the one tablet that was left and tasted it in the back of her throat before she could wash it down. She drank a second glass of water, rinsed it, and went out onto the deck through the kitchen.

She was still there fifteen minutes later when she heard Peter calling her from the living room. She turned and saw him, dressed now—too dressed. He draped a tan suit jacket over the back of a chair and disappeared into the kitchen. He called her again and Maggie said, "Here." She slid the screen door open. Peter came back into the room. He was wearing a yellow silk shirt and smelled of cologne when he came closer.

"What did you do with our drinks?" His voice was still cheerful.

"Sorry, I forgot them. Why are you dressed like that?"

He went to the bar. "I'm taking you out to dinner."

"Out?"

"Got to, the cupboard here's pretty bare."

She watched him pour white wine for her and a long vodka for himself. "I'm not that hungry," she said.

"No? Wait'll that sea air hits."

"I can always improvise," she said. "Whatever you've got lying around."

"My idea's better. It's nothing special, so don't panic. What you've got on is fine."

She looked down at herself, and whether she looked fine or not was beside the point. *I don't want us to be alone*, was what he really meant. "You really don't have to entertain me," she said.

He brought her the wine. "Part of the package deal." He touched glasses, barely looking at her, and walked away.

Maggie put the glass down without drinking and picked up her bag. "Let me pull myself together, at least."

Peter was looking out at the ocean. "Go ahead," he said, without turning. She saw him check his watch. Almost out of the room, she stopped.

"Pete?" She raised her bag. "Your room?"

"What do you mean, my room? Where else?"

They were already in the car when the phone started ringing in the house. Maggie heard it first; it was coming through an open window on the ocean side. Peter listened for several rings, then opened his door and started to run toward the house. The ringing stopped. Peter came back to the car and said, "Every time." He turned the key in the ignition. When the car pulled out onto the road, the ringing began again, a lot longer this time.

He took her to Twiggy's, a noisy bar near Amagansett, where there were no tables except for one crowded with friends of his whom Maggie had never met before. They stayed for two rounds, Maggie nursing a white wine, and when he put her on the spot and she had to say not just to him but to everybody, "Of course I don't mind," stayed on for a dinner of hamburgers and french fries. She smiled a lot and looked interested and made, she was sure, no impression at all. Afterwards they went with two of the couples to a new disco—just for a look, Peter promised her, but the look stretched to an hour at least. It was an evening completely unlike any they had ever spent together, with an energy and drive in Peter that was just short of manic at times.

"What are you on, anyway?" she asked him at one point, and he said, "A natural high," as though she hadn't been serious.

On the dance floor, suddenly, she found herself breaking into a cold sweat, and her head started to spin. She stayed as long as she could, then told him calmly, "I'll be right back," and left him dancing with the Rowans. She walked slowly, trying to keep her balance above the noise and the lights, reached the ladies' room, and locked herself in a stall until the nausea and the shakes and the terrible sense of anxiety had passed.

"What's the matter?" Peter asked her when she came back.

"I don't know. Nerves. Look, would you mind a lot if we left? I'm not up to this right now."

The air helped, and the quiet, and not having to watch Peter perform so desperately; not having to smile, either, at a bunch of strangers whose faces were blurred in her mind already. She moved closer to him in the car, and when he said, "Better now?" it was gentle and calming, almost his old voice back again. She closed her eyes on it, nodding against him, feeling the knot inside her loosen a little.

It was almost two when they got back to the house. Peter started a wobbly circuit of the living room, turning off lamps. At the bar he stopped and held up a bottle of brandy. "Nightcap, short one?"

"Uh-uh." She touched her stomach and gave him a small, apologetic smile.

"It'll help you relax." Maggie shook her head and yawned. He poured for himself.

"Pete?"

He raised his head and listened to Maggie moving closer behind him. He stood still a moment, not weaving at all now, then turned, his shoulder brushing against her.

"Kiss me?" she said.

She waited and watched herself in his eyes which were a watery blue, the pupils enlarged. He leaned forward and without putting his arms around her, kissed her softly on the mouth. Maggie's eyes were still closed when he pulled away.

"I'll be with you in a minute, okay?" he said.

"Okay."

He turned and picked up his drink.

Maggie went into the bedroom, took off her clothes and hung them, and took a long shower, hot and then cold. She dried herself with a big black towel Peter had used, and found the terrycloth robe hanging behind the door. She put it on, then started searching through drawers and cabinets for his hairdryer. She found a bottle of aspirin in the meantime and put it on the sink. There was Valium in the same drawer, and a few Seconals and a jumble of small pill bottles. Valium was a lot closer than aspirin to what she needed, but she had been drinking and she couldn't remember, if she ever knew, what the Valium mix would do to her. She replaced the bottle and as she did, the name at the bottom of another label leaped up at her. ELLIS. She turned it. SUSAN. And felt her heartbeat quicken. The name was on something called Doriden too, and Ritalin, and a few other bottles with different-colored pills whose unpronounceable names Maggie had never seen.

It wasn't finding the pills that was unsettling, or the fact that Peter had kept them the way he had kept Susan's clothes in the guest room; it was coming upon that name so unexpectedly. Bringing the past back again when she was most vulnerable to it, making it an insistent presence. Like Gail in her apartment.

She closed the drawer and stared at her foggy reflection in the mirror, almost seeing Susan's face, the face in the photo, covering her own.

Then the phone rang, just twice, and she heard Peter's voice distantly, and knew right away it was Gail at the other end. She went to the bedroom and listened, hearing only the changing tone of his voice—surprise or alarm, she couldn't make out which—but none of the words. Water ran down her forehead into her eyes. She raised her arms and passed the sleeves of the robe over her hair. Then she took a step out into the corridor.

Peter was at the far end of the living room, standing, facing the stone fireplace wall. She saw him move a few paces, back and forth, holding the receiver close with both hands, then sit hunched forward on the edge of a chair. His face was turned away from her; there were no sounds at all, as hard as she listened, just a slight movement of his head as he whispered into the phone.

Gail. Inevitably Gail.

Maggie came back into the bedroom. She forgot about the dryer; took a smaller black towel off the bathroom rack and rubbed it slowly over her hair. What was Gail telling him at—she looked at the clock—two-ten in the morning? And still telling him, with Peter listening in that same hunched-over position, ten endless minutes later? It was about Maggie, of course, but that didn't matter so much, she expected that, what mattered was that Peter was listening—he wasn't walking away from it the way he had walked away from Maggie.

She put the towel back and brushed her hair in front of the mirror, counting the strokes to try to empty her mind. But it came again anyway—that feeling, a sour tightness, just below her chest. She made the strokes harder, faster, but the feeling only deepened, until she put both her hands on the edge of the sink and pressed down hard, holding her breath. When it passed she opened the drawer, found the bottle of Valium, and took one.

Behind her, outside, a screen door slammed shut. Two-thirty. The deck lights went out. Maggie pulled her hair back and wound a rubber band around it. She could hear Peter walking on the deck, the heavy, hollow sound approaching, then moving away, then stopping altogether. She turned off the bathroom light.

Peter was leaning against the railing, shadowy in the light spilling out from the living room. He turned and watched silently as Maggie came out of the house; then when she was beside him, looked away, at the ocean.

"I found some Valium," she said; "at least that's what the label said. I took one."

"Did it work?" His voice, like his face, was lifeless.

Maggie breathed in and closed her eyes a moment. "Not yet."

"Give it awhile." He was silent.

She moved closer. "I heard the phone ring." She waited.

"It was Gail."

"I thought it might be." She pulled the robe around her tighter, and held herself, her arms pressing against that point just below her chest. "Does she know I'm with you?"

"She knows."

"She was upset, of course," Maggie said. She saw his hands, clasped, moving on the rail. "What did she say?"

"She wants me to end it—us. Stop seeing you." He said it wearily, the words a little slurred.

"Does that surprise you, Pete?"

"No. Maybe just the way she said it."

"Does it convince you? That's a lot more important to me."

"I don't know."

Maggie blinked. "You don't know?"

"No. I've got to think about it."

She tried to see into his face, to make him look at her. "Because Gail *wants* it?"

"Because—" He stopped and raised his hands, which were pressed together so tight they were trembling—even in the dark she could see that. He brought them back down on the rail. "—I can't put her through something like this again. Can't—punish her like this."

"Punish her?"

He took a deep breath and held it, steadying himself, and then pushed himself away from the railing. He walked to the end of the deck and came back halfway. The light was on him now, on Maggie too, facing him. "You called Creegan today," he said suddenly, and it was a different voice, cold and controlled. "Why?"

It took her a moment. "It was a mistake," she said.

"What did you want to talk to him about?"

"About . . . Susan," she said quietly.

"And Gail. You were going to tell him that, weren't you?"

She shook her head. "It doesn't matter; I didn't talk to him. Gail must have told you that, too."

"That doesn't mean you're going to let it drop though, does it, Maggie?"

"How can I?" She started toward him. "Pete, this time listen to *me*. Whether you believe it or not, one way or another Gail is going to get me out of your life. I'm exactly what Susan was to her, the same kind of threat, and nothing's going to change that. Not as long as we're together."

She was directly in front of him, searching his face and trying to find something she could remember in it. She felt his hand touch her arm. "Then Gail's right," he said softly, and she could hear—in his voice, not her imagination—enormous sadness. "The way

Gail's . . . always right." His hand tightened on her. "*Pull out,* Maggie, for Chrissake, get away from it!"

"Let go, you mean, the way Gail wants me to let go."

"The way I want you to let go." His hand fell away from her and made a helpless gesture that gave the lie to everything he was saying—*forcing* himself to say. For Gail. He started to walk away, toward the living room first, uncertainly, then moved instead in the direction of his bedroom.

Maggie called, "Pete?" and he stopped without turning. "What'll that do? Make the truth any easier to live with? For either of us? I'm sorry, but we don't have any options anymore. Do we?" She thought he was about to turn and say something, but instead he went into the bedroom and slid the door shut behind him. She watched him take off his shirt and throw it on a chair, then move out of view.

She stayed on the deck, out of the light, and watched the breakers rolling in; tried to drug herself with the sound of them, because the Valium wasn't doing anything for her, not yet. There was a quarter moon out throwing some light on the vast and deserted beach.

She was right—there were no options, especially not for Peter; no way he could go on protecting Gail and living with the memory of Susan's death. She knew him too well now, had seen him too vulnerable.

She took deep, deep breaths of air and tilted her head back, letting the damp breeze wash over her face. There were lights left on in the living room and kitchen; the doors were wide open. She went inside, closed the glass doors and locked them, and turned off the remaining lamps. Peter's bedroom door was open, light falling into the corridor. Moving closer, she saw something else—a thin line of light under the closed door to Gail's bedroom. She stopped and stared at it, breathing faster, even though she knew it wasn't possible—Gail *couldn't* be in the house with them. She moved forward and looked into Peter's room.

It was empty, his clothes hanging off the chair. The bathroom was empty, too.

He was in Gail's room.

Maggie listened. There were no sounds anywhere in the house; just the steady sound of the surf. She waited, and then forced herself out of the room, into the corridor. Toward that pencil line of light. She touched the door and let her hand slide down to the knob.

She couldn't call his name, couldn't find the voice to do it. She turned the knob and pushed slowly. Saw the pictures, and two steps later, to her left, saw Peter lying on Gail's bed, face down, naked, the silk spread twisted under him. She stood frozen, watching him lying still, his arms spread wide.

It was the one part of the truth she had never allowed herself to admit, had fought however insistent it had become. But it was in front of her now, as clear and devastating to her as though Gail were in the bed with him.

He knew she had come into the room—had to have heard and to know she was seeing it finally. What he wanted her to see. All the reason he could find for her to let go. His head lifted and his face, buried in the pillow, turned to the wall, away from her. She could see from the movement of an eyelid that his eyes were open, staring.

She whispered his name in the sealed-in silence of the room, aware not only of him, but of all the faces, the years of Gails and Peters, watching behind her. *Over now . . . over. . . .* She kept repeating it to herself, trying to convince herself and let the words carry her toward the bed. Wanting to say it to him—*would* say it to him, to that vulnerable part of him that would believe her and trust her. She stood beside him and looked down at his face, and saw what *she* believed and trusted, and loved, *still.* She bent down and her hand, when she touched him, was trembling.

"There were times, though . . ." she whispered, so close that he had to see her now, ". . . when it was me and not Gail . . . me you were making love to, not her . . . weren't there, Pete . . . weren't there?"

She kissed him and then she drew back, undid the belt, and let her robe fall to the floor. Peter's eyes were still dull, as if they weren't seeing her at all, but something traced a quick, deep line across his forehead.

"Don't, Maggie. . . ."

She hesitated, then sat on the edge of the bed. "Why not, Pete?" She leaned over and stroked his hair. "You wanted me to know, didn't you? All right, I know, I think I knew all along. It didn't change anything and it still doesn't, not between us."

She looked across the bed at the night table with things on it that were unmistakably Gail's. She got up and walked around the bed to Gail's side and felt the silk spread cool under her as she eased herself down beside him. She lay still awhile, as still as Peter—breathing in as lightly the sweet, deep fragrance of Gail that was everywhere. She touched his neck and moved her hand slowly down his back. He stirred and she heard him murmur something into the pillow.

Her hand slid around him, under him, and spread flat against his chest.

He made another sound and it was her name, it was *Maggie* he was saying, faintly at first, almost pleading. And then saying it again, only stronger this time, a warning in it, "*—don't.*"

Her hand kept moving lower though, and she felt him, soft—even with her touch, still soft. And then he pressed down on her to stop the insistent stroking. "Let me," she said. Her lips brushed his shoulder, and she felt his skin wet against her face. Then the weight on her hand lightened a little and he slipped off. She rolled onto her back and watched Peter raise himself and turn slowly toward her. He looked at her. She could see no warning in the look, nothing distant, just that softness coming into his eyes again—which meant she was right, she was right all along. She tried to draw him down, but he pulled back and said quietly, "I can't, Maggie."

"Can't?" It was a whisper. "Why not?"

"Not here."

"Because it's her room?"

"Not here."

"What's that matter, Pete? What's it matter?" She kept saying it and pulling him closer; it was easier now, with all his resistance going. "It's what you want. I know it is. I know it."

He was on her. His arms slid under her back and held her. And then he began moving against her, slowly pushing himself between her legs. Maggie's eyes closed and her head rolled back and forth over the pillow. And as ready as she was for him, it happened with such a sudden, hard push into her that it left her too breathless even to cry out. It happened again and again, each thrust deep and punishing.

Her hands tightened on his back, pulling him down against her to bury the cries. He must have become aware of the pain finally, must have felt it even without the cries, because he stopped suddenly and looked almost stricken. He lifted her face and caressed her, and when he began to move again, it was gently, as though he were someone completely different now, making love to her, not just driving himself into her.

Now if only she could hear it again the way she had before—her name, gently and pleading. Here, in Gail's room, Gail's bed. *Maggie.* Especially when she felt him quicken and then stop suddenly and shudder all through his body.

He lay still, and when she touched him, drew in his breath sharply and shuddered again, lightly, and then not at all. His breath was warm and wet on her neck, and then he rolled off her and lay staring at the ceiling.

Maggie raised her arms and pushed the hair back off her face. The room was hot and airless, and once again she became aware of that sweet smell of Gail all around her. And Gail watching her dimly from the pictures across the room. A drop of sweat slid down her side onto the silk spread that was warm under her. She looked at Peter, still staring up, and if it weren't for the Valium and the wine finally working on her, the presence of Gail they were both conjuring up would have been even stronger and more disturbing.

"Pete?" She moved closer to him and lay her arm across his chest. "Hold me."

He lowered his head and looked at her vaguely a moment, then gently brushed her arm aside and swung his legs off the bed. He sat on the edge, bent forward, rubbing his eyes. Maggie propped herself up on one elbow and reached out to touch the space between them. "Pete, are you all right?"

He dropped his hands and stood up. "Sure I'm all right," he said without looking back at her. He walked, almost stumbled, across the room and groped behind the closed drapes for the cord. He jerked the cord down, opening the curtains wide, then slid open the glass and screen doors, quickly, as though something noxious had to be let out of the room. Maggie reached down and found the terrycloth robe on the floor beside the bed. She covered herself against the cool breeze and watched Peter leaning against the doorjamb, looking out. She called him twice before he heard her; then he turned his head so that he was facing the pictures on the dressing table.

"Can we talk?" She waited. "Pete?"

"What—?" He looked away from the pictures. "I need to walk on the beach awhile."

"Do you want me to come?"

"No," he said quickly. He went outside, stopped, and called back over his shoulder. "Fix the bed, will you?"

Maggie saw him enter his bedroom from the deck and come out a minute later wearing his denim shorts. She listened to the sound of his footsteps fading down the wooden steps to the beach.

She pulled the robe higher, up to her shoulders, and let her eyes travel slowly around the room. It was just that, she told herself—a room, with a presence in it that had no existence outside her own mind. They had made love before, she and Peter, in this house, just beyond that wall, and with Gail a *real* presence then—with no premonitions, no regret, and no guilt. She tried to pretend it was no different now and closed her eyes on the room. When that didn't work, she tried to distract herself with the sounds outside and with the awareness that she was shivering in the breeze.

She got up groggily, fumbled with the robe, put it on, and went out to the deck. The only other light anywhere was coming from Peter's bedroom. She crossed the deck and turned on the outside spots which reached slightly beyond the footing in the sand. She stood against the rail, scanning the empty beach, and leaned far forward to see beyond some plantings obstructing the view to her right.

Peter was nowhere, and the confused state he was in when he stumbled out frightened her even more than being alone in the house with Gail knowing she was there. (Why was she thinking about Gail now? Gail was in the city. Peter had said that, hadn't he? She tried to remember.) She paced to the other end of the deck and stood with her hands cupped around her eyes to block out the spotlights.

And then she saw him, or thought she did—a dim figure standing at the edge of the water, outlined briefly against the white of a breaker. Maggie lowered her hands to her mouth and called out to him. The shape of the figure changed, or moved. She called again, but her voice had to be lost in the sound of the surf, so she went to the steps and climbed down quickly. At the bottom she saw that the figure had disappeared below the slope of the beach. She walked beyond the light, and halfway to the water, saw him again; really saw him this time, in the surf, dragging himself out. She cried out his name and the sound reached him and startled him. Maggie walked faster. The sand became wet and firm underfoot, and then the surf was rolling around her ankles. She stopped and waited for him to come closer, then wrapped her arms around him and squeezed, so tightly that he took hold of her wrists and eased himself free.

"Let me get my breath," he said. He coughed and pressed his hands against the sides of his head, combing his fingers through his hair. She followed him onto the dry sand and watched him drop exhausted to his knees.

"I'm sorry," Maggie said, and she was just as breathless. She knelt beside him and touched his arm. "I didn't know what had happened to you. I was getting frantic, really I was."

"Why? What did you think I'd do?" Maggie shook her head. "I told you, I wanted to be alone awhile." He exhaled heavily, and let himself collapse into the sand.

"I know." She wiped the water off her face and dried her hands on the robe, which was gritty with sand. "I'm panicking, I guess. I don't mean to."

"I'm not going to let anything happen to you, Maggie," he said.

"I'm not thinking about that." Her hands kept rubbing against the robe, her body rocking back and forth. "Pete—I know what this is doing to you—"

"I suppose you do. Hell, I'm not keeping it much of a secret. That's not going to change things though, is it?"

She lowered herself beside him. "There's no other way, Pete. No way you can go on protecting her."

"No," he said quietly, with that enormous sadness in his voice again. He watched his fingers tracing lightly in the sand. "I didn't think it would happen again. But it's no different, *Christ*"—his fingers tightened into a fist and ground out the even pattern of lines—"no different. It's everybody back to GO." He was silent, and then he pushed himself up to his knees. The front of his body from his shoulders down was coated with sand. He gave a few quick sweeps of his hand and sat back on his heels staring at the ocean. "I don't know how to do it yet," he said dully. "I need time. Okay?"

"Okay," Maggie said, almost voiceless. She sat up, and the robe spread open slightly; she tightened it. "I know what it is, Pete—the real panic I'm feeling." She waited for him to look at her; he kept staring straight ahead. "What are you going to let this do to us?"

"I don't know," he said. "I'm not letting myself think that far ahead." He looked at her finally, his face too shadowy for her to read. "You don't honestly see us surviving it, do you?"'

"Yes, *yes*, of course I do!" Her body shook with the cry. Peter looked at her impassively, and before she could touch him, pulled back and rose to his feet.

"I'm sorry, Maggie," he said, "it just doesn't seem that important to me right now." He brushed more sand from his shoulders, bent and slapped at the back of his legs.

Maggie tried not to react, not to show herself hurt, or even reasonable and understanding; nothing to pressure him into any more words that he obviously wouldn't mean.

Peter straightened and looked back at the distant house which was the only point of light anywhere on the bluff. "It's late," he said, and seemed to start toward it; instead he turned, as if remembering Maggie, but walked past her without even a slight pause, and headed for the water. Maggie watched his even pace change and his body pull through the surf. He stopped and poured handfuls of water on his legs and back. She got up shakily. There was sand in her hair, under the robe, all over her. She shook her head and ran her hand under the collar of the robe, walking to the water and letting it wash over her feet.

Peter was moving away from her into deeper water, whether he saw her or not, she couldn't tell. She kept her eyes on him though, watching him duck under a wave and take a little too long to surface. The darkness was making her uneasy, and the fact that he was out there alone and going deeper; and if anything should happen she wasn't a strong swimmer, not at all. He dove under a wave just before it broke, and as soon as he disappeared, her voice worked like a reflex and shouted his name. She waited, searching the darkness, then took a step forward, lifting her robe as the foam rose to her knees.

Finally he surfaced, probably no more than a few seconds later, but too many for her. He saw her motioning him toward her and calling, *"Please?"* Another wave hit him in the back and pushed him forward. When it reached Maggie, she winced at the cold against her thighs and let the skirt of the robe, already wet, fall.

Peter moved in slowly, and about ten feet away from her he stopped and waited silently for Maggie to speak.

"Pete? Please come out, will you?" She gestured him forward.

"I will in a while," he said, and she pleaded, "Now?"

He hesitated, then moved a few swaying steps closer, still keeping himself out of reach. "What are you so afraid of?" he asked.

Maggie gave a broad sweep of her hand. "This . . . aren't you?" She smiled nervously and after a few seconds saw that he was smiling back at her—actually smiling—and then holding his arms out to her and urging her toward him, gently, as though trying to calm a frightened child. He was making it work on her: with that smile and that calm gesture, soothing all the fear and anxiety out of her. She fought the push of the surf and fell against him, barely conscious now of the rising shock of the cold.

The words came out in a rush. "You didn't mean any of it before, I knew you didn't." She pressed closer. "And I was right, wasn't I?" She lifted her face and saw that the smile was gone; but that didn't matter, not with his arms closing around her. "Don't do that to me again, ever."

"You don't let go, do you, Maggie?" he said. All she let herself hear in it was affection and, finally, something like acceptance.

"No. Not when I've found something this right. You can't blame me for that, can you?"

A wave hit them and Maggie stumbled against him. Peter's arms tightened around her, holding her steady, even after the undertow had passed and her footing was secure again. "I'm okay," she said, but his grip was tightening uncomfortably now. "Pete?" She tried to pull away a little to catch her breath. "Pete?" she said again. The look on his face had changed, become distant again, not on her at all. She brought her hands between them, against his shoulders, and pushed. Peter blinked and looked at her face. "You don't let go," he said, and something frightening had come into his voice. He freed her suddenly and she fought for air, for just a few seconds because his hands went to her wrists, squeezing, and she thought, *"My God!"* and right away tried to block out the terrifying idea. But she couldn't; he was pulling at her, harder, hard enough to snap her wrists if she didn't bend, dragging her farther out and saying over and over, *"Let go, Maggie, let go. . . ."*

And, my God, it was happening, it was happening to her.

His hands shot up to her shoulders, and the cry of astonishment and terror burst out of her just as he pushed and her head went under. She came up choking, and when for just a moment his face came into focus, she saw it again—that savage, terrible look he had turned on Joanne Ellis. She screamed. The open robe twisted around her and floated up as Peter leaned forward and pressed down again with all his weight. She fought him, tearing at his back with her nails. His head jerked back with the pain. He threw himself down on her, forcing her lower, submerging his face to do it, until she was struggling less and less, and finally not at all. Still he held her under. When he let go, the robe floated up and billowed on the swell of a wave.

Peter choked. He staggered away a little and felt his insides heave. He bent forward and vomited. When he looked back, the robe was still floating above Maggie's body. He pulled it free and dragged it behind him as he stumbled out of the water onto the beach. Lines of blood were running down his back. He fell to his knees on the dry sand, his arms tight, tight against his middle.

At five-thirty in the morning, which had been as fast as she could drive out to East Hampton, Gail left the car in the driveway and ran into the house. She searched through all the rooms until she found Peter sitting in a chair near her dressing table, wearing only his cut-off jeans, which were still wet. She stopped abruptly in the doorway, and when she saw that dazed look in his eyes, said with quiet dread, "Where is she, Pete?"

His lips moved soundlessly at first, and then his eyes closed and the sound came out, barely above a whisper, "I'm sorry, Gail. . . ."

Gail—her face white—didn't move from the doorway. "It . . . happened?"

Peter opened his eyes. He shook his head. "I didn't mean it to."

"But it *happened*?" she said, her voice rising.

Peter nodded, and Gail leaned her head against the doorjamb and said quietly, "Oh, my God, no."

"I tried, Gail—really. But it just—" He covered his face and strained to find the word, "—*went* on me again, I couldn't help it."

"Why?" she cried. "Pete, *whatever* she thought about Susan, there's nothing she could have done, you know that. Do you think *I* would have told her if I wasn't sure of that?"

"It wasn't what she could've done, Gail." He lifted his face and looked from Gail to the bed which was still rumpled. Gail followed his look. "It wasn't that. . ." His voice died.

Gail moved out of the doorway, toward the bed. She lingered beside it, touched it, then came toward Peter. "Nothing would've mattered, Pete, nothing would've happened to us. Has it ever? Has it?"

"No."

"Then *why*?"

He looked frightened and helpless, a face from out of one of the earliest snapshots on the dressing table. His arms went around her waist and his lips pressed against her. Gail stroked his hair, and when she looked down, her eyes caught the smears of blood blending into the flowered pattern covering the chair.

She saw the gashes in his back and gave a small cry. And thought immediately—*her fingernails, his skin under her fingernails. Where was the body?*

She left Peter in the room and went outside, scanning the beach from the deck until she saw in the first light the white of the terrycloth robe in the sand. She went toward it, looking back constantly at the gray outlines of the houses on the bluff. Peter had come out to the deck and was watching. She bent down and examined the robe, handling it carefully, then walked the deserted beach several hundred feet in both directions. There was nothing else visible.

Peter was waiting when she climbed the steps to the deck. "Nothing," she said and kicked off her shoes caked with sand. He followed her inside and waited in the living room while she put on a pot of coffee and paced the kitchen, trying to order her thoughts.

"I'm going to handle it myself this time," she heard him call out. She stopped pacing and looked out at him. "I don't want you involved in it, not again, Gail—you or Michael. Okay?"

Gail thought a moment. "Better put a shirt on," was all she said.

She brought in coffee—black and strong—and made Peter sit beside her and drink it, and answer all her questions, which she asked coldly, with no emotion: where they'd been and when, and exactly how he remembered it happening—every detail of it.

Sitting silently, she poured another cup of coffee and drank it, then drew a deep breath and carried the phone closer. She dialed, all the while looking at her brother. Through the entire call she looked at him.

"This is Gail McCabe on the Shore Road," she said into the phone, sounding frightened and out of breath. "I want to report an accident, a drowning. Could you come out here right away, please? Thank you."

She lowered the receiver and turned to Peter. "We'll have to call Michael soon," she said, and waited for him to nod, which he did, finally, grudgingly.

"He's not going to do it, Gail, not this time."

"He'll do it."

His look became soft and adoring. He raised his hand and touched her face. "You're always there. . . ."

"Always," Gail said. "Always."

She let him draw her close and kiss her until she could feel his control going. She pulled away from him and leaned forward on the couch. Peter's hand slid down her back and rested.

The game board was on the coffee table in front of her. She studied it, tilting her head to read the colored squares on the opposing three sides. More absorbed, she slipped to her knees and reached for one of the pawns. Peter watched her and then slid off the couch and crawled to the position opposite her.

Gail look up, puzzled. "What's the game?" she asked.